W9-BTZ-287

DISCARD

A TASTE OF REALITY

KIMBERLA LAWSON ROBY

A TASTE

OF

REALITY

WILLIAM MORROW *wm* *An Imprint of* HarperCollins*Publishers*

This is a work of fiction.
The characters, incidents, and dialogue
are products of the author's imagination and
are not to be construed as real.
Any resemblance to actual persons, living or dead,
is entirely coincidental.

HarperCollins books may be purchased
for educational, business, or sales promotional use.
For information please write: Special Markets Department,
HarperCollins Publishers Inc.,
10 East 53rd Street, New York, NY 10022.

FIRST EDITION

Designed by Kate Nichols

Printed on acid-free paper

Library of Congress Cataloging-in-Publication Data

Roby, Kimberla Lawson.
A taste of reality / Kimberla Lawson Roby.—1st ed.
p. cm.
ISBN 0-06-050565-6 (alk. paper)
1. African American women—Fiction.   2. Discrimination in
employment—Fiction.   3. Female friendship—Fiction.
4. Women employees—Fiction.   5. Married women—Fiction.
I. Title.
PS3568.O3189 T37   2003
813'.54—dc21   2002070138

03 04 05 06 07 WBC/RRD 10 9 8 7 6 5 4 3 2 1

In loving memory of my mother

Arletha Stapleton
May 11, 1944–November 3, 2001

You were the best mother in the world,
and you are in my heart always

9/03

A TASTE OF REALITY

CHAPTER 1

I DROVE MY PEARL WHITE Lexus SUV into the subdivision and sighed with much confusion. I sighed because even though I was living "the good life," I wasn't all that happy. My marriage was more than shaky, my career was heading nowhere, and I spent most of my time wondering how everything went wrong. I even wondered why this solid-brick three-level dream house was no longer important to me and why now, it was merely a place to lay my head.

After pulling around the circle drive, just past the front door, I eased the gear in park and turned off the ignition. Then I stepped out onto the concrete, grabbed my handbag and briefcase, and pushed the door shut. It really was a gorgeous day, and now I wished I could spend the rest of the evening relaxing on the deck. But if I wanted to finish updating the new-hire handbook by next month, I knew I had to keep working on it at home for a couple of hours each night until then. But I didn't mind, because in human resources, overtime was very necessary.

I unlocked the front door and walked inside. I went through the two-story foyer, passed the sunken great room, and headed into the kitchen, where I set my belongings down on the double island and picked up today's mail. The central air was kicking with full force, and that of course meant that David had finally arrived home from one of his many weeklong business trips—one that included this past weekend. He was a successful vice president at a Chicago pharmaceutical sales company, but somehow it was hard for me to believe that spending so much time away from home was truly necessary.

I dropped the stack of bills, magazines and clothing catalogs I've never ordered from back onto the island, went down the hallway and into our master bedroom suite. David was sitting in bed, leaning his back against two king-size pillows, watching something on television. But he looked at me almost immediately.

"Hey," I said as a peace offering, because we really hadn't spoken since arguing two nights ago.

"Hey, how's it going?"

"I'm okay," I said, but couldn't help remembering how things used to be when he arrived home from his business trips. He'd call me twice each of the days he was gone, send me flowers without warning and would call me at work, letting me know that he was back at home waiting for me. But things always seem to have a way of changing. So have we as man and wife.

"So how was work today?" he asked, glancing at the television and then back at me, waiting for a response.

"Same ole, same ole." I kicked off my pumps and shed the jacket to my periwinkle linen pantsuit. "Although, they did repost the same HR manager's position I applied for six months ago. I heard this afternoon that the guy they gave it to is moving to Arizona."

"You thinking about going for it again?"

"I don't know. I don't even know if it's worth the hassle."

"Meaning what?" he asked. "A hassle in terms of all the responsibilities that come with a managerial position or the hassle of having to apply for it again?"

"I mean the hassle of having to prove myself all over again to a group of men who totally ignored the fact that I was qualified the first time."

"Well, for one thing, I don't think that sort of attitude is going to help you one way or the other," he said, and then looked away because he knew we'd argued about this very thing not so long ago, and that I resented his position regarding it.

"I don't want to be pessimistic about this, but based on what happened last time around, I just don't know if Jim and Lyle believe I can do the job. I was clearly the most qualified, yet they still gave it to a white guy who only had an associate degree and had *never* worked in human resources. Even though I had an M.B.A. and over three years of HR experience." I removed my panty hose and wondered why he never tried to sympathize with how I felt about anything.

"I'm not saying you shouldn't be upset about what happened before. But what I am saying is that maybe this time will be different if you go into the situation with a little more confidence in your superiors and with more of an open mind. I know you think they treated you unfairly, but maybe you just need to give them a chance."

"You know what, David?" I said out of mere frustration. "Just because you have the job of your dreams and have never had to experience job discrimination doesn't mean that it doesn't exist."

My feelings were so hurt. I couldn't believe my own husband, the man I loved, was trying to defend the same people who had passed me over for a promotion without any justifiable explanation.

"In all honesty, I can't confirm whether discrimination really exists or not, but since I've been pretty successful with climbing my own career ladder as a black man, it's hard for me to see what so many woman and minorities keep complaining about. Maybe it did go on back in the sixties, but things are different now. They're much different," he said matter-of-factly.

If I hadn't heard him with my own ears, I never would have believed that any black person could say such a thing. I was trying not to argue with him, but he was making it more difficult by the minute.

"You've been successful because you've always kissed up to the right people," I said before I knew it. "David, you've been a yes-boy for as long as you've been in pharmaceutical sales, and sometimes even I can't tell if you're black or white. Pretty much, it depends on what day of the week it is, where you are and who you're talking to."

"So what are you saying?" He sat all the way up and swung his legs over the side of the bed. Which meant I'd struck a serious nerve with him. But I didn't care because he knew I was telling the truth about him.

"Let's just leave this alone," I said, and pulled open the dresser drawer. "Because I really don't want to fight with you about this."

"No, I want you to tell me what you mean, since you know me so damn well."

He was steaming, and I could tell from his tone that this argument was only going to escalate. What I was planning to say next wasn't going to make things any better.

"Tell you what? That you didn't start out this way, but now you've completely lost your identity? That you've forgotten where you came from? That somehow along the way you've become so blinded that you think every black man and woman in America is experiencing the same success as you? That some of your white colleagues make derogatory jokes about black people on a frequent basis and you actually laugh louder than they do? I mean, what else do I have to point out for you to understand what I'm saying?"

"A joke is a joke, and just because you don't have a decent sense of humor, that's not my problem."

I laughed and sighed at the same time, because I couldn't believe he didn't get what I was trying to tell him.

"David, some of your friends even use the word nigger to your face and then pretend like it's okay because they're only joking around. And I can't tell you how sick I get every time I hear the president of your company insist that you just aren't like *most* black people. I mean, what exactly does that mean? What are *most* black people like anyway?"

"You're impossible," he said, picking up the channel selector. "And as far as I'm concerned this goddamn conversation is over. Shit, now I hate I even bothered asking you how your freakin' day went."

"I hate that you asked me, too, David, because it's not like you care about how I feel, anyway."

"I do care. But I don't understand why you can't quit and stay at home like a real wife should. Especially since I gave up all the luxuries I was used to when I moved all the way out to this backwoods city where you grew up. But the whole time we've been married, you've never gone out of your way to do anything except what's convenient for you. And hell, if you want to know the truth, I'm embarrassed to tell people that you work. So I don't know why you can't just join some organizations or sit on a few boards, like every other executive's wife."

"So that's what this is all about? Me giving up all my dreams so I can sit at home and do nothing? Because you knew when you met me that I wanted a career, and that the money you made wasn't going to change that. My mother raised me to be self-reliant, and that's why I didn't rush to get married before I was thirty. I was always up front with you about that. And I can't help it if now you don't like my independence."

"The bottom line is that you're not available when I need you to be for corporate dinners or even sex for that matter. All you do is work ridiculous hours, trying unsuccessfully to prove how good you are, and then you scream how tired you are when you get home. So I'm telling you now, things can't continue going the way they are, and I think it's time for you to decide what your priorities are."

"My priorities are the same as they were when you first asked me to marry you. And what about your own work schedule? You're hardly ever here, and when you are you're always planning the next business trip."

"Well in case you hadn't noticed, Anise, I'm a very well-paid executive. And that means I don't have the luxury of blowing off my responsibilities the way some people do. My job requires much more than just sitting behind some desk making a few phone calls."

"So exactly what are you trying to say?" I asked.

"That given the menial jobs you've always had, I don't expect you to understand what it takes to walk in my shoes."

"I don't believe you, David. I can't believe you've become so vain that you don't even care what you say to your own wife."

I gazed at him for a split second and then turned away because the last thing I wanted was for him to see my eyes watering. I couldn't fathom why he was diminishing me the way he was. I knew things weren't that great between us, but this cruel, insensitive criticism he was dishing was totally uncalled for.

"Oh, so now you don't have anything to say?" he asked.

"No, I don't. And as a matter of fact, I'm finished with this conversation altogether."

"Well, I'm *not* finished. And if you don't do something about rearranging your priorities real soon, we're both going to be sorry."

"Is that some kind of a threat?" I asked.

"No, because I don't make threats. At forty years old, I don't have to. But more importantly, at thirty-six, you need to think about having a baby before you're too old."

What he didn't know was that I wasn't planning on having any children at all. I'd thought about it when we were first married and was actually looking forward to it, but the one thing I'd learned over the years was that it was illogical to bring a baby into an unstable situation. We weren't even getting along with each other, so how on earth were we going to be good parents to an innocent newborn baby?

"If you think I'm going to give up my career and do nothing except have a houseful of babies, I don't know what to tell you."

"Oh, so it's like that?"

"Unfortunately, it is," I said, standing my ground.

"Then you won't ever hear me bring it up again."

David walked out of the bedroom, and while I felt like I'd won this latest quarrel of ours by unanimous decision, I didn't feel much like a heavyweight champion. He was too calm, and I could tell that I'd lost just a little more of him and part of the love he once had for me. Which hurt terribly, because there was a time when we both loved each other hard—when we both thought that life wasn't quite worth living if we couldn't be together. That feeling lasted five long years, but these last twelve months had played another tune, one that we were no longer able to create beautiful lyrics to. We both kept trying, but the rhythm just wasn't the same as it once was.

Maybe we were never meant to be together from the beginning. But I didn't want to believe that theory, because I did know how love felt. I could still remember the first day we met. We were at a pool party that was being given by some mutual friends of ours, Sam and Theresa, over in Olympia Fields, a predominantly black, upper-echelon south suburb of Chicago. I'd met Theresa at a four-day human resources convention in Oak Brook, and we'd continued to stay in touch ever since. David knew Sam because Sam had been one of his pharmaceutical clients when David was a sales manager. Theresa had always tried to play matchmaker for me since the time we met and couldn't wait to introduce David as soon as he'd arrived at the party. I knew then that I was strongly attracted to him, and it was pretty obvious that he felt the same way about me. It wasn't love at first sight, but we clicked from the very first moment we laid eyes on each other. We spent most of the evening together and exchanged phone numbers before leaving. He called me daily, and I was always smiling from ear to ear whenever I heard his voice. His work schedule and the fact that he lived almost ninety minutes away kept us from seeing each other during the week, but it didn't take long for his visits on Saturdays and Sundays to evolve into extended overnight stays. He began arriving on Friday evenings and never left my condo before daylight on Monday mornings.

We dated all of six months before he surprised me with a two-carat diamond solitaire engagement ring. I immediately told him yes, that I would marry him, and we took lifelong vows the very next year. He'd really wanted to keep his residence in the Chicago area, though, not just because he worked there but because he loved the suburb he lived in. I would have liked being closer to Chicago as well, but I just couldn't bring myself to leave my mother or most of my relatives who lived in Mitchell, a city with barely 150,000 residents. We'd always been such a close family, and the thought of living in a different city from the rest of them made me uncomfortable. Had I made the move, I knew I would have been extremely unhappy, so David, against very strong wishes, agreed on moving here with me and had been commuting ever since. He loved me that much, and I had the utmost respect for his giving up the lifestyle he was so accustomed to living. Mitchell was a wonderful place to reside and a great place to raise children, but it wasn't Chicago. There was no Magnificent Mile, no large-production plays, no concerts with A-list entertainers, and no exquisite art galleries. But again, it was a wholesome, quiet place to live, and I was happy to be here. David, on the other hand, wasn't, and now I was pretty sure that this was part of the reason he was so distant and almost preferred going on business trips as opposed to being at home with me. Our lifestyle was, well, boring by his definition, but I, on the other hand, perceived it as comfortable living. However, I was born and raised here, and I learned a long time ago that we all get used to what we get used to.

Sometimes love just isn't enough. Sometimes so much more is needed, and I couldn't help wondering how long it was going to be before David flashed a news broadcast my heart wouldn't be able to handle. I guess I did still love him, but there were so many days when I honestly didn't like him at all. Not to mention that he obviously felt the same way about me.

I honestly didn't know what it was we needed to do to make things right again. But if it had anything to do with me swallowing my pride and forgetting about work altogether, that wasn't an option.

I just couldn't see myself doing that.

Not for him.

Not for any one person I could think of.

CHAPTER 2

I LEANED BACK in my chair and read the job announcement for the third time. I wasn't sure if I was expecting to read something different in comparison to what I'd read the first two times or not, but more than anything, I guess I was still debating whether I should even bother applying again. The fact was, I really did want a career in human resources, so I didn't see how I could possibly pass up this opportunity. Especially since the city of Mitchell only had five decent-sized, industrial corporations to begin with and opportunities like this only presented themselves on rare occasions. Actually, my company, Reed Meyers, a screw manufacturer, was the largest.

I skimmed the posting one last time and finally found the courage to go meet with Jim, vice president of human resources. I walked over to his office and knocked on his door, even though it was already open. He was sitting at his shiny mahogany desk, jotting down some notes inside what looked like an employee's folder.

"Hi, Anise, what can I do for you?"

He had a pleasant smile on his face.

"Can I speak to you for a minute?"

"Sure, come in and have a seat."

I closed his door before sitting down.

"Whoa," he said. "A closed-door meeting? This must be pretty serious."

"Somewhat," I said, wondering where and how I should begin.

"Everything is okay with work, isn't it?"

"Yes, everything is fine. But I do want to talk to you about the HR recruiting manager position that you're trying to fill."

Jim leaned back in his chair nonchalantly, staring at me and waiting to hear me continue.

"I know I applied for it six months ago, and now that Jason has decided to leave so quickly, I'd like to apply for it again."

"Well, I guess my only concern or question is whether this position is really the one you should be applying for. You seem to work so well with the people in the shop, and I think it has a lot to do with the fact that both your parents worked in factories. You really do know how to relate to these people. They love you, Anise, and I would hate to see you leave your current position in order to take one that may not be as rewarding."

I wanted to choke over what he'd just said. What did he mean, I knew how to relate to *these* people? And what in heaven's name did my parents' occupations have to do with my career in HR?

"The shop employees are wonderful, and I love working with them, but I came to Reed Meyers to work with all people. You know that I stressed my interest in recruiting the last time this position was open, so I've had more than enough time to think about my goals. Working with employee benefits is fine, but I'd also love working with potential employees who are interested in joining our company."

"Well, I still think you should be sure about what you want to do before submitting the official application. Because who knows, maybe Elizabeth's job will open up at some point, and you'd be interested in managing the benefits area instead. Or I can tell you right now that Frank Colletti is being groomed for a position in operations. He'll be the youngest VP the company has had in years, so while this information is strictly confidential, I wanted to share it with you so you know that his position will probably open up sometime in the near future."

What was he talking about? Hadn't he heard me say that I was interested in *this* position and not one that *might* become available? I couldn't believe he was still trying to persuade me to move in another direction. Then there was this comment about Frank Colletti being groomed. Frank was a gorgeous Italian, whom I liked a lot and had great respect for, but I didn't see how they could secretly decide that he deserved a top-management position. Especially since he worked in training. Yes, he was the director of training, but to my knowledge hadn't worked in any other areas of the company and didn't have a graduate degree. Not that he shouldn't be groomed for a better position, but why weren't they grooming other managers and directors inside the company along with him? Namely women. But it was my guess that they didn't think women belonged in VP positions either.

"I appreciate your suggestions about both the other departments, but what I really want is to apply for the recruiting position. So what I'll do is complete the internal application form and place it in your mail bin. Or better yet, I'll give it to your secretary," I said, letting him know that my decision was firm.

"It's your call, but I have to tell you that we're already considering two other employees for this promotion, and that we'll have no choice but to choose the best-qualified candidate when it's all said and done."

I stood up. "You know, Jim, that's all I'm hoping for."

He stared at me in silence as I walked out of his office.

Shortly afterward, Lorna caught up with me and followed me into my own office. She was the only true friend I had here at the company. My best friend Monica was my best friend in the whole world, but Lorna took close seconds.

"So what did that asshole Jim have to say," she asked, shutting my door and pushing her white blond hair away from her face. I'd told her first thing this morning that I was going to make my interest in the promotion known to Jim before lunchtime.

"He acted as much like a jerk as he always does, and he made it very clear that he doesn't think I should apply for the position," I said with disappointment, and while I hated admitting it, I felt like sobbing. My mom raised me to be a strong, confident woman, but this entire scenario was starting to wear on me emotionally. I didn't want anything that I didn't deserve, but what I did want was to be treated fairly. What I wanted was for Jim and Lyle to look past my color and gender, if that was the problem, so they could see me for the person I truly was. So they could see that I really was qualified to carry out the responsibilities of a manager in the highest possible capacity.

"Anise, I hope you're not going to let them get away with passing you over again. Enough is enough, and if they don't promote you, then they won't leave you with any other choice except to file a discrimination complaint with EEOC and a private attorney if you have to."

"I know, but I'm really hoping that I won't have to do that."

"You may not have a choice. And if you ask me, Jim, Lyle and the rest of their white-collar KKK buddies need to be brought to their knees."

I wasn't sure why Lorna was so upset, because even though she'd been vocal in the past about the way women and minorities were treated, she seemed completely outraged today.

"If I have to, I will, but I'm not going to consider any legal proceedings until after this selection process is over with," I agreed, trying to convince myself that everything was going to work out and that maybe I was worrying about nothing. "Oh, and before I forget, Jim insinuated that Frank might be getting promoted, so since you're the top training specialist, you'd be next in line for his job when he leaves it."

Lorna folded her arms and looked at me in silence. Something wasn't quite right, but I wasn't sure what was wrong with her. Especially since the possibility of being promoted should have been fabulous news to her.

"Anise, I've never told anyone what I'm about to tell you, but if what happened to me will make you go forward with filing a lawsuit, then it will be worth it for all of us."

"What? What are you talking about?" She'd piqued my curiosity.

"When I first came to Reed Meyers four years ago, Jim had just been transferred here from the Raleigh plant, but his wife stayed behind until their children finished the school year. Then, when she'd finally sold their home, she joined him five months after he'd gotten here."

"And?" I said, anxious to hear what she was getting at.

"He came on to me immediately, and when he found out that I wasn't interested in him, he started harassing me in other ways. Like the time I arrived at work ten minutes late, and he told me that if I couldn't get to work on time, then I should look for another place of employment. And, Anise, it was the first time I'd ever been late for work since I started here. Then he sat in on a training session that I did on time management, and contradicted every point I made to the class. But the worst part of all . . ." she said, pausing and swallowing hard. Then she took a deep breath. "The worst thing of all was when I worked late one evening compiling the new training manual. You know our offices are at opposite ends of the department, but he came down to my office when he realized I was still working. He made a couple of sexual comments as soon as he walked in, but I ignored him. But then he walked behind my desk and caressed my hair. He kept saying how beautiful my blond hair was, and then he started stroking it. I was so terrified, but I didn't move. I just kept praying that he would go back to his office and leave me alone. But he didn't. And . . ."

Lorna burst into tears, and I walked around and sat in the chair next to her. I pulled some tissue from the Kleenex box, handed it to her and then placed my arm around her shoulders. I couldn't believe what I was hearing. She and I had been close for a good while, but she'd never hinted at anything like this before. It bothered me that she was so shaken up, and I was afraid to hear the rest of the story.

She sniffled a few times and wiped her eyes. "This is so hard, Anise, but I can't keep this to myself any longer."

"And you don't have to. You know you can trust me with your life," I promised her.

"He went from stroking my hair to stroking the side of my face. Then he said he'd been more than patient with me, but that now it was time for me to stop playing games with him. He said he didn't like being teased, and that it was time for me to stop pretending I didn't want to be fucked. Tears rolled down my cheeks, so I closed my eyes. But when I did, I heard him opening the zipper to his pants. I begged him to stop, but he pulled his dick out and rubbed it across my lips. I tried to leave my seat, but he forced me back down in it. He told me that if I didn't open my mouth and do what I was told, that I wouldn't have a job to come to the next morning. But right when he finished telling me that, we both heard a door slamming shut on the opposite end, and he zipped his pants back up and left my office."

"Oh my God, Lorna. When was this?"

"Right before his wife moved here."

"Has he approached you again?"

"No, but he pretty much told me that since I wasn't willing to cooperate, I could forget about ever getting any promotions, and that if I tried to leave and go work for another company, he would make sure they knew how incompetent I was as an employee. And, Anise, I have a daughter to take care of. I don't have a master's degree like you, and it's not that easy being a single parent when your ex-husband deliberately misses child support payments just to punish you."

I was flabbergasted. Rarely was I speechless, but Lorna had told me something I never would have expected even from Jim. I'd heard how ruthless and conniving he could be, but I never would have pictured him harassing anyone sexually. The man was vice president of human resources, for God's sake.

"I can't believe he would stoop this low," I finally offered. "I am so sorry that you had to go through this, and I wish there was something I could do to help you."

"You can. I'm not as strong as you, Anise. But if you go forward with filing a discrimination lawsuit, I'll find the courage to tell EEOC and whoever else what Jim did to me. There's no way I can afford to lose my job, but if there is more than one of us making a complaint, they'll be afraid to fire either one of us."

Lorna had obviously analyzed this whole lawsuit situation very carefully, and while I heard what she was saying and believed wholeheartedly that she should go to the police and have Jim arrested, I was still hoping they'd give me my promotion. I didn't want to drive over to Chicago to visit EEOC or any other equal opportunity enforcement agency unless I absolutely had to. I was hoping that I'd get my job and be able to push all of this anger, frustration and humiliation behind me. I wanted Lorna to do the same, but I wasn't so sure she'd be able to forget about any of this until Jim had gotten what he had coming to him.

"That's probably true, although I think it'll be best to wait and see what happens with my situation first," I said. "But regardless of how things turn out, I think you still have to go to the police. And maybe you should even think about telling Lyle or Tom, too."

"If I go to the police, it'll be my word against his, and on top of that, they'll want to know why it took me four years to file charges. And if I go to Lyle or Tom, what difference is it going to make with both of them being friends with Jim? No, that's not the way to go. And while I know you won't want to hear this, I have to say what I honestly feel. There's no question that you are the most qualified person for that management position, but I really doubt that you're going to get it. I'm not trying to be negative or trying to undermine your confidence, but I know these men all too well. We can bring them down, though, Anise. You're a black woman who's being discriminated against because of her skin color and gender, and I'm a white woman who has been sexually harassed by an executive of this company. So it's not like they can say we're both screaming racial and gender discrimination or that we're both claiming that we've been sexually harassed and are being forced to work in a hostile working environment. We both have separate claims, and I'm willing to bet that if we both come forward, there will be others who'll find the courage to tell what has happened to them, too."

She had a point. Actually, a few good points, and I had to admit that she was right about what we were obligated to do. I'd already experienced discrimination at Bradford, the company I worked for prior to joining Reed Meyers, so if this was the same case here, I knew I'd have to help break the cycle. The evidence would be as obvious as Alaskan icicles if they denied me a second time, and now I knew I would have no choice but to file a complaint against the company if I wasn't promoted.

But how was David going to react to something like this? We hadn't spoken to each other this morning before leaving for work, but I was hoping that this latest blowup of ours would quickly pass. I couldn't deal with all the frustration here at work and at the same time participate in angry debates with him. What I needed was someone to talk to, someone to help me through these very trying times. I needed someone to be there for me tonight, and since I knew David wouldn't be home until late, I decided to call my girl Monica to see what she was up to. I was hoping she and her husband Marc didn't have anything important planned for the evening, which was a possibility, since their daughter had already finished finals at the private school she attended and had gone to Houston to spend part of the summer with Monica's parents.

But if Monica wasn't available, I would go visit Mom instead.

Mom was one of the few people who knew exactly what to say when times were tough.

It would be a blessing to spend time with either one of them.

CHAPTER 3

ONICA HAD ANSWERED my phone call on the second ring and told me that Marc would be teaching a continuing education course at one of the community centers this evening. So I'd driven straight home from work and changed into a pair of stonewashed jeans and a black T-shirt. Now, I was walking up her classic brick walkway, preparing to ring the doorbell. She must have seen me pull up, though, because she opened the door without delay.

"Hey, girl," she said, reaching out to hug me. We hadn't seen each other in maybe a couple of weeks, so I was elated to see her as well.

"Hey, how's it going?" I asked, embracing her.

"You know, things really couldn't be better, Anise," she said with no hesitation, because she really was experiencing a very joyous time in her life. She'd married Marc about a year ago, and he'd proven to be the most caring husband and stepfather I knew. She was truly living her life to the fullest, and it filled my heart to see her so happy. Life hadn't been the greatest when she was married to her first husband, so this made her even more appreciative of Marc.

"I'm so glad to hear that everything is going so well for you," I told her. "I wish I could say the same."

I hated always having such a woe-is-me sort of attitude whenever I spent time with Monica, but I couldn't help it. I just couldn't seem to find a positive way toward dealing with my problems.

"Why? What's going on?" she asked, giving me her full attention.

"What isn't? My marriage is still falling apart, and I'm pretty sure there's going to be extreme drama at work in the near future."

"Don't tell me they're trying to keep you from making manager again?"

"That's exactly what they're trying to do, and I'm worried about it because I'm not going to sit back and take it this time."

"Wait a minute. I want to hear the details regarding this, so let's go sit out on the patio," Monica said.

"That's fine."

"Do you want something to drink?" she asked, opening the refrigerator.

"I'll take some lemonade if you have it."

"We don't have any that's fresh-squeezed, but we do have some cans of Country Time."

"That's fine with me."

Monica grabbed two cans of pink lemonade, pulled two glass mugs from one of the cupboards and filled them with ice from the refrigerator's built-in ice dispenser. I scanned the recently remodeled kitchen, which was beautiful, but I couldn't help but wonder how we could be such close friends, see eye to eye on almost every social and personal issue, but have vastly different tastes in decorating. I was modern with a flair for anything that was contemporary, but she was strictly traditional. I loved exquisite leather, but she loved cloth of almost any texture. She purchased a ton of cherry wood pieces, but each of my wooden pieces showcased the new-washed look.

But no two people were the same, and that's what made the world a lot more interesting.

We strolled through the double-glass patio doors, sat our drinks down on a small table, and positioned our bodies on two matching chaises.

"So now. What exactly is Reed Meyers up to this time?" Monica asked.

"You remember that HR manager's position they didn't give me six months ago, right?"

"Yeah."

"Well, Jason has already given his notice and is leaving the company."

"You've got to be kidding? After only being a manager for six months?"

"Yep. So I took yesterday and today thinking about it, and figured I would go in and talk to Jim about applying for it again."

"And what did he say?"

"Girl, he was so discouraging and had the audacity to say that the reason I work so well with the shop people is because my parents worked in a factory environment. He actually said that's why I can relate to them."

"That's ridiculous."

"Don't I know it."

"Well, it's either the fact that he doesn't know any better or that he flat out believes he can make whatever racist comment he wants to. But either way, he has no right talking to you like that, nor does he have the right to deny you a promotion that you clearly do deserve."

"Oh, he knows better, but just doesn't care. They think I'm overstepping my boundary by trying to get into management. I'm good enough to work with factory employees, but not corporate managers or executives. And I'm telling you, Monica, I'm so sick of it I don't know what to do."

"I know and rightfully so."

"It's all so disturbing, and, girl, I actually lost sleep over this last night. Not to mention my issues with David."

"So I take it things still aren't better with him either?" Monica asked, because I'd been telling her about our marital problems for quite a few months now. She always looked at the bright side of most everything and kept insisting that things would eventually get better between us.

I wasn't so sure about any of that.

"No, they're not better at all, and when I got home from work yesterday, we ended up arguing like enemies. He just doesn't think my work issues are a big deal, and he made it pretty clear that he wants me to quit work, become the wife of some boring executive and have a baby."

Monica laughed quietly. "So you *did* tell him that you're never going to do that, right?

I couldn't help but laugh with her.

"No, and I don't think I will for a while, because not only does he want me to have a baby, but two years ago I heard him telling his brother that it's a wife's duty to have a child. He's so old school when it comes to marriage. But I'm not the type who could ever be happy sitting at home watching the housekeeper clean the house and wash our clothing every other day while he's gone, and then spend the rest of my day watching soap operas, talk shows or playing a game of bridge with the type of women he thinks I should mingle with. That's just not me, and there's no sense in me trying to pretend like it is."

"I hear what you're saying, but I think you need to be honest with him."

"I always have until this getting-pregnant business came up again. And really, having a baby wouldn't be that bad if we were still happily married the way we used to be. But all I keep thinking is how I'll give up my career, have a child or two, and then shortly thereafter he'll decide that he doesn't want to be with me any longer. Monthly child support payments just ain't somethin' I could learn to live with, and I think all children deserve much more than a part-time relationship with their father."

"But look at Tamia. She sees her father all the time, and Marc treats her like she's his own daughter."

"I know and that's wonderful. But you and I both know that Xavier and Marc are not the norm. They're like best friends, and that's why Tamia is such a happy child. She doesn't ever have to feel like she's without any of you. So if somebody could guarantee me that David would be there all the time for our children even if we divorced and would get along with my new husband, then that would be different."

"First of all, you shouldn't even be thinking about getting a divorce. You should look at your marriage as something permanent. Everybody has problems in their relationships, but nothing is too hard to work out."

Monica did this all the time. She saw everything as a fairy tale, and I always made it my business to point out why she was wrong in her thinking. This of course was one of my worst personality traits, proving people wrong, and the one thing she didn't like about me on most days. But nobody was without fault, and what mattered was that she still loved me like a sister, anyway.

Still, I couldn't resist making my next comment.

"Then why did you divorce Xavier, if marriage is supposed to be so permanent?" I asked, smiling.

"Whatever, Anise," she said, dismissing me.

"That's what I thought."

We both laughed until she spoke again.

"But seriously, you and David can work this out if you want to. It's not like either of you are sleeping around with other people, like Xavier was. And as far as I'm concerned, any other disagreement or problem can be fixed."

"Maybe. But who's to say whether it can be or not, because we both know every man isn't like Marc."

"No, I admit, he is a wonderful person. Almost too good to be true when I dwell on it for too long. Sometimes when he's sleeping, I stare at him and wonder what I did so great for God to bring him into my life. I don't think I've ever been happier, but the tough part about being this happy is that you spend at least a quick moment every day wondering when it's all going to blow up in your face."

"You shouldn't think that way, because we all deserve some happiness."

"I know, but every now and then, I can't help thinking about the fact that he had a drinking problem before I met him. He hasn't even drunk beer since I've been with him, but still, I sometimes worry about it."

"I can understand that, but you just have to believe that everything is going to be fine."

Monica opened her mouth to speak again, but the phone rang.

"Shoot, I forgot to bring out the cordless. I'll be right back," she said, darting into the house.

A warm breeze swept across my face, and I closed my eyes savoring the moment. I sighed when I thought about the problems in my life. If my grandmother were still alive, she'd tell me to say, "Hallelujah anyhow." She'd tell me that I should stop complaining and thank God for waking me up in my right mind, for giving me all the necessities I need to survive and for keeping me in good health. Which I did all the time, because I was extremely gracious toward His blessings. But even though I wholeheartedly believed that God never placed any more on us than we could bear, it really was starting to feel like it. I was so terribly overwhelmed, and for the most part, just plain miserable. I kept asking myself what happened to the life I lived barely two years ago. I wasn't having much success with my career back then either, but at least I'd just started a new position at Reed Meyers, and David and I were happier than ever. We did everything together, and we took more trips to Jamaica, Mexico, and Hawaii in one year than most couples did in a lifetime. Then I became consumed with trying to get ahead in the business world, and David started working much longer hours, sometimes calling to say it was too late to drive all the way home, and that it would be more convenient to grab a hotel room instead. His company was generous enough to pay for it, but I noticed that his overnight stays in Chicago eventually became more frequent as time went on and his two-day business trips turned into weeklong conferences. I'd questioned him a number of times about how limited his time was at home, but he always responded by telling me that traveling was part of the business, and that he had no choice in the matter.

I didn't know whether he was telling the truth or whether he used those excuses as a means to disguise what he was really up to. I knew he was upset about my not getting pregnant, but it just seemed to me that there was something else bothering him. Like there was something or someone else distracting him. Maybe it was just my imagination or maybe even the guilt I kept feeling for not doing everything I could as a wife to make him happy. But I couldn't avoid the fact that he wasn't being the best husband either. The least he could do was give me the support any husband should give any career-oriented wife who was possibly being shafted by her employer. I had basically remained the same in terms of my values and morals in life. He, however, had changed completely with this whole why-can't-I-be-white mentality, and I didn't see how I could ever get used to it, now or in the future. But maybe he'd be willing to change if I calmly explained how derogatory his thinking was. Maybe I needed to spend more time focusing on my own faults as well and doing everything I could to try and be a better wife. Maybe it was time I stopped dwelling on my career issues for a while and spent more time acknowledging what David needed as my husband.

Monica stepped back onto the patio with the cordless phone in one hand and closed the door with the other. She laid the phone near our drinking glasses and eased her body back down on the chaise.

"That was Mom calling," she said.

"Really? How are she and your father doing?"

"They're both fine, and from what it sounds like, they're spoiling Tamia worse than they did last year. Which means she'll have to be brought down to the proper level when she returns home. They let her get away with murder, and somehow she fixes her little mind to think that the rules are the same here in Mitchell."

I laughed because I remembered doing the same thing as a child when I visited my grandparents.

"You know how it is when grandchildren spend time with their grandparents," I said. "It's hilarious if you ask me."

"Yeah, because you were probably one of those same brats yourself."

"You're right, and I must say I'm proud of it."

We laughed and continued talking about everything imaginable. We enjoyed our time together, and I hated when the sun finally rested to the west of us, because it meant I had to go home and face David. It meant I had to prepare for another awkward evening in my own household. But there was no sense in trying to prevent the inevitable.

So I went home and vowed to do all I could to make things right between us.

It wasn't even nine, but surprisingly, David was already home. When I walked into the kitchen from the garage, he was sitting at the wrought-iron-trimmed breakfast table eating ice cream. I glanced at him and then away, unsure if he was still angry.

I sat my purse on the island the way I always did when I arrived home and turned toward the hallway leading to our bedroom. My first thought was to ignore him, but my heart was too heavy to continue this silent combat we were unnecessarily engaged in.

"Hello, David," I said, stopping in front of him.

"Hi." He spooned another helping of ice cream from the bowl in front of him.

"David, how long are we going to go on like this?" I asked.

"Go on like what?"

"Like this. Giving each other the silent treatment, arguing like we hate each other, and not spending any quality time together."

"I don't know. You tell me."

He wasn't helping the situation in the least.

"I know we don't agree on a lot of things, and that we've grown somewhat apart, but I don't want us to continue like this. I want things to be better between us. I'm miserable all the time, and I'm tired of feeling all this pain."

He looked at me but didn't respond.

"Don't you have anything to say?"

"Not really, because every time we have a conversation, it always turns into a sparring match. So what's the point?"

"The point is that I'm tired of going through this day in and day out. I'm having all these problems at work, and then I come home to either an empty bed or an argument with you. And I'm telling you, David, it's becoming way too much for me to deal with. Sometimes I feel like I want to scream or like I'm having a nervous breakdown. I feel like everyone is against me. I know you don't understand my job situation, but I'm still your wife, and the least you could do is be here for me," I said with tears in my eyes. "Do you hear what I'm saying, David?"

"I'm sorry." He stood and walked toward me. "I'm really sorry."

He pulled me into his arms, and I cried the way I'd wanted to for weeks. It felt good being held by my husband, the man I'd been so happy with and so in love with in the beginning. I wished we could erase all the disagreeable moments we'd shared and start our marriage from scratch. I wished we could make things better than they ever were.

I lifted my head from his shoulder and gazed into his eyes. "David, I don't want us to continue the way we are, because I do still love you. I know it may not seem like it, but I do. I need you more than you realize, and I need you to love me back."

He was speechless, but he looked at me in the most genuine way. Then he rested the palms of his hands, one on each side of my face, and kissed me. I tried to remember the last time we'd been this intimate, but I couldn't.

He kissed me aggressively, almost like he wanted me to know he was in control, and I loved every second of it. We'd been struggling against each other for so long that I'd forgotten what it was like to be with my own husband. I'd forgotten what it was like to be with a member of the opposite sex.

Finally, he pulled away, took my hand and led me into our bedroom. I kicked off my sandals, and he pulled my T-shirt over my head, unsnapped my bra and kissed my lips again. I pushed down his khaki shorts and removed his polo shirt. We kissed erotically for a long time, until he leaned my body back onto the bed and removed the jeans and satin underwear I was wearing. He kissed me passionately again, and I moaned when he took one of my breasts into his mouth and massaged the nipple of the other. He pushed both my legs above my chest and eased inside me. He stroked in and out of me, maybe six or seven times, and then he bellowed with pleasure almost instantly. We both breathed deeply. Him, from having the orgasm he'd just experienced, and me from trying to have one myself, before it was too late. I was somewhat disappointed, but tonight I was just happy to feel so close to the man I was married to.

David rested on top of me for a few minutes and then pecked me on the lips. "It's really been a long time, hasn't it?" he asked, smiling.

"Too long. Way too long for two people who are married."

"All I can say is that I'm sorry."

"I'm sorry, too. And more than anything, I want to try and save our marriage. We both have things we need to change, and no matter what's going on with our careers, we have to make a conscious effort toward spending more time together."

"I agree."

"Maybe we should take a trip somewhere," I suggested.

"Maybe. Maybe we can plan something for next month."

"I'll check with our company's travel service tomorrow."

David moved his body to my side, and I laid my head on his chest. He caressed the top of my head in silence for a long while, and I could tell he was deep in thought. But I didn't say anything because I didn't want to spoil the moment. I felt more relaxed than I had in months, and I was thankful that we both wanted to reconcile and keep our marriage intact. We'd been through a lot and would have to work hard to fix things between us, but I was willing to do whatever it took. I was independent and, yes, even stubborn at times, but I wanted to make David happy again. I wanted to be more like the wife he wanted me to be. I wanted our relationship to exceed both our expectations.

We held each other close, and I finally spoke.

"I love you, David."

"I love you, too, and more than anything, I want you to know how sorry I am for everything," he said, sounding more apologetic than I'd ever heard him in the past.

"I'm sorry, too," I said, and raised my head to look at him.

Then I kissed him like it was our final opportunity to be together. Because from this moment on, I wanted us to live each day as if it was our last.

CHAPTER 4

DAVID HAD LEFT bright and early this morning, and while I wanted to take a hot, soothing bath in the Jacuzzi, I settled for a shower because I was running late. We'd held each other most of the night, and it felt good being able to sleep hour after hour without tossing and turning with anger and worry. Lately, David had been turning his back to me and sleeping so close to the edge of the bed that a tiny tap on his back would have sent him crashing to the floor.

There were many mornings when he hadn't even told me he was leaving, and the only way I knew was that I heard the security system beep three times when he opened the door separating the garage and kitchen. Something he never would have done a year ago, because he always kissed me before going out. He'd been acting almost like he didn't have a wife, like he lived alone, like I didn't even exist. I'd felt so empty without him, and I hadn't been sure how much longer I'd be able to tolerate his hurtful rages of silence. But things were finally changing, and I couldn't have been happier. I couldn't wait to schedule our much needed getaway to wherever.

I finished drying myself from shoulders to toes, smoothed roasted hazelnut lotion across my body and sprayed on a splash made of the same scent. In my walk-in closet, I pulled out my navy blue skirt suit. I'd decided last night that today would be the day I completed the job bidding form, printed a copy of my résumé outlining all of my in-house accomplishments and submitted my official application package to Jim. I knew he wasn't going to be happy, but he would just have to deal with it. There was a chance that things were going to get ugly, but I decided that somehow, it was going to be well worth it in the end. The way I saw it, there were only two ways to go with this. They could either promote me or give the job to someone less qualified, and I could either be happy with their decision or file a discrimination lawsuit against them if they didn't do what was right. I preferred an amicable outcome, but I was willing to fight Jim, his supervisor, Lyle, and Reed Meyers all the way to the finish line if I had to.

Traffic wasn't as bad as I'd expected, so I ended up arriving at work just before seven. I sat in my office reviewing everything on today's agenda, and prepared my application package for Jim. Then I knocked on my supervisor's door so I could inform her about my interest in another area.

"Come in, Anise," Elizabeth Weeks instructed, and beckoned with her hand. "I'm on hold with my bank, but it shouldn't take too long for me to finish up with them."

"No problem," I told her, and sat down in one of the chairs in front of her desk.

"Well, can you send me a copy of last month's statement, because I never received it," she said when the bank representative returned to the line.

She paused for a few seconds as she listened to the person she was speaking with and then said, "Thank you for your help, and I look forward to receiving it in the mail."

"Good customer service people are obviously very hard to find," she said as she hung up the phone.

I laughed, but didn't comment one way or the other because I remembered being in customer service during college, and while there were some incompetent representatives, there were just as many irate customers who jumped the gun before allowing us to do our jobs. Some callers never even allowed you to hear what their question or complaint was, which made it hard for us to give the best possible service.

"So what's going on these days?" Elizabeth asked. "I hear you're interested in the HR recruiting manager's position."

"Well, I was hoping to have a chance to tell you about it myself, but I see Jim already beat me to it."

"He didn't say much, but he did tell me that you came to his office to discuss your interest in it."

"I thought about it all yesterday, and I've decided that I am going to apply for it again. I really hoped that I would get it six months ago, but without going into any of that, I feel like I should try for it again."

"I don't see anything wrong with you trying to get promoted, but what I do want is for you to make sure that you want to report to Jim Kyle. I've reported to him the whole time I've been here, and just between you and me, he's not the easiest person to work for. He's a perfectionist, but the worse thing about him is that he hates women. And please don't think I'm trying to be offensive, but he's not too fond of any person who's not the same color as him."

I was really shocked to hear Elizabeth confess to me what she knew about Jim. But, I must admit that from the first day I met Elizabeth during my interview and as soon as I was hired and began working for her, it became evident that she didn't have a racist bone in her body. She saw my credentials for what they were, and it never mattered to her that I was African-American. I appreciated her kindness and how fair she was to me as an individual, and while I hadn't thought too much about it before today, it was going to be hard leaving her department and going to work for the likes of Jim.

"I know he's not the most honorable person in the world, but I can't let him stop me from going after the job I really want. I've always wanted to be a recruiter, and I know I deserve to be promoted into management. I'm not sure how this is all going to work out, but I have to go with what I feel."

"I totally understand, and you have my blessings. You are an outstanding employee, so of course I would hate to lose you, but I would never try to stand in your way when it comes to getting ahead."

"I really appreciate hearing you say that, and I want to thank you for being one of the best supervisors I have ever had."

Elizabeth smiled at me.

"Well, I guess that's it, and what I'm going to do now is take the application material over to Jim. I'd told him that I would place them in his in basket, but if he's in his office, I'm going to give them to him personally."

"Good luck," Elizabeth said.

"Thanks," I said, and left her office.

Jim's door was closed, so I asked his secretary if he was with someone. She told me no, called him on the phone to let him know I needed to speak to him and then said I could walk right in.

"So how are things going, Anise?" he said, smiling.

I didn't know if he was being sincere or not, but I was going to keep an open mind like David suggested.

"Everything is fine, but I just wanted to bring you my bidding form and résumé personally."

"So you're going against my advice and applying for that corporate management position, huh?" he asked, but wasn't smiling the way he'd been at first.

"Yes," I responded. "I am applying for it."

What I wanted to ask him was why he had such a problem with considering me for a management position. I wanted to make him see that I was more than capable of doing a good job if he gave me a chance.

But I stood in silence, trying to show him some respect.

He leaned forward, rested his arms on his desk and said, "Well, it's like I told you yesterday, this is your choice, but we will still have to offer the job to the most qualified candidate."

"I totally understand that, and I would never expect you to give me something I don't deserve. I know you didn't think I was the most qualified a few months ago, but I really hope that you and Lyle will take my educational background and work experience into consideration this time," I said as calmly as possible.

"I guarantee you, we'll be considering each applicant in the same manner." He spoke with slight irritation. "And since we want to start the interview process sometime next week, I'm sure my secretary will be calling you to schedule a time fairly soon."

"I really appreciate you considering me," I said, and left.

Not twenty minutes after I returned to my office, I received a phone call from Lyle asking me if I had a few moments to meet with him. Which was strange, because it wasn't often that any person in the company heard from the vice president of operations directly. He would ask his executive assistant to get someone on the phone or summon someone to his office from time to time, but he never made direct contact himself.

As I hurried through the benefits, training and corporate recruiting departments, in that order, I passed Jim's office and headed down the long hallway that led to the executive offices. Jim was an executive, too, but it made better sense to have his office at the end of HR and not completely in the same area where the other VPs and executives were located. The recruiting area for factory employees was at the exact opposite end of the department, just past my office, so he had access to it as well.

I felt somewhat uneasy about meeting with Lyle, not because he made me nervous, but because I didn't want to confront him in a knock-down-drag-out argument. I was tired of explaining

myself to the powers that be, and this whole scenario was grow-
ing old.

I walked up to his executive assistant's desk, but before I could
speak she said, "Lyle is expecting you, so please go right in." She
had a beautiful smile and was dressed in the most professional red
suit I'd seen in a long while. Which meant she hadn't purchased it
here in Mitchell. It looked more like something you could find in
stores on Michigan or State in Chicago or in one of the better malls
in the suburbs.

"Thank you," I said, smiling. "Your suit is absolutely gor-
geous."

"Well, thank you," she said, and I walked into Lyle's office.

"Close the door, please," he said with the same pleasant smile as
Jim. I couldn't tell if his was genuine either, but I knew I'd find out
in a matter of seconds.

I did what he told me and took a seat in front of him. "You
wanted to see me?"

"Yes, I did. Jim called to let me know that you were applying for
the corporate recruiting manager's position, and I wanted to speak
to you about it."

I listened but didn't respond. I wasn't sure what he expected me
to say.

"I know you applied for it six months ago as well, and we ended
up giving it to Jason. And now this time, we're going to be in the
same situation of having to review the qualifications of each candi-
date so that we can make the right decision."

I nodded my head in agreement but still didn't speak.

"Jim said that he mentioned the benefits manager position and
that Frank Colletti might be promoted from his training director
position in the very near future. I know you told him that you
weren't interested in either one, but I really wish you would rethink
your decision, because we would have no problem with moving you
into either one of those slots. I'm not telling you that you *might* get

one or the other, I'm telling you that you would without question. We'd still have to go through the normal posting and bidding process for other internal candidates who might be interested, but those are just technicalities."

I wanted to laugh out loud. I couldn't believe Lyle was sitting here admitting that they decided who they wanted in a certain position before they even knew who was going to apply for it. They did it when they passed me over six months ago, and now they were scheming and trying to figure out a way to give the corporate recruiting job to someone else—not to mention their plan to get me into a position that wasn't even available.

I gazed at him waiting for him to continue, but he didn't.

So I took the plunge and said, "I've already made my position very clear with Jim, and while I appreciate your offer, I'm really not interested in managing the benefits department. And even if I were, Elizabeth has never mentioned one word about wanting to leave Reed Meyers or about applying for another position within the company. And as far as running the training department, I have no interest in that either. What I want is to be a recruiting manager who's responsible for recruiting salaried professionals and executives. I've wanted to do that for a long time."

"Well, there are two HR specialists who do quite a bit of recruiting for clerical openings and professional positions, so it's not like you'll spend your entire day recruiting employees."

"No, but I'll be supervising everything that those specialists do, and I'll be completely responsible for all management and executive recruiting."

"But you've worked in benefits the entire two and a half years you've been here. And if I might add, you've done a helluva fine job the entire time."

"Thank you, but if you're so happy with my performance, Lyle, then why don't you think I'm capable of doing the same in recruiting?"

I was becoming a bit agitated, and I could tell he was surprised at my expression and tone.

"There's no need to get upset, Anise. I'm just trying to get you to see my point. I don't want you thinking that the only way you're going to move up to management is to apply for the first management position you see posted."

I refused to make any further comments because I couldn't guarantee what I might say next. Whatever it was, though, I didn't think it would be something Lyle wanted to hear.

He leaned back into his chair and folded his arms across his chest. "All I'm asking is that you take a couple of days to think about this."

"I appreciate you offering to give me more time, but I don't think I need it. I've already given my application to Jim, and I thought that was all I needed to do."

"We're not trying to be the enemy here, Anise. What we want is for you to make the best career choice. We want you to be happy with whatever job you have, and it just seemed like benefits or training might be better departments for you to manage."

"I appreciate your concern, but corporate recruiting is really what I want to do," I said as pleasantly as I could.

"Then that's all I needed to know. We'll be doing interviews next week, and shortly after that we'll be offering the job to the most qualified person, which just might be you," he said, smiling.

I didn't know why he seemed to be having such a change of heart, but I was happy about it just the same.

"All I want is to be given a fair chance, Lyle. That's all. And like I told Jim, I would never expect you to promote me into a position that I'm not qualified for."

"I'm glad you feel that way," he said. "And I hope you know that the only reason I asked you to come see me was because I wanted to be sure that you wanted this job for the right reasons. At first, I thought you were just looking to be promoted to any management position, but now I realize that your interests really do lie with recruiting."

"I really appreciate hearing that."

"Thanks for coming, and we'll be in touch," he said.

I turned and walked out of his office feeling somewhat better than I thought I would. I still couldn't be sure of what was going to happen, but I was hoping for the best.

I prayed that Jim would have a change of heart the same as Lyle had.

CHAPTER 5

AVID HAD CALLED MY OFFICE to say he wouldn't be home until late, so Lorna and I made last-minute dinner plans and decided to meet at Antonio's after work. Normally, advance reservations were required, especially on a Thursday night, but fortunately Lorna knew the owner's wife, and we were seated as soon as we arrived.

I loved this restaurant—the atmosphere and the food. The entryway's focal point was a mesmerizing waterfall surrounded by beautiful multicolored stone. The marble flooring was something I wished David and I had chosen for our own foyer at home. It was the one place residents always chose whenever they wanted to impress someone visiting Mitchell. They specialized in Italian food, but they also served the best steaks in town.

We scanned our menus by candlelight, and I decided on the rib eye. Lorna had vowed to give up red meat two months ago, so she ordered meatless baked lasagna instead. Now we were eating fresh tossed salad covered with ranch dressing.

"So Lyle turned soft on you, huh?" Lorna asked, slightly chuckling.

"I wouldn't say that, but I really think he understood where I was coming from."

"Maybe. But I still wouldn't let my guard all the way down, because both Jim and Lyle have been known to say one thing and then do another. Especially Jim."

"I realize that, but I'm trying my best to stay positive."

"But what if you don't get the job? What if they give it to someone who isn't more qualified than you all over again?"

"Then we're going to have a problem, because I do know what my rights are. And if they force me to, I'll do everything in my power to exercise them legally."

"Good for you, because I have a strange feeling that you're going to have to."

"I hear what you're saying, and even though I know you don't think Lyle and Jim are on the up-and-up, I still have to stay hopeful. I mean, it's not that I'm trying to dismiss what you've been telling me, but if I don't stay open to all possibilities, I'm going to worry myself crazy."

"I understand, but I just want you to be aware of how they tend to operate, Anise. I feel bad about you having to deal with this crap all over again, but you've got to be prepared for what we both know might happen with this."

"Yeah, but I guess I'd like to know who they could possibly give it to besides me. Because I know they wouldn't have the audacity to hire someone outside the company."

"Maybe not, but I heard from Jim's secretary that Kelli Jacobson is one of the people who applied for it."

"What!" I said, louder than I should have. The couple sitting at the next table glanced over at me, and I felt somewhat embarrassed.

"Yep. She did. And another gal over in public relations submitted a bidding form yesterday."

"How can they even consider Kelli when she started out as an HR assistant doing strictly clerical work? And even though she's an HR specialist for corporate benefits, she's only been doing that for one year."

"I know, but if I had to guess, I'd say the job is as good as hers if she wants it."

"But how? I know she's been with the company for four years, but two of those years were clerical. And even though she spent her third year working as an HR coordinator, she worked more closely with training and special events than she did anything else."

Lorna raised her eyebrows and said, "But do you really think any of that is going to mean a damn thing when it comes to Jim and Lyle's final decision? They'll find a way to justify giving it to her no matter what. I've seen them do it too many other times, and you saw it firsthand when they gave that job to Jason over you."

"But why in the world would they do that? And how can they just keep getting away with it?"

"They won't after this. Not after you sue their bigoted asses."

I took a sip of ice water from the long-stemmed crystal goblet and sat it back down on the table. I was outraged. I knew both Jim and Lyle had made it pretty clear that they would have to promote the most qualified candidate, but deep down I wanted to believe that person was me. It had to be if we were talking about educational background and previous work experience. But hearing Lorna tell me that Kelli Jacobson was in the running placed me just a bit on edge.

"And wait a minute," I said. "What college or university did she graduate from?"

"Well, I know she has a one-year secretarial certificate from Mitchell Community College, but I think that's it."

I laughed like a confused madwoman. But nothing was the slightest bit funny.

"I know," Lorna continued. "But the thing with Kelli is that she's kissed mega ass since the first day she started working at Reed

Meyers. She agrees with any and every thing Jim has to say, and I've seen her do it with Elizabeth, too. Hell, Elizabeth is the person that you and she both report to, but you'd swear she reports directly to Jim with as much time as she spends smiling in his face."

"You think they're messing around?"

"Who's to say, but Kelli is barely one cubic centimeter from being poor white trash, so I really don't think so."

I smiled because it always amazed me when I heard Lorna and some of my other white friends label someone as poor white trash, and I was equally amazed when we as black people called certain African-Americans the word nigger. The latter was even more interesting, because we'd fought for more than a century trying to prevent all other nationalities from calling us that. But with everything I could think of, there were always unwritten laws and tiny exceptions to every rule.

"I still don't see how they could just give it to her, because it says right on the job posting that nondegreed applicants must have five years of solid HR experience. And I don't see where two years of clerical work can be counted as solid anything when we're talking about a managerial position. Plus, she's only been with the company four years."

Lorna reached across the pure white linen tablecloth and covered my hand with her own. "Anise? Honey? We could go on and on about this for the rest of the evening, but it's not going to change anything. I'm not in a position to make any waves, but what I do know is that you have to start planning your recourse. You can't dwell on Kelli Jacobson or that job. You've got to figure out a way to bypass the emotional aspects of this and start speaking with an attorney."

"I just can't do that. Not yet, anyway, because I really feel like I have to give them the benefit of the doubt until they make their decision. And it's not like I'm overly anxious to go to court anyhow. As a matter of fact, I've never had to go to court for anything except a traffic ticket," I said, sighing with much grief.

The waiter refilled our water glasses and removed our almost empty salad plates.

"More rolls?" he asked in a deep voice that reminded me of a guy I went to college with.

"No, not for me," I answered.

"I'm fine as well," Lorna added.

"Just let me know if you need anything, and your dinners will be out shortly."

"Thank you," Lorna told him with a flirtatious look on her face. He smiled and walked away.

"Wouldn't you like to get wild on a Saturday night with him?" she asked me, laughing.

"Please. I guess he looks good enough, but I'm a married woman, remember?"

"Too bad for you. Because I'd love to teach him a few things or two."

We both cracked up.

"He looks like he just stopped nursing from his mother, if you ask me," I teased.

"Yeah, and that's why it would be so easy to train him. You can make them do all the right things in all the right places when they haven't been out in the world for too long."

"Train them to your own liking, huh?" I said, encouraging her.

"That's right."

"You're a mess," I said, but I wondered how Lorna could be so outgoing and so open when it came to desiring certain men—well, actually a lot of them—but seemed terrified when she'd told me about her run-in with Jim. I understood how she might have been afraid when the incident actually occurred, but I just couldn't see her keeping quiet about it. But maybe I really didn't understand as well as I thought I did and had no right judging her, since I'd never been sexually harassed myself.

We finished our meals and discussed everything from her

fourteen-year-old daughter to the fact that she really hadn't been happy for a good number of years. She talked about wanting to find a man who loved her and her daughter and one who would be committed for life. She'd dated a ton of no-goods, and was starting to believe that there wasn't much else to choose from. I insisted there was, and tried to make her realize that timing had a lot to do with everything. Some people were happier early in their lives and miserable later, while others were just the opposite. But regardless, there were going to be some bad times that we all had to deal with whether we wanted to or not.

When the waiter left the check, I looked at the total and slid fifty dollars inside the leather folder. Then we walked out to our vehicles, said our good-byes and drove away from the parking lot.

I wondered if David had arrived home yet, but my question was quickly answered when I opened the garage and saw that his Escalade was nowhere in sight. Working late was part of his normal schedule, and it wasn't like he hadn't called to inform me, but I was still hoping he'd be home somewhat earlier tonight. It was only after eight-thirty, and since there were times when he didn't arrive home until after ten o'clock, I knew I had to be patient.

I disarmed the security system, closed the door behind me and went down the hallway to our bedroom. I sighed when I realized I'd forgotten to grab the mail from the mailbox, and dreaded walking down the long driveway to get it. Still, I removed my suit, threw on a pair of lounging pants with a matching shirt and prepared to go retrieve it. But first, I lit five peach-scented candles, three across the dresser and one on each nightstand. When I finished, I removed all eight decorative pillows from our bed and neatly pulled back the comforter. I knew David would be tired after working so many hours and from driving home, so I decided the least I could do was create a relaxed atmosphere for him. We'd shared such a peaceful evening the night before, and now I wanted to continue in that mode indefinitely.

When I remembered the mail again, I opened the door and stepped onto the front porch, but halted when I heard David turning off his ignition inside the garage. I hadn't even heard the garage door opening while I was inside, but that wasn't unusual, since the garage and our bedroom were on completely different sides of the house. I wanted to start the evening off right with him, so I decided to go offer my wifely greeting before he came into the house.

But as I moved closer, with no shoes on, I could hear him talking. I hadn't heard him slam any doors shut, so I assumed he was still sitting inside the truck with his windows down, because the closer I walked toward him, the more audible his conversation became.

I stopped dead in my tracks when I heard him say, "I wish I could have stayed longer too, because you know I really enjoy being with you. We understand each other, and I appreciate that." Then he paused for a minute, I assumed waiting for the other party to speak, but for me, time stopped completely. I didn't know if it was that I couldn't believe what I was hearing, or if what I was hearing was unbelievable. I really couldn't decide one way or the other, and while I contemplated back and forth, he spoke again.

"Yeah, she's here, but she doesn't know I'm home yet. And I really hate having to face her, because I don't want this reconciliation she's all of a sudden pushing for. I tried pretending like I did, but there's no way I can keep doing that."

He paused again.

I stood there stifled, unable to move an inch.

"I really want to," he continued. "Believe me, I do. But you know I can't just walk out on her that easily. Things like this take time when there's so much property involved. And it's like I told you tonight, it would be much better for me if she leaves, or if she is the one who files for a divorce. But now, she's making things harder by wanting us to work things out. And in all honesty, I don't know what's come over her."

"You might as well tell your *bitch* that she can forget about me leaving or filing for a divorce," I said, walking inside the garage where he was sitting.

He flinched sharply when he turned and saw me, and it was obvious that he didn't know whom to speak to next. Me? Or the whore he was having an affair with.

"Damn," he said. "I've gotta go, okay?"

"Oh, so now you need some bitch's permission to hang up your own goddamn phone?" I yelled as loud as I could.

"Anise, please."

"Please my ass, David. You were stupid enough to get caught, so why don't you deal with this like a man?"

He unlatched his door and tried to open it.

But I shoved it back closed.

"Why are you being so childish?" he asked in frustration.

"Childish? You're the one sneaking around like a child with some other woman."

He sighed deeply. "Are you going to let me out or not?" he asked.

"Yeah, you can get out all right. And while you're at it, you can pack every goddamn thing you own and move your ass out of this house altogether," I screamed, and walked out to the street to pull out the mail. It seemed silly, but that was the real reason I'd come outside in the first place.

When I arrived back inside, I closed the front door, stormed into the bedroom, dropped the mail inside the armoire and started in on him again.

"So how long has this shit been going on, David?"

"Long enough," he answered boldly.

"Oh, really now? And when exactly were you planning to tell me about it?"

"When it was necessary, I guess."

I laughed like I was deranged. "When it was *necessary*? You are so damn full of it, you know that?"

"Look, all I can say is that I'm sorry. But before you continue on this rampage, I want you to know right now that I love her, and that I'm not about to stop seeing her."

My body went numb.

I wanted to know the identity of this person who had snatched my husband from me without my knowing it. I wanted to know why he'd made love to me when he knew he wanted someone else.

"Who is she, David?"

I waited for him to say something, anything. But all he did was stare back and forth between me and the suit he was hanging up.

At that moment, I wished I had never laid eyes on him a day in my life. I knew our marriage had been falling apart, but I didn't think David would actually go this far. I had my faults, some that really needed to be worked on, but nothing should have been so terrible that he sought comfort in someone else's bed. Especially since he'd just made love to me the night before. I was so hurt over what I'd just learned, but in a sense, I had been aware all along of those unusually long business trips and late-night meetings. Maybe I had believed what I wanted and hadn't taken the time or energy to notice what any intelligent wife should have known by instinct.

He slipped on his pajama bottoms and strutted toward the bed. I was disturbed by the thought of another woman holding him. Consoling him. Making love to him. The fact that he was no longer exclusively mine, suddenly made me ill.

I didn't know if my pain was a result of him messing around or the fact that he'd gotten away with it for so long without me knowing. I did love David, but the truth is, I really hadn't liked him as a person for quite some time. Maybe I was only hurt because no human being ever wanted to be replaced under any circumstances. But I was still hurt just the same.

When I heard the phone ring, I glanced toward my nightstand but didn't bother answering it. David didn't look in that direction or at me. Instead, he pulled the covers back and climbed onto the pillow-top mattress we'd made love on barely twenty-four hours before.

I didn't say another word to him, because I didn't see what else there was we should say. Not to mention the fact that I was smothered in a blinding state of shock. I didn't see why we should argue about someone I didn't know or someone he wasn't planning to give up.

I didn't see a reason to shed tears or continue throwing a fit.

I decided I would wait for him to tell me when he was leaving and exactly when I should expect the divorce papers in the mail. I decided that this was the best way to handle everything without going insane, and the best way to prevent myself from doing something unthinkable.

But who was I kidding? Because there was no way I could continue sharing a bed with a man who had voluntarily betrayed me.

"You know, David? What I want you to do is get your shit, and get the hell out of this house. Not tomorrow, not next week, but right now."

He looked at me like he didn't recognize who I was. His mouth hung wide open in total astonishment.

"What do you mean, you want me to get out?"

"I mean exactly what I said. I want you out."

"And you think just because *you* want me out, I'm actually going to go?"

"No. Because, actually, *you* don't have to do anything you don't want to. But I think you should know that your life is going to be in terrible danger the very moment you drop off to sleep," I said, glaring at him with no sign of sanity.

"You don't scare me one bit, Anise," he said, throwing the bedcovers away from his body and stepping onto the carpet. "But just so I don't have to deal with your ignorance for the rest of the evening, I'm going to spend the night elsewhere."

"Yeah, that's what I thought. And if you want the rest of your things, I suggest you get them out of here while I'm at work. That way I won't have to see your sorry ass."

"Whatever, Anise."

"As a matter of fact, I want them out of here by the end of this week."

"Look," he said. "I'll get my things out of here on my own terms and not a minute sooner."

"Suit yourself," I said, walking past him and into the bathroom. "But if I were you, I would get them out before something bad happens to them."

"Just try it, Anise. You hear me," he said, coming down the hall toward me. "Because if you try to destroy anything of mine, you'll regret it for the rest of your life."

I stared at him in a rage I'd never felt in the past, and before I had time to think, I took both my hands and swept every toiletry from the top of his vanity onto the floor.

Glass shattered everywhere, and I could tell he wanted to strangle me.

"What the hell is wrong with you?" he yelled. "Have you lost your fuckin' mind?"

"No, I haven't lost anything, but if you don't get out of my sight, more than this is going to happen."

"You know what? I'm not even going to stoop to your level of idiocy, because all this means is that you're hurt. You're hurt because I don't want your black ass anymore," he said, and then walked away.

I would never admit it to him, but he was right. His words and adulterous actions had cut me right down to the bone, but I knew I had to be strong in his presence. I knew there would be more than enough time for me to fret when he was gone.

He threw a few pieces of clothing into a duffel bag, threw on a nylon sweat suit, picked up his briefcase and walked out of the bedroom. I didn't follow behind him, but soon after, I heard him open the back door and then back out of the driveway.

I sat down on the edge of the bed in deep thought. I wasn't sure exactly what to think or how to feel at this very moment, but I knew it was best for David to leave. I knew it was better for us to keep our distance for the time being, and that our marriage was probably over for good. Of course, there were couples who separated and eventually reconciled. But somehow I knew we wouldn't fall into that category.

I knew that there was no chance we'd be getting back together.

It was simply a fact.

CHAPTER 6

WOODFIELD MALL was as busy as always for a Friday afternoon. Mom and I had left Mitchell not even an hour ago, but were now driving around the parking lot searching for a place to park. We were willing to walk as far as we had to, but there weren't any open spaces that would accommodate us. So finally I decided to wait at the beginning of any aisle until someone was ready to leave. We sat for a couple of minutes until a middle-aged woman and two teenage girls entered their car. They pulled out, we pulled in, left the vehicle and headed toward Marshall Field's lower-level entrance.

I'd gone to work at 7:00 A.M., but with everything that had happened last night with David, coupled with this constant worry I had about my career, I'd asked Elizabeth if it was okay for me to take a half day of vacation. She'd told me to get my things and go, and I hadn't hesitated to leave right at eleven. Mom had told me earlier in the week that she was taking the entire day off, so I called to see if she wanted to drive over to Schaumburg to do some shopping. It wasn't that I was looking for anything in particular, but I felt this need to go somewhere other than Mitchell. I needed alternate scenery, and I wanted to tell my mom what was going on with my marriage. She knew it was in trouble, but she had no idea that David was in love with someone else, or that we were no longer living together.

I'd wanted to tell her as soon as she drove to my house and then again while we were traveling on I-90, but I couldn't. I knew she would understand, because she understood everything else I had ever gone through, but somehow this thing with David, his sleeping with another woman, made me feel like a failure. I felt as though this unidentified woman had better qualities than me if she'd been able to take him so easily.

But most of all, I didn't want to tell her that his philandering could be partly blamed on me. I truly had forgotten about our marriage, the family he wanted to have and what was really important to him. He wasn't the supportive, loving husband he once was, but I feared that I'd helped push him toward being unfaithful, and I regretted it.

We walked through the first set of double doors and felt the central air sweep across our faces. It was at least ninety degrees outside and the coolness felt refreshing. We continued walking until we arrived in the handbag section and decided this was a good place to browse.

"This is really cute, isn't it?" I asked Mom, and then lifted the black-and-tan bag from a group of designer purses on top of the counter. They were priced 40 percent off, which meant these particular styles were likely being discontinued.

"Actually, it is. Kind of small, though, because you know how much stuff you like to pack in every purse you get," she said, and we laughed.

"Isn't that the truth?"

I wrapped it back around the silver hook I'd taken it from, and we strolled over to the nondesigner section—the only section my mother was willing to purchase from.

"What I need is a new work purse," she said as soon as she saw a midsize shoulder bag. "Something that's not too fancy, but nice."

"What about this one?" I asked, passing her a black leather bag that caught my attention.

"That's not bad, but it's not really what I'm looking for."

We scanned a couple of other racks but didn't see anything we were all that interested in.

"So do you want to shop some more in here, or go out into the mall?" I asked her as we continued walking.

"You still need to go to the M•A•C store don't you?

"Actually, I do, because I need some more of that Oh Baby! lacquer for my lips and some Chestnut lip liner for my Coconutty lipstick."

"You love that stuff, don't you?"

"Ever since Leslie and I went shopping downtown at Nordstrom two years ago, I've been hooked," I said, referring to one of my college dorm mates. "I'm just sorry it took all these years for me to realize how wonderful their products are. No other line can compare, although I do buy some things from Lançome that are also good."

"For years, all black women had was Fashion Fair, but now there's Iman, M•A•C and really just about every line I can think of carries makeup that we can use."

"Times have actually changed with some things, I guess," I said, thinking about Reed Meyers.

"So still no word about the job you're trying to get?"

"No. I applied for it, though. And while I'm hoping I get it, I know I have to be prepared either way."

"And you should be. We didn't have some of the laws that exist now when I was coming up, and even with the ones we did have, they really weren't being enforced. No one has the right to discriminate against you or anyone else, and if that's what your bosses are up to, then you have to stand up for yourself. Even if it means hiring an attorney."

"My friend Lorna, at work, keeps telling me the same thing, so that's exactly what I'm planning to do if things don't turn out the way they should."

Mom had certainly changed over the years. She'd worked at a corrugated box manufacturer for three decades and never complained about much of anything, at least not to any of her supervisors. She went to work, operated her machine and then came home. She did this every Monday through Friday from seven to three-thirty and sometimes worked five to eight hours on Saturdays, depending on how their workload was running.

She and my father had divorced when I was a junior in college, and since I was an only child, she didn't have anyone else she could spend her time with. She visited her two older sisters fairly often, but for the most part she spent her free time alone. She'd wanted another child, a daughter if she'd had her choice, but the doctors had found cancer in her uterus about a year after I was born, and she'd had no alternative but to have a hysterectomy when she was only in her twenties.

We walked into one of the women's specialty shops and took a look at some of the summer clothing they were showcasing.

Mom walked toward the back of the store, picking up a couple of things to try on as she went along, and I pulled two pairs of shorts from a rack at the front. Not long after, I added three shirts to my arm and a beautiful dark lime suit that I thought was perfect for work. I saw one of the salesgirls asking customer after customer if she could take the items they'd gathered and start a fitting room for them. I didn't think much of it until I noticed that some of those customers had entered the store well after Mom and me. The second strike was when the clerk paraded past me so she could explain today's sales promotion to a woman who'd just walked in. The third was when she marched right past me again and asked another customer if she was finding everything okay. I hadn't been asked any questions, hadn't had any promotional information explained to me and hadn't been relieved of this load of merchandise I was holding.

But I didn't say anything, because before I went off, I wanted to see if Mom had been treated any differently.

I stepped close to where Mom was standing and heard her asking Ms. Rude and Inconsiderate if she could try her selections on.

That's when I intervened.

"Mom, you mean to tell me that you've been carrying those clothes around all this time and no one has asked you once if you needed a fitting room?"

"No. Not one person."

I turned to Ms. Rude and asked, "So is there some special reason why you've been asking every customer in this store if you can help them in one way or another, but you haven't bothered to offer any customer service to the two of us? The only two black women in the store?"

"Oh. I'm sorry," she lied unconvincingly.

"No, you're not. And I want to see a manager."

"Nancy, is Lisa in the back?" the clerk yelled to her coworker who was running the cash register. She yelled in an irate tone.

"I think she is," the other salesperson said with a shameful look on her face, and then returned her attention to the customer she was helping.

Ms. Rude turned abruptly and walked into the back room. A minute later, a short, well-dressed woman with beautiful brunette hair approached us.

"Hello, I'm Lisa, the store manager. Is there something I can help you with?" she asked, smiling.

"As a matter of fact there is. My mom and I have been in this store longer than some of the people who have already had a dressing room started for them, and I want to know why."

"Rachel, can you answer this lady's question?" she asked, turning toward Ms. Rude.

At least we knew what her name was now.

"I don't know," she answered with a frown that said, Why are you asking me this stupid question? "It wasn't like I missed them on purpose. They looked like they were just browsing, anyway—"

"How were we just *browsing* if we were picking up things from the rack so we could try them on or purchase them?" I interrupted.

"Rachel, it's our responsibility to help every customer who comes through that door," Lisa said matter-of-factly. "We don't assume anything, and we treat all of our customers with the highest respect."

Rachel stared at Lisa as if she hadn't heard a word she'd spoken. She stared like she was still going to treat the next black person the very same way when the opportunity arose.

"Well, I'll tell you this," I said. "You can take all of these and put them back where we got them." I shoved both my stack and Mom's into Rachel's arms, and she had no choice but to take them.

"Lisa, I appreciate you taking the time to come speak with us, but you can thank your little salesperson here for losing our business. And even if I walk by here in the future and see an outfit that I absolutely have to have, I won't be coming in here to buy it. Neither will anyone else I know who shops in this mall if I have anything to do with it."

"I am really sorry that this happened, but I can guarantee you that this *will* be taken care of to your satisfaction. So I do hope you will reconsider."

I assumed she meant that Rachel was going to be fired, but I would still have to be in dire need before I dropped any of my hard-earned money in here again.

"I'm sorry, too," I told her. "Mom, are you ready?"

Mom nodded, and we left the store in a fury.

"It doesn't look like those laws you were talking about are making that much of a difference, Mom. Some of these people are crazy, and it makes you wonder what type of households they were raised in."

"Well, some of these young people are only racist because of learned behavior. Their parents hated blacks and their parents'

parents felt the same way. If no one breaks the cycle, then the problem will never go away. But not every white person is like the girl back in that store, because I have many white friends I would trust with my life and who would do anything for me. Which is why I raised you to like people for who they are and not because of their skin color."

"I feel the same way about Lorna and some of the women who live in our subdivision, but there are still so many people who hate that we shop in the same stores or eat at the same restaurants as them. It makes me so angry, but you just don't know, Mom, sometimes it makes me feel like crying. Sometimes the thought of never having a chance to be treated equally tears my heart apart, because it's so humiliating. It's like we're fighting a losing battle to be treated fairly."

"I know, but you can't give up, because too many people lost their lives trying to fight for our rights."

We continued walking, and I realized that this latest incident of bias had us walking through a crowded mall talking about racism and equal opportunity. I didn't even feel like shopping any longer. Not at any store I could think of.

"Do you wanna just leave?" I asked.

"I'm ready whenever you are. You know I'm not the biggest shopper in the world anyway, and I only came so we could spend some time together."

I was already depressed, still up in the air about my marriage and my job, and now this had dampened my spirits even further.

We left the mall without stopping to eat as we'd planned on doing. When we made it to my SUV, we hopped in and drove away from the senseless episode we'd just experienced. Leaving wouldn't erase what had happened, but at least we'd be able to move on to something else.

We entered the tollway, and I decided that it was best to tell my mother straight out about David and me. I'd managed to feign a genuine smile for hours, but she hadn't noticed once that anything was wrong. Usually she sensed when something wasn't right, but I'd worked hard at disguising my problems because I didn't have the courage and because I'd wanted us to enjoy our time together without worry. But so much for enjoyment, something we'd obviously been deprived of, anyway.

"I found out last night that David is seeing someone else."

"You what?"

"He's seeing another woman, and he made it very clear that he's not going to stop."

"When did all this come about?"

"I don't know, and he wouldn't give me any details."

"You should have *made* him tell you."

"I guess I didn't press the issue because it really doesn't matter to me when it started."

"Who is this woman?" I could tell Mom was becoming upset.

"He wouldn't tell me that either."

"And you're just going to leave it like that?"

"Actually, I am, because there's nothing I can do about it. I tried to reconcile with him two nights ago, and that never made a bit of difference to him. So, as painful as it is, I know I can make it without him if I have to. David and I have been moving further and further away from each other for a long time, so really, I should have seen this coming before now."

"How did you find out?"

"I walked outside to get the mail right after I came home from Monica's and heard him talking to someone on his cell phone. He was still sitting in the garage with his engine turned off, but hadn't closed the garage door."

"Lord Jesus," Mom said, sighing. "What are you going to do?"

"Nothing. Because it's pretty clear that he wants to be with someone else."

"I just don't believe this is happening. The least he could have done was stand by you until your job situation was taken care of."

"He doesn't care about any of that. And if you ask him, he'll say that my career is part of the reason why he strayed in the first place.

Which I have to agree with to a certain extent, because it has been my priority for a long time."

"That still doesn't give anyone the right to mess around."

"Maybe not, but this is what the reality is, and I'm willing to live with it if this is what he wants."

"You're taking this a lot better than I would be."

"I know, Mom, but David and I don't love each other the way we used to. It's almost like we love each other but we're not *in* love any longer."

"I just hate to see anyone going through a breakup. Especially my own daughter. When your father and I separated, it was the hardest thing I ever had to deal with, and I don't wish the way I felt on anybody I can think of. Not even that girl back at that store."

"I know it won't be easy, but this is out of my control."

"So have you spoken with him today?"

"No, I haven't seen or heard from him since he packed his stuff and left."

"Packed his stuff and left? As in for good?"

"Yeah. And I doubt he'll be back except to get the rest of his things."

"I can't believe he just up and left you like that."

"Actually, he didn't have a choice, because I told him to get out or else."

"I'm so sorry that all this is happening" was all Mom could say.

We rode in silence for almost twenty minutes as Chicago's V103 played two of Luther's new cuts back-to-back. She was hurting for me the way any mother would, but I vowed to overcome this the same as I had overcome every other obstacle in my life. She'd raised me to be strong, independent and self-confident, and while she worried about how I was going to make it on my own, she would soon learn that the reason I'd be able to was that she'd taught me how to survive, regardless of the situation.

In time, I was going to be just fine.

CHAPTER 7

T WAS MONDAY MORNING, and it had taken every ounce of willpower I had to tear myself out of bed, take a shower, get dressed and drive to work. David hadn't made any attempts to call, so I'd had a load of time on my hands to do a whole lot of thinking. I'd weighed everything out and had come to the same two decisions I'd shared with Mom on Friday: I wasn't moving out of our house, and I was filing a lawsuit against Reed Meyers if they forced me to. I was sure the reason David hadn't called was that he still regretted being caught the way he had been, and that he wanted to make me feel so alone that maybe I'd get lonely enough to pack my bags and go live with my mother. But I wasn't going to make things that easy for him. I would agree to a divorce if he filed, but the dissolution of our marriage was going to mean fifty-fifty from top to bottom. I'd worked just as hard as he had to obtain all that we owned, and he wasn't going to simply push me aside, move on and allow God knows who to take my place.

I'd convinced myself all weekend that I didn't care who the next

Mrs. David Miller might be, but deep down I was being destroyed by curiosity. I wanted to know if she was his secretary, one of his coworkers, a colleague or possibly a client, but I finally realized last night that what I wanted to know most of all was whether this mistress was a white woman. Successful black men did this all the time. They always started out with black women, who were good enough as long as the men were still struggling to build their careers. But once their bank balances escalated and their image needed to be upgraded, successful black men jumped ship. Sometimes they tried to keep the obvious on the down-low by marrying a biracial or even a Hispanic woman, but eventually they went all the way and found a beautiful white woman—the prize they'd been working so hard to secure. For years, I wondered why a huge majority of the black NBA, NFL and MLB players thought it was so important to marry outside of their race. If it was strictly for love, I totally understood and agreed with their decision. But what I finally figured out was that marrying a white woman announced loud and clear that they'd finally arrived in terms of status. It made them feel more important and like they could finally receive just a tad more respect than they'd ever had with a black woman.

I saw nothing wrong with any two people of any race becoming man and wife so long as they were madly in love with each other. But when the marriage was based on status, I didn't agree. I'd formed this opinion the same day I asked my forty-year-old cousin why he'd suddenly made a change in preference. He'd always dated black girls in high school, black women in college and then married a black woman who paid all the bills the entire time he attended medical school. But five years ago, he divorced his first wife and married a white woman. He'd looked me straight in the face and told me that there was so much more his new wife could do to help his career. He was invited to all the VIP parties and dinners, his practice was better than ever, and if it hadn't been for his new wife, there was no telling what his children would have ended up looking like. Not to mention the fact that their hair would have been much too nappy.

He'd convinced himself that he was no longer black, and I remember telling him how pathetic he was and how at some point in his life he would be reminded of who he really was.

It wasn't six months later when someone mailed him an anonymous note saying: WE HATE NIGGERS AND EVEN WORSE, NIGGER LOVERS. SO WHY DON'T YOU DO THIS NICE NEIGHBORHOOD A FAVOR AND MOVE BACK TO WHEREVER THE HELL YOU CAME FROM.

He hadn't been emotionally stable ever since.

The phone grabbed my attention when it rang, and I reached over to answer it. "Anise Miller."

"Anise, it's me," David said in a low tone.

"And?"

I wasn't going to make this conversation simple.

"I really don't know where to begin," he said, pausing.

"Well, I can't help you with that, David."

He blew a sigh of frustration.

Then he spoke.

"I didn't mean for you to find out like this. I was going to tell you, but it seemed like the more I got involved with her, the harder it was to face you."

"Well, the damage is done, and while you were having, I'm sure, such a fun weekend, I sat at home alone, thinking about the fact that our marriage is over."

"All I can say is that I'm sorry. I wanted things to turn out differently, but they didn't."

"So why are you calling now?"

"I want to explain all of this to you."

"What is it that you think you need to explain? How many different positions you've screwed her in?"

"Anise, please. Why do you always have to be so boorish?"

"Boorish?" I laughed, but my tone was sarcastic. "Since when did you start using *that* as an everyday word?"

"It's in the dictionary, isn't it?"

"So is antidisestablishmentarianism, but I don't go around using it when I'm talking to my friends and family members."

"Just because you don't know what it means, don't—"

I interrupted him. "It means rude, ill-mannered, impolite, crude, uncouth—do you want me to continue? Hell, you're not the only person in America who graduated from college with honors. I know you think you are, but the joke is on you."

"See, it's this very type of thing that made me find interest in another woman."

"What? You mean because I don't take any shit from you, and I call you on every ignorant comment you make? Or is it because I don't act white enough for you?"

"Maybe if you did, you wouldn't be crying over a damn job every single year."

"Well, if I have to act like someone else to get promoted, then I'm S-O-L, because I'm never going to disown who I am. I'm intelligent, professional and experienced at what I do, so that's all that should be considered."

"Hmmph. But you see none of that has made any difference, now has it?"

"Look," I finally said, losing patience. "If there's something you want to say, then say it. Otherwise I need to get back to work."

"Let's just forget it. Pretend like I didn't even call."

"Fine. I will."

I prepared to hang up, but deep down I wanted to know who this new love of his life was. So I asked.

"David?"

"What?"

"Who is she?"

"Why does it matter to you so much?"

"Because I think I have a right to know."

"What do you want to do, harass her? Because I don't want her dealing with anything like that."

That pissed me off.

"First of all, neither you nor she is worth the trouble," I shot back, but it hurt knowing that he was more concerned about her feelings than he was about mine.

"Her name is Christina, and I met her at one of the golf courses I go to."

"Oh really? Well, at least now you have a woman who likes to play the game."

"She doesn't play. She works inside the clubhouse."

"So what are you saying?"

I knew exactly what he meant, but I wanted to hear it from him.

"I'm saying that she works at the golf course, and it doesn't matter to me that she doesn't have a degree like you."

"You finally found someone who will do whatever you want when you want her to, didn't you?"

"I guess I did, didn't I?"

"Did you finally get your white girl, too?" I spoke sternly.

"As a matter of fact, I did."

Even though I half expected it, his words struck me like a flying baseball.

"I know that's not what you wanted to hear, but I can't help that I've always preferred white women," he said. "I grew up with white people. I went to school with them, and that's who I feel the most comfortable with."

"Then why did you marry me, David?" I heard myself ask.

"Partly because I really did fall in love with you, and partly because I knew my colleagues weren't ready to see me with a white wife six years ago."

"So are you saying you used me until you realized you didn't need me anymore?"

"I didn't use you, but the longer we were together, the more I realized we weren't compatible. Although I was willing to try and make it work if you gave me a baby and stopped being so obsessed with having a career."

"How could you make love to me the other night, knowing that you were in love with someone else? I mean, how could you be so cruel?"

"Because I felt sorry for you, and whether you believe me or not, I really feel bad about all of this. I never meant to hurt you like this, and I never expected to fall in love with someone else while I was still married to you."

"I hate you for doing this to me, David," I said, determined not to shed any tears.

"I'm really sorry for everything, Anise. You have to believe that."

I dropped the receiver on its base without saying good-bye and closed my eyes. Tears rolled down my face. My heart ached terribly, and I wondered why he'd acted as though he wanted our marriage to work. I wondered why he'd used me for sex, or worse, why he'd made love to me out of pity. I couldn't help thinking about how ironic it was that I'd just been thinking about my idiot cousin, and now David had fallen into that same category.

I pulled myself together in the ladies' room, finished a few action items in my office and went down to the company cafeteria. I'd considered going out, but I had far too much work and didn't need to waste time walking out to the parking lot, driving to a restaurant and then waiting for my meal to be served. Apparently a good number of other employees were on the same wavelength, because the cafeteria was certainly busier than usual.

One of the servers positioned a plate on top of the counter with a tuna entrée, and I sat it on the blue tray I'd grabbed at the beginning of the line. I moved along and tried to resist reaching for a slice of southern pecan pie, but didn't see why I should deny myself. I had a lot on my mind and was dealing with enough stress to justify all the calories and fat grams I knew it was saturated with. Which is why I picked it up. I was five nine and still wore a comfortable size ten, so it wasn't like I was overweight, anyway.

I filled a glass with Sierra Mist, paid the cashier and located a seat by the long wall of windows. I'd barely had time to open my napkin full of silverware when Frank Colletti, the training director, walked up to the table.

"You're not expecting anyone for lunch, are you?" he asked, looking as handsome as ever.

"No."

"Do you mind if I join you?"

I was hesitant, because Frank always made me feel uncomfortable. It was the type of discomfort a man inflicts upon you when he looks at you the wrong way and you are 100 percent sure he wants to be more than just a friend, coworker or acquaintance.

But against my better judgment, I said, "Sure, why not."

He placed his tray on the table, which contained a sub sandwich and chips, and then took a seat in front of me. I wondered why I hadn't seen him in line, but now I knew he'd purchased his lunch on the other side of the cafeteria where they sold sandwiches and snacks.

"So how's everything going?" he asked, smiling.

"As well as they can be, I guess."

I didn't know Frank well enough to confide what I was going through. More important, I didn't know how I was going to tell a white man that my life was being turned upside down because my white superiors were possibly trying to discriminate against me and my husband had left me for a white woman. I just didn't see how he could possibly understand, and there was a chance he might be offended by what I was thinking.

"I'm glad to hear it, because you don't look like everything is going well. But I guess looks can be deceiving," he said, and took a bite from his sandwich. It was clear that he knew something was bothering me.

I chewed a forkful of casserole but didn't comment.

"I'm not trying to pry, but sometimes it's better to talk to some-one you don't know all that well than it is to your closest friends."

I smiled to myself, because prying was exactly what he was doing.

"Okay," he said, raising both his hands in surrender. "I'll talk about something else, because I can see you don't want to go there with me."

"It's not that."

"What is it then? Because if you're worried about me repeating anything you say, you don't have to. I'll die with whatever you tell me."

I couldn't help but grin at his humor.

"See, I knew I could raise your spirits. And I wasn't going to leave here without seeing you smile."

I appreciated his empathy, and I couldn't help but notice how attractive he was. Like a lot of Italian men I knew, he was tall, fine-looking and had stunning black hair, and now that I was looking into his eyes, I had to admit that there was a certain amount of chemistry between us. Which I didn't want to think about, because there was no way I could date outside of my race or commit adul-tery. David was doing both, but he and I were not the same. At least I didn't think we were.

"So how's the training department?" I asked, changing the subject.

"Oh, I get it. That's a hint, right? You're telling me on the sly that you don't want to discuss anything that has to do with you."

"No, I'm simply asking how your department is coming along."

"If you say so," he said, smiling skeptically. "It's fine. We're implementing some new programs and planning to hire two addi-tional trainers in the coming months."

"Good for you."

"How's the benefits section? Jim was telling me this morning that you applied for the HR manager's slot again."

I nodded and wondered why Jim thought it necessary to discuss my career decisions with anyone other than Lyle and Elizabeth, my current immediate supervisor.

"Why was he telling you that?"

"He was saying that they had three candidates for the position, and that he really wanted to give it to you, but his hands might be tied."

"His hands might be tied how?"

"He said something about Kelli Jacobson having more seniority with the company and in the department than you do."

"You know, Frank, I won't even say what I'm thinking, because I might regret it. But all I know is that they're going to be sorry if they don't do the right thing."

"Say whatever you feel like saying. I'm all ears," he said.

"Why? Did they ask you to see if you could get me to back down like a good little girl?"

Frank stared at me with no specific expression and kept quiet.

"Actually, I was joking, but you're acting like they really did ask you to talk to me."

"They did."

"They what?!"

"They wanted me to tell you how wonderful my job is and how I thought you would be perfect for it once I'm promoted. Jim said he had a feeling you were under the impression that he and Lyle were trying to discriminate against you, but that they weren't. He told me that they wanted you to be in the job they feel you're best suited for and the one they believe will make you the happiest."

I felt my blood roaring. What nerve they had, asking another employee to assist them with their scheming. I didn't know whether to be angry with Frank or not, but apparently he wasn't buying into what they were attempting to do, because he wouldn't have told me about any of this if he was.

"But, Anise," he continued, "I want you to know something right now. I don't agree with any of what they are trying to do to you, and under no circumstances would I do anything to hurt you."

I didn't know whether to believe him or not. My intuition told me that I could trust him, but there was no way I could be sure.

"Well, since Jim will be expecting you to report back, what are you planning on telling him?" I wanted to know.

"Whatever you want me to."

"Yeah, right," I said, looking away from him.

"I'm serious. I'll tell him whatever you ask me to."

"Okay, then tell him I said to go to hell."

Frank laughed. "I understand how you feel, but I was thinking of something a little more subtle. Something more along the lines of why you don't want the training position. Because we don't want him finding out that I gave you the heads-up on what they're trying to do."

"I know, but I'm just so pissed about this. Jim has been a thorn in my side ever since I told him I was going to apply for that job again. I don't mean to offend you, Frank, but Jim is one of the most racist white men I have ever worked with. And the only reason he's going to such great extremes about this is because they'd rather close the company than see a black woman in management."

"I agree with you completely. I've been here much longer than you, and I've seen some pretty crafty stuff happen with a few employees. And don't ever think you're offending me about any of this, because they're the ones who are wrong. Not you."

I cut a bite of pecan pie and was raising it to my mouth right when Kelli Jacobson slithered over to our table.

"Well, well, well," she said. "Since when did the two of you start having lunch together?" The tone of her voice was sarcastic.

My first thought was to ignore her, but I realized this was an opportunity to speak with my lovely competitor.

"Hi, Kelli. So I guess we're both going for that corporate manager position, huh?"

"I guess so. And may the best woman win. Good luck," she said as she walked away.

She was flippant and acted as though she'd already been told the job was hers, and I didn't like it.

"I can't believe she even applied," Frank said.

"She applied because Jim wanted her to."

"Well, if I were you, I wouldn't let that worry me too much until the decision has been made."

"That's easy to say, but there's no way I can simply forget about how Jim keeps trying to manipulate me. And the worst part of all is that Lyle called me into his office to discuss my interest in the job and almost made it seem like he was behind me. So of course I couldn't help but think that maybe he was going to convince Jim that I was the best qualified for the job. He seemed so genuine when I left his office."

"Really?" Frank said.

"Yes, so I guess I don't understand what's going on with either one of them."

"I can imagine, because it does sound like the two of them are giving you mixed signals. And while I don't have any answers for you, I do want you to know that I'm here if you ever need someone to talk to. All you have to do is say the word. We can even do it over dinner sometime if you want."

He was making me feel uncomfortable again.

"No, I don't think so," I answered.

"Why not?"

"Because even though I'm separated—" I said, and paused. I couldn't believe I'd let that slip.

"You're separated?" he asked.

I looked away from him and didn't respond.

"Anise, I am really sorry. I didn't know."

"Actually, there's no need to apologize. But I would appreciate it if you don't mention this to anyone else."

"Of course not. I would never do that."

"And as far as your dinner invitation, I'm still going to have to pass, because it wouldn't be right."

"Even if our relationship is solely platonic?"

"Yes, because I'm still married."

I would never admit my true feelings to Frank, but with David not caring about our vows one way or the other, I did have this growing desire to pay him back for what he'd done to me. Which was the real reason I knew it was best that I not go to dinner with Frank or any other man I was attracted to.

"So what you're saying is that having lunch here at work is fine, but the reason you don't want to have dinner with me at a restaurant is because I'm white."

"No, that's not it at all," I lied.

"C'mon, Anise," he teased.

"I'm serious. That's not it."

"Okay, then tell me this: Have you ever been seen in public with any white man in the past?"

"No."

"Then that's what it is."

I didn't know what else to say, but I wished he wouldn't look at me the way he was right now.

"I need to get back to work," I said as an escape.

But he disregarded what I was saying.

"If you ever change your mind, the offer still stands. And before you even start thinking it, I want you to know now, that I don't make it a habit of asking every woman I come in contact with to dinner. Especially women I work with and especially women who are married. And I'm only offering because I realize what you may be up against here at work, and because you may need someone in your corner before long. I know Lorna is a good friend of yours, but it won't hurt to have a friend like me who knows how Jim and Lyle tend to think."

"I really appreciate hearing that," I told him. Then I gathered my tray and stood up. I was still at a loss for words, but I finally said, "See you later, Frank."

"Bye, Anise."

I walked over to the conveyor belt, put my tray down and left the cafeteria. A handful of thoughts scattered through my mind, but the one that stood out the most was the one I didn't want to acknowledge.

I couldn't deny the fact that I really was attracted to Frank, and that I'd had to double my determination in a major way in order to decline his dinner offer. I'd wanted so badly to say yes, and I felt guilty about it. I felt guilty because even though my marriage was on the rocks, in God's eyesight, I still had a husband.

But even if I had been single, there was still a very serious problem with this picture.

Frank Colletti was a white man.

He was the type of man I was beginning to hate, thanks to Jim, the type of man I couldn't be sure about, thanks to Lyle, and the same race as the woman who'd taken my husband. But as much as I'd rather die than admit it, he was someone I could see myself being with.

So what was I going to do now?

CHAPTER 8

I JUST SPOKE TO Frank," Jim said to Lyle as he closed Lyle's office door.

"And?"

"Anise is still obsessed with this recruiting promotion."

"Did he explain why training would be a better area for her?"

"He says he did, but all she said was that she wasn't interested in training or any other department."

"Hmmm." Lyle was disappointed.

"This shit really gets me," Jim said. "Why can't she just cooperate and do what we tell her? I mean, who is she to tell us who we have to hire and promote? If we don't want her in that recruiting position, it should be as simple as that."

"But you know it's not. I don't want her in recruiting either, but it's those damn equal opportunity laws I'm worried about. And believe me when I say that Anise Miller wouldn't think twice about slapping a discrimination lawsuit on us."

Jim pursed his lips in disgust. "And that's the very reason I'm so sick of all these ridiculous laws the government keeps passing. First, it was women's rights, and then it was this racial crap. Even if a company wants to have all white men with no women or minorities, it ought to be just fine. Women belong at home taking care of their children anyway."

"I wouldn't go that far," Lyle said humorously. "Because if it weren't for women, who would we get to schedule our calendars and make our coffee?"

Jim chuckled. "You do have a point there, but with the exception of that, I don't see any other positions that we really need them in. And when you hire these women, it's always just a matter of time before they start talking about having a family. It used to be that they got six weeks for maternity leave, but now that Family Leave foolishness is in effect. Every woman at Reed Meyers who's had a baby in the last year has opted to take three months off. Hell, I say if a person wants that much time at home, then they should quit altogether and let someone else have their job. Someone who has their priorities in order."

"I agree," Lyle said, clasping his hands together. "I think we're going to have to do some rearranging and make some other openings available. That way, maybe Anise will reconsider applying for something else."

"Maybe. Because quite frankly, I'm becoming a bit tired of all this unnecessary time she's forcing us to spend on one job opening. Kelli Jacobson isn't the classiest woman, but I'd much rather have her in the position than someone who is barely one step away from living in the ghetto. Hell, you'd think Anise would just be happy we hired her at all, because you know I never wanted her here in the first place."

"Isn't that the truth? But it's not like we really had a choice with some of the factory workers making such a fuss over the fact that there weren't any minorities in human resources."

"Well, regardless of who complains this time, I'll be damned if I'm going to let someone like her have that corporate recruiting position," Jim professed. "Because the next thing you know, she'll be recruiting God knows what kind of people into this company."

"That you can be sure of, so if we can't find a position we can open up right away, then we'll just have to create one. All we have to do is make the education and work experience requirements match hers. That way the posting is bound to grab her attention."

"I'll get started on this, but I sure hope these are the last few days we'll have to spend with this," Jim said, standing.

"I hope so, too, because I'd really like to see you get Kelli moved into that position so we can post her current one as soon as possible."

"I'll check back with you later this afternoon or sometime tomorrow."

"That sounds fine," Lyle said, lighting his cherry wood pipe and taking two initial puffs. Then he relaxed his body against the high-backed chair he was sitting in.

Jim leaned his head back in deep pleasure. He'd left work later than usual and had spent all afternoon trying to find a new strategy—one that would allow them to give Kelli Jacobson that management position. He hadn't made much progress, but on his way out to the executive parking lot, a whole new scheme had come to him. It had appeared from nowhere, and he couldn't wait to work it all out on paper first thing tomorrow morning. He'd promised Kelli weeks ago that she could have the next managerial slot that was posted, and with the way she was performing oral sex on him right now, he knew he couldn't disappoint her.

Kelli moved her head forward, backward and then in half circles. Jim moaned with desire and Kelli increased her momentum. Jim could feel himself swelling with every stroke, but he wanted to hold out a little while longer, until he was rock hard. She tightened her lips, but as soon as she did he pushed her away.

"Get up, you little bitch, and take this monster dick like a real woman should."

"Okay, Mr. Tarzan," she said in a timid voice.

He forced her onto the hotel bed, she rested on her hands and knees and Jim plowed into her with all three inches. She groaned loudly, but Jim paid her no mind. He maneuvered himself in and out of her and then pushed with more force than when he'd entered her initially.

"Oh my goodness, Mr. Tarzan, you're way too big for me."

Jim slapped her on her buttocks and left his handprint plastered in red.

"Shut up, you little whore, and take this the way I taught you."

"Okay," she said. "I'm so sorry, Mr. Tarzan."

"You'd better be sorry, or you won't be getting any more of this gigantic dick."

"Please don't deprive me of it, Mr. Tarzan. I'll be good."

"Oh no! I think I hear Jane swinging through the jungle," he said, and rolled his eyes toward the top of his head, all the while pushing himself in and out of her with intense speed. He moaned with pleasure and she grunted with what he was sure was pain.

He continued pulling and pushing her buttocks until he climaxed. She yelled loudly and he breathed uncontrollably. She flattened her stomach across the bed, and he lay to the side of her, trying to calm his heart rate.

Kelli was the best. She dropped down on her knees every time he told her to, and she didn't mind doing it here at the hotel, in his office or in his company car. About a year ago, he'd asked her if his dick was the biggest she'd ever had and she'd made the mistake of telling him no. So he'd had no choice but to threaten taking away her job if she didn't tell him the truth. He'd made her tell him that she was lying, and that not only did he have the biggest dick she'd ever had, it was the most enormous one she'd ever seen.

He'd then decided that he would be Tarzan from here on out, and she would be the mistress that Jane never arrived in time to see.

"Guess who I saw eating lunch together this afternoon?" Kelli said, pushing her long blond hair behind her left ear and turning toward him.

"Who?"

"That bitch Anise and Frank Colletti."

"Is that so?" Jim responded, but didn't think it was necessary to tell her he'd set the whole thing up.

"Yeah, and it made me sick just watching them. She thinks she's hot shit, and I can't wait for her to find out that I'm getting that job she wants so badly. She actually brought up the fact that we both applied for it, and I wanted so desperately to tell her she was wasting her time."

"I understand your frustration, but don't you even think about telling her anything. Everything I discuss with you is confidential, and it has to stay that way."

"I know, I know. But it was just that she had that smug look on her face like she had just as much right to be working at Reed Meyers as we do. And they looked way too comfortable."

"Comfortable how?"

"You know. Like they've known each other for twenty years or something. It made me sick, because all I could think was that Frank might actually be interested in her sexually. You do know that he pretty much dates only black women, don't you?"

"Frank dating black women? I doubt it," Jim said in disbelief.

"Okay, but I'm just telling you what I've heard in the past."

"Well, if he is, he can just forget about that promotion Lyle is wanting to give him. As a matter of fact, he'd better not be, or he'll be out of a job altogether. Lyle will go through the roof. Lyle's daughter married a black, and he cut her clean out of his will because of it. He and his wife haven't seen or heard from her in over ten years, and if you ask Lyle, he'll tell you that he doesn't even have a daughter."

"Yeah, I'd heard rumors about that, but I never knew if it was really true," Kelli said, rubbing her foot slowly up and down Jim's leg.

"I tell you, what is the world coming to?" Jim said, sighing. "But I will say this. We might not be able to control what's going on everywhere else, but we sure as hell can control what goes on at Reed Meyers. And that's exactly what Lyle and I plan on doing."

"I'm glad to hear it," Kelli said, and kissed Jim up and down his neck. "So are you sure the job is going to be mine?"

"I'm positive," he said, closing his eyes. He enjoyed what she was doing to him, but he hoped she knew a fifty-year-old man couldn't rise again so quickly.

"I think Jane is gone, Mr. Tarzan," she said, moaning.

"No, I don't think she is," he said, trying to tone her down.

"Yes, I really think she is, because I saw her swing right past us with Cheetah."

Jim kept quiet and tried to ignore her until she forced her nipple inside his mouth. He inhaled it roughly and squeezed the other one so tightly that she jerked. Her breasts were 42Ds, and since her frame was so tiny, they were the first thing any man noticed as soon as he laid eyes on her. They drove him wild, and she always used them against him. She made him suck them for long periods of time, and sometimes she even got off with the assistance of her own fingers while he did it.

He'd slept with five different women inside the company, but Kelli Jacobson was, by far, the best he'd ever been with. She made him feel like a man, and she recognized how massive his dick really was even though none of the others would admit it.

Jim enjoyed watching Kelli climax again, and when she did he got up and went into the bathroom. Kelli followed him shortly thereafter, and then they both showered, dressed and drove to their respective homes. Jim drove far east to his mini-mansion, and Kelli drove to her less-than-luxurious apartment on the southeast side of town.

CHAPTER 9

'D BARELY SAT DOWN at my desk when Frank stuck his head inside my doorway.

"Hey," he said.

"How are you, Frank?"

"I'm good. What about you?"

"I'm okay, I guess."

"At least you have that beautiful smile on your face today," he said, and then turned away when someone called out his name.

"Hey, I'll see you later, okay."

"See ya."

I was sort of glad to see him. I'd dodged him as best I could ever since we'd had lunch a week ago, but he'd made sure to attract my attention as often as he could. Even if he didn't say anything, he winked and smiled in a way that he shouldn't have, or watched me walk by until I was out of sight. It had gotten to the point where I almost expected it. In all honesty, I wanted him to do it. I wanted any attention he was willing to give me because I was now sleeping alone in a cold bed.

David never called, and I was sure he was living with his new woman. I told myself that I didn't care, but my emotions still zig-zagged around the clock, and there were moments when I thought I was losing my mind. I was sad because it hadn't bothered him to leave me. I was angry because things still weren't the way they should be at work.

I hadn't shed any more tears, but I kept wondering when I was finally going to explode. Everyone had a breaking point. I knew I would be no exception. I'd kept to myself for the most part, but Mom and Monica made sure they called me every day. Mom even brought me dinner on Saturday and sat with me for a while, and Monica convinced me last night to meet her at the gym this eve-ning. But the highlight of the week was about to take place in thirty minutes. Jim's secretary had called me on Friday and scheduled my interview for 3:00 P.M. today.

Mom had tried talking me into going to church yesterday, because she really thought prayer and worship would make me feel better, but I took a rain check instead. Now, though, I wished I had listened to her, because my stomach was tied in knots. I'd told myself this morning that all I had to do was walk into Jim's office, answer his questions, ask some of my own and then leave with my head held high when it was over. But that was easier said than done. I didn't like Jim, and Jim clearly didn't want me applying for the position. So how were we going to deal with each other during this pointless interview process? I was sure he and Lyle had already made up their minds and were only doing this for documentation purposes. But a small part of me was still hoping that they'd decided to give in and promote me.

I wasn't being naïve.

I was just trying to stay positive until this was over.

Finally, I gathered together my leather portfolio. Jim's office was at the opposite end of the department, but today it seemed as if it was just around the corner. Before I knew it, I was standing in front of his secretary with no true recollection of how I'd gotten there.

She smiled and told me to go right in, the same as she'd done in the past.

"Have a seat, Anise," Jim said as soon as I entered.

"Thank you."

"I guess this is a little awkward for both of us," he began.

"Yes, I guess it is." I wondered how I was going to get through this.

"This won't take very long, but I do have a short list of questions that I'm asking each candidate."

I wondered if he was asking each of us the same exact questions.

"What is it about this position that gave you the most interest?"

"The idea of being able to meet people who don't work for the company but who are interested in doing so, and the idea of working with internal candidates who are applying for management and executive positions. I also like the idea of playing a part in finding the most qualified people and matching them with the appropriate jobs."

"But you do know it's not always as simple as that, and that this job is not always the most glamorous, right?"

"Yes, but no job can be wonderful all the time."

"And you do know that while you'd be hiring people, you'd also be responsible for terminating employees if it became necessary. And you'd also have to send out rejection letters to candidates who aren't chosen for a particular position."

"I realize that, but one of the things I like about human resources is that it allows you to interact with people on all levels. I love working with people, and I think that will help when I'm faced with the responsibility of having to terminate or reject someone."

"Maybe, but somehow I still think you're seeing this job through rose-colored glasses."

"Well, unfortunately, I have to disagree with you."

Jim gazed at me and then at the sheet of paper in front of him.

"Where do you see yourself in five years? Still working here at Reed Meyers? Still living in Mitchell? Or do you have plans to relocate if something better comes along?"

"If I'm selected for this promotion, I would hope to still be working as the corporate HR recruiting manager or in your position if you're promoted to operations."

Jim grunted in disbelief.

He was making this more difficult by the minute.

"Do you have any questions for me?" he asked without interest.

"Actually, I do," I said, pulling out my list of five questions. "How many candidates applied for this position?" I knew the answer, but I wanted to hear him tell me.

"Three." No elaboration.

"Am I the last person to be interviewed?"

"Yes."

The look on his face said that I was wasting his precious time. But I continued.

"I know the low portion of the salary range is around forty-eight, the mid is around fifty-eight, and that it tops out at sixty-eight. Right now I'm earning just over thirty-eight thousand dollars, so would I start right at the beginning of the range, or is there a chance I would start somewhat higher than that?" I knew that going from thirty-eight thousand to forty-eight would mean a twenty-six percent increase, and that they'd never start me out any higher than that, but I still wanted an answer. I wanted him to know that I was aware not only of their hiring and promoting practices but also of their pay scales, because last night it dawned on me that they could be discriminating against employees in that respect, too.

"Probably," he said.

But since I didn't know which part of my question he was answering, I said, "Probably, meaning . . . ?"

"Probably, meaning you would definitely start at the beginning of the range."

I couldn't believe how irritated he'd become, but I continued.

"I found quite a few HR manager training conferences that are coming up and was wondering if you'd allow me to attend one of them if I'm selected?"

"Maybe. We'd have to make sure it was beneficial for both you and the company."

At least he'd spoken a full sentence this time. But I wondered how he was going to respond to my final query.

"Since I'm the last person to be interviewed and I'm the only candidate who has a bachelor's degree, master's degree and four years of solid HR experience, how soon do you think you'll be making your decision?"

"You are really a piece of work."

"What do you mean by that?" I spoke strongly.

"Never mind. We'll be making our decision within the next week or so."

"Can you tell me why it's going to take so long?"

"Because we have to evaluate everyone's qualifications thoroughly. And if that's all you have for me, then I guess this interview is over."

"You know, Jim," I said, standing up, "this is the first interview I've ever had where the person asking the questions didn't take any notes after I answered them."

"I don't think any two people conduct interviews the same way."

"Maybe not, but then I guess since you know I'm the most qualified candidate, it's not like you needed to take notes anyway, did you?"

I turned and walked out without looking back, and at that moment I knew I might as well start searching for a Chicago attorney. I'd have to go to Chicago because too many CEOs, attorneys and physicians in Mitchell golfed and ate dinner together. There was a risk that someone would be paid off, and I couldn't chance that.

I arrived back in my office and, once again, hadn't noticed anyone or anything. I was shutting my door but Lorna stopped me. So I let her in and then closed it.

"So how did it go?"

"Not too well. Not well at all," I said sadly.

"Dirty bastard. I knew he was going to do this to you."

"He hasn't done anything yet, but I do think you were right when you said they would never give me the job."

"Did he try to intimidate you?"

"He tried to, but it didn't stop me from asking him every question I wanted an answer to. He was very rude the entire time, though, and you know, Lorna, it really hurts to know that he's treating me this way because the color of my skin is not acceptable to him."

I felt my eyes filling up. I'd felt humiliated and unappreciated a number of times while working at Reed Meyers, but today was worse than any time I could remember. Jim had basically looked me in the eye and silently told me that my qualifications didn't matter, that he was going to choose who he wanted to, and that there wasn't a thing I could do about it.

Lorna pulled a couple of tissues from the box on my desk and passed them to me. Then she reached out her hand. "Honey, you've got to do what I told you. You've got to fight for what they're trying to take from you."

I sniffled and wiped my face, but I was too shaken to talk.

"Do you hear what I'm saying to you, Anise?" she asked softly.

I nodded in agreement.

"Good. This is not going to be easy, but I promise you, it'll be worth it in the end. It will stop them from getting away with all this bias."

I listened but didn't speak.

So Lorna said, "I have an afternoon class that I have to get ready for, but are you going to be okay?"

"I'll be fine," I told her, but I knew I wasn't telling the truth.

"Are you sure?"

"I'm sure. Go do what you have to do."

"Honey, call me if you need me, and even if you have to get me out of my class, that will be fine too."

"Thanks, Lorna," I said, and forced a smile on my face.

She closed my door behind her.

As soon as she did, I bawled like a teething baby.

. . .

Monica had left me a message, wanting to make sure that I was still meeting her at the gym. But after my session with Jim, I was no longer in the mood for working out, so I told her that maybe we could go tomorrow. She asked me about what was going on the same as she always did, and when I told her about my interview, she said she'd be at my house as soon I arrived home from work. I was glad because I didn't feel like being alone. She'd even called Mom and asked her to drive over as well. The three of us sat downstairs in the family room.

"I know I always say this, but things really will get better with time," Mom tried to convince me.

"I agree with you, Emma," Monica added. "Things always feel much worse than they actually are."

I listened to both of them and wished I could believe what they were saying. I wanted to so desperately, but hearing that everything was going to be okay, that God would eventually work things out, and that time could heal all wounds wasn't exactly brightening my spirits. However, I knew they meant well.

"I hear what both of you are saying, but the fact is, David has left me for another woman, and Reed Meyers is going to deny giving me a promotion for the second time in six months. My marriage and my career are my life, so what am I supposed to do now that both of them are ruined?"

"Honey, even though David is gone now, it doesn't mean he's gone for good," Mom said.

"But, Mom, even if he did want to come back, I don't even know if I could forgive him. And I can tell you right now, I will never be able to forget it."

"Never say never," Monica chimed in. "Although I do understand why it will be hard to forgive him. Especially since he left you for a white girl."

Monica had lost her first love to a white girl when we were in college, and had despised interracial dating ever since.

"What the two of you keep forgetting is that, yes, I'm hurt, but it's not because I'm desperately in love with David or that I can't live without him. It's more because he fell in love with someone else, and I didn't have an alternate plan like he did."

"I hate seeing you go through this," Monica said.

"I hate it too," I said. "But this is the reality."

"Why is it that men can't be satisfied with one woman for longer than a few years?" Mom asked. "Some can't even be faithful from the start of a relationship let alone anything else."

"Not every man is like that," I said, because I was still convinced that it truly was possible to be happily married until death.

"No," Mom responded. "You're right. Not every man is like that, but every decent black man I know is either married or in a long-standing relationship. Which is also why I would have no problem crossing over if the right white man came along."

"What?" I said.

"What nothing," she said as serious as could be. "You know I've never had a problem with interracial dating anyway."

"I know, but you've never said you were interested in doing it yourself."

"Well, when you get to be fifty-eight like me, all you want is to be happy. And if being happy means I have to date a little differently than I have in the past, then so be it."

Monica frowned. "Emma, I just don't see how you could do that. I mean, isn't it enough just knowing that white men forced themselves on slave women, and that white women secretly had sex with our men, who sometimes lost their lives for it? Because I know you saw *Mandingo*."

"Girl, nobody's thinking about that. This is the twenty-first century. I'm not saying I agree with what went on in the past, because I don't. But I'm not going to spend the rest of my life dwelling on it either, because I haven't had a decent man in my life since I divorced Anise's father. And that was fifteen years ago."

"I guess, but I could never date anyone other than a black man. Even if it meant spending the rest of my life alone."

"It's easy to preach that when you have a *good* black man like you do," Emma continued.

"But even if I didn't, I wouldn't go that route," Monica said, trying to convince her.

"Uh-huh," Mom teased. "I bet."

I laughed as they seesawed back and forth like mother and daughter, but I wasn't about to side with either one of them. Two weeks ago, I would have agreed with Monica in a heartbeat, but my new feelings for Frank had changed my way of thinking.

They kept debating, but we never discussed the interview I was so upset over this afternoon. Which, as I recall, was the main reason the two of them rushed right over here. They'd come to console me, but now they were making me laugh, and for the time being, I felt a lot better. My problems were still unresolved, but I knew Mom was right about what she'd said earlier.

Things would get better with time.

They had to.

CHAPTER 10

S o how much more are they going to take out of our weekly paychecks?" Tony, one of the drill operators, asked me regarding the additional life insurance plan we were now going to offer through a new company.

I was conducting a benefits Q&A session for the hourly employees in the manufacturing break room. Elizabeth and I had decided last year that it was a good idea to schedule something each quarter so employees could express their concerns.

"It will depend on your age, sex, health and how much additional coverage you choose. Every person's situation will be different, but the schedule of premiums for individuals and families is listed on the sheet I'm passing around right now."

"What if I mark down that I'm twenty-five even though I'm fifty, do you think I could get away with that?" Tony asked, and the entire first shift roared.

I laughed right along with them, because the shop employees always knew how to have a good time. They didn't take things as seriously as we did in the office. They were laid back and totally down to earth. Most of us were stuffy and spent far too much time trying to compete with each other. I loved working with them, and Jim was right when he said "those people" loved me. They loved me because I had worked hard to make their lives at Reed Meyers as comfortable as possible. Maybe Jim was right about something else, too. Maybe I actually did connect with them because my parents worked in factories. But that still didn't give him the right to keep me in a particular position.

"No, Tony, I don't think you'd be able to get away with that, so I don't think that's a good idea."

"Just checkin', ma'am," he said, still enjoying himself. "Because I'll bet the premium on a twenty-five-year-old is much cheaper than what it'll be for an old buck like me."

We all chuckled again, but I thought I'd better start winding down the meeting. We'd been in here for forty-five minutes, and I'd already gone over everything I needed to.

"Well, if that's it, then I just want to remind all of you again that open enrollment begins in less than two weeks. If you choose the same health carriers, then your enrollment will automatically renew and you won't have to do anything. But if you decide to go with another plan, then you'll have to complete the appropriate forms to do so. Representatives from each insurance company will be here during the first week, so if you have additional questions, you can ask them at that time. Also, there will be a Merrill Lynch rep on hand for those of you who are interested in starting a 401(k) plan, and if you already have an account, you can increase your percentage at that time as well. Actually, you can make an increase on an existing account anytime throughout the year, but a lot of people like to do it during open enrollment, because the reps are here to answer questions."

Everyone sat at attention and a few employees spoke among themselves. I'd scheduled this meeting at the end of their shift, and they were obviously ready to punch out.

"Well, if there aren't any other questions, then I guess that's it."

"Thanks, Anise," Billy said with a southern Kentucky drawl.

"Yeah, thanks, Anise," Willy spoke loudly with the same tone of humor.

Billy and Willy were two of my favorite people because they joked around all the time. There was never a dull moment, and even though Billy had told me how his parents "hated Jews and coloreds," he always assured me that he and his twin brother Willy didn't feel that way. They'd grown up in a small Kentucky town but had decided as teenagers that they didn't care what color a person was so long as that person treated them decent. I so appreciated hearing him say that, and it was a good feeling to know that they'd been brave enough to break that continuous cycle my mother always spoke about.

The meeting adjourned, I gathered my material together, chatted with a couple of employees and headed back through the plant. When I arrived at the door leading into the HR department, Elizabeth opened it and then allowed it to close. I was sure she could tell that I was headed inside, so it surprised me when she didn't hold the door open.

I was about to find out why.

"Jim wants to see you in his office," she said.

I stared at her because I didn't like the expression I saw on her face.

"Did he say why?" was all I could muster.

"He asked me to let him tell you what's going on, but I'll at least tell you that it's about the job you applied for."

My stomach turned flips. I knew immediately that it wasn't good news, because Elizabeth was still standing here with no smile and no indication that I was going to be promoted.

"They gave it to someone else, didn't they?"

"I'm sorry, Anise, but I really do think it would be best if you spoke with Jim first, and if you want to talk afterward, I'll be in my office."

I didn't even respond. Not because I was angry with Elizabeth, because I knew she meant well. The truth was, I was speechless.

It didn't take me five minutes to drop off the meeting material in my office and walk down to Jim's for what seemed like the hundredth impromptu subpoena in the last month. I knew there was a reason why eleven days had passed since he'd interviewed me, but I'd still stayed hopeful. I'd even decided that I wasn't going to let it consume me day in and day out. At least not until I heard from him one way or another.

But now the time had come, and I didn't want to hear the decision I knew he couldn't wait to tell me.

"Hi, Anise. You can go right in," his secretary said. But this time she didn't smile so readily. I could tell she wasn't being rude, but her inability to look me straight in my eyes told me that she already knew what I was about to discover.

I went in and took a seat without being instructed to.

"I'll get straight to the point," he said.

He was so arrogant that it made me ill.

"Elizabeth has been offered a position with another company and has decided to leave Reed Meyers. So now that I have two managerial positions open, I'm going to have to do some major restructuring of the entire department and reevaluate everyone's responsibilities. Which means I'm going to have to place the position you applied for on hold."

For the first time in my life, I knew why disgruntled employees woke up on any given day, drove to the parking lot of their previous employer and shot everyone in sight. I was feeling temporarily insane *again,* and I thanked God I didn't own a gun.

"Lyle and I feel real bad about having you wait all this time for an answer, and then now having to tell you this. So we agreed that since you are obviously the most qualified candidate for Elizabeth's job, we would have no problem offering it to you."

"Why would you think I'm qualified for Elizabeth's job, but you've never thought I was for the HR recruiting one?" I asked.

"Because you've worked in benefits for two years, you've reported to Elizabeth the entire time and you've even carried out some of her responsibilities when she couldn't be here."

"Yeah, but so has Kelli."

I could tell he didn't have a rebuttal, and I wondered what he was going to conjure up as a scapegoat.

"You're good with benefits. You're good with handling all the questions and concerns that people have. Kelli is a people person too, but I think you're a better fit for the job."

"Really?"

"Yes, and since I don't know when we'll be filling the other position, this would give you a chance to be promoted to management in the next couple of weeks or so."

"Well, I'm still not interested."

"How could you not be?"

He looked shocked, and I wondered, did he actually believe he could dangle a ten-cent lollipop in front of me when I craved Godiva chocolate?

"I've told you more than once that I'm not interested in continuing a career in benefits, I'm not interested in being a training manager and I'm not interested in any other area besides HR. So I guess I don't have a choice except to wait for you to release the recruiting position from hold. Which isn't a problem for me because I have all the time in the world."

In reality, it was a problem. It was a major problem, because I suspected this job was only being placed on hold to frustrate me. What they wanted was for me to lose patience and either take Elizabeth's job or leave the company. They'd succeeded in frustrating me, but I wasn't about to resign. I was in this for the entire ride whether they realized it or not.

"I understand your position, but if I were you, I would rethink all of this very carefully. I know you want the recruiting manager's position, but I have to remind you that we'll still be selecting the most qualified candidate when the time comes. And I'd hate to see you miss out on that position as well as Elizabeth's."

"I appreciate your concern," I said, standing up, "but I'll take my chances."

"Your choice," he responded.

I left his office fuming.

They'd made it clear that they didn't want me in recruiting, and for a while I'd thought part of the reason was that they didn't want me knowing the salaries of corporate employees. But if he was practically shoving Elizabeth's job down my throat, then that wasn't the case, because as benefits manager, I would have access to information on everyone who worked for the company. So now I knew that Jim and Lyle's mission was primarily to keep me out of a job that would give me the authority to recruit qualified women and minorities into corporate positions that were vacant.

The roadblocks were being stacked against me at an alarming rate, but I fought hard, trying to stay strong. I wasn't sure what depression felt like, but I had a feeling that this stirring in the pit of my stomach and my sudden desire to crawl into a hole were likely qualifiers.

It was almost four-thirty, and although I usually kept working until five or six, I grabbed my things and walked out.

I told Elizabeth I was leaving for the day. When she asked if I still wanted to talk, I told her maybe tomorrow. I didn't even bother saying good-bye to Lorna or anyone else.

All I wanted was to escape. I drove to the one place where I wouldn't have to speak to anyone. I drove home, where I would be safe.

I'd been lying in bed for two full hours, trying to deal with my disappointment. Which was fine, because in the midst of it, I was minding my own business. I wasn't bothering a soul, but now here David was standing inside the doorway, staring at me in silence. I had no idea what he was doing here. I hadn't seen him in weeks, and I wondered what was so special about tonight.

He continued standing, I'm sure in hopes that I would say something—anything. But I didn't.

"What's wrong with you?" he asked.

I glared at him.

"Oh, so you can't even talk to me, I guess?"

I turned my head away from him and nestled into my pillow. I didn't want to hear any new explanations he might have for cheating on me, and I didn't feel like arguing with him. What I wanted was for him to leave me alone, or even better, go back to the woman I was sure he was shacking up with.

"At some point, Anise, you really are going to have to grow up," he said, and strutted into what used to be his walk-in closet. He'd cleaned out just about everything he had the day Mom and I had gone shopping, but there were still a few of his items on some of the shelves.

I knew it was killing him that I was ignoring him, but it served him right. He didn't deserve any conversation from me, and if he wanted someone to talk to, I couldn't help him.

"You know, we really did have everything, and every bit of this separation is all your fault," he said. "You and that damn career ruined us, and the sad part is, you're probably still obsessed with it."

He was badgering me for no reason, and I was quickly becoming tired of it.

I heard him walk out of the closet, but I didn't raise my head to look at him.

"Anise, why are you doing this?"

I sat up, faced this man I no longer had one ounce of respect for and said, "Why are you bothering me?"

"I'm trying to keep things pleasant between us, so I'm sorry if you feel like I'm *bothering* you."

"David, I've had a very bad day. I'm trying to deal with some things that happened earlier, and I refuse to participate in another screaming match with you. You haven't been here, and you haven't called, so why are you here harassing me now?"

"I tried to call you a week or so ago, but you blew everything out of proportion. All I wanted to do was apologize, but you wouldn't even give me a chance."

"But I don't need you to apologize. You made your decision to be with someone else, and I'm dealing with it."

"You don't even care about any of this, do you?" he asked, folding his arms.

"Why should I spend all my time thinking about the fact that you're sleeping with another woman? Our relationship was basically over anyway, so if you're expecting me to roll on the floor in tears, it's not going to happen."

"You know? That really sickens me. I've seen you shed tears over other shit, but now you're sitting here telling me that I'm not worth it."

"What are you talking about? Are you saying that you *want* to see me torn up emotionally?"

"At least then I would know that our marriage meant something to you."

I laughed, but didn't find any of this amusing. I'd done that a lot with him lately.

"David, you had the affair and then decided you weren't going to stop. So I'll ask you again: Why are you bothering me?"

"I'm asking because you haven't tried to contact me once since the day I moved out."

"Why should I try to contact you? You're the one who messed around and got caught. Not to mention the fact that I have more important things to worry about than you and your mistress."

"Don't pretend like my moving out isn't bothering you, Anise, because if it wasn't, you wouldn't be lying in bed on a hot summer day while the sun is still shining."

I hated to drop his ego down a notch, but he left me no choice.

"Yes, I'm upset, but it doesn't have anything to do with you. I've already gone through my sad and angry moments regarding our marriage, but today I'm dealing with something different. Something you couldn't care less about, and something I don't care to discuss."

"I hope it's not that same old Reed Meyers saga again?"

"Whatever, David," I said, and went over to the extra tall armoire, opened the doors, pulled out the TV selector and powered it on. Then I sat down on the bed and flipped through the channels. There wasn't anything on I wanted to see, but this was the only thing I could think to do to avoid him.

"What is it now? They've given that job to someone else?"

"Why in the hell won't you just leave me alone?"

"Because you're my wife, and I'll be damned if you're going to make it seem like I'm no big deal and that our marriage never even existed."

"What are you talking about?" I asked. "I mean, exactly what is it that you expect me to do?"

"First I started taking on more overnight projects, then I started attending more five-day training conferences, but I still didn't get your attention. Now you've found out that I'm seeing someone else, and that hasn't made any difference either."

He was becoming more and more unbelievable with every breath.

"No, the reason you did all those things was because you couldn't control me. You wanted me to do everything except the things I wanted to. I am who I am. My mother raised me to be strong, and she made sure I knew how to take care of myself in case some man left me the way you have. So if you're waiting for me to apologize for that, you'll be waiting for the rest of your lifetime."

"You being so strong and independent is what caused all of these problems."

"No, you trying to control me like some child and not being able to is what happened."

"You just don't get it, do you?" he said.

"Oh, I get it, but I'm not sweating it," I told him.

"You may be riding on your little high horse now, but you'll come down off of it when you realize what you've lost."

"Honey, don't flatter yourself," I said.

He turned sharply and stormed out of the bedroom mumbling. I thought I heard the word bitch, but I knew I must have been mistaken. For his sake, I had better be.

"David, what did you just say?"

"I wouldn't worry about it."

"No. Repeat what you said."

"I don't want to hurt your little feelings, so let's just forget it."

"You are so freakin' spineless."

"Okay. I'll tell you exactly what I said. I called you a crazy bitch. Happy?" He was now standing inside the bedroom again with a self-satisfied look on his face. He was proud of what he'd just called me.

"That's real good, David. And I hope you're happy about the way you just disrespected me, because there are a lot of things I could say to hurt you, too, but I won't."

"Yeah, right. Like what? Because I know for a fact that I'm the type of man every woman in America dreams about."

"Hmmph. If you only knew."

"If I only knew what?"

"That those same women you're talking about would rather die than have a jerk like you."

"What the hell is that supposed to mean?"

"That most women wouldn't dare have a man who can't fuck."

"I knew I shouldn't have married your little nappy-headed, double-chocolate-looking ass in the first place."

"My hair isn't nappy" was all I could say.

"Only because you spend sixty dollars every few weeks drenching chemicals through it. But if it weren't for that, your shit would look ridiculous."

I was wordless. It was bad enough that I was being humiliated by a white man at work because of the color of my skin, but now my own husband was making me feel the same way in my own home. He obviously thought being high yellow gave him the right to do that.

"I bet you'll think before you speak next time, won't you?" he said, pretending to look through one of our dresser drawers for nothing.

I wanted to shoot something back at him, but I couldn't. I was too stunned.

But he continued delivering his speech.

"And you keep wondering why you can't get ahead at any company you work for. My guess is that they probably feel the same way I do. Certain jobs at certain levels have to be filled with people who portray the right image. It's not about your ethnic background, it's about your physical characteristics. Because no matter how many expensive suits or hairdos you wear, your skin is never going to be light enough. You may be attractive for a dark-skinned sister, but, sweetheart, that's not going to help you."

"David, just get out," I screamed, stepping onto the carpet and moving toward him. "Get out before I do something crazy."

He moved away from me as quickly as I approached him.

"Don't worry, I was leaving anyway." He reached for the doorknob when we arrived in the kitchen.

I grabbed the glass sitting on the island and slung it against the door.

He jerked his head away from it and stepped back.

"You are so *stupid*," he yelled.

"No, you're the stupid one. Especially if you stay here."

"You're just mad because you know I'm right about your dark skin and the way you look."

I pulled a huge butcher knife from the wooden block on the granite counter.

"I'm giving you one more chance to get the hell out," I said, and moved closer to him.

This time he left without comment.

I was so furious I felt as if my head was going to crack wide open. But my feelings were hurt as well because of the way he'd spoken to me, and what bothered me the most was that David, for the first time, had shaken my confidence. He'd made me feel self-conscious about my looks and like I was a disgrace to all women. He'd made me think long and hard about my career expectations, and I was terrified that he might be telling the truth. What if he was right? What if my skin really was too dark? What if my hair really was too coarse? What if being black meant I could forget about all my hopes and dreams?

What if Reed Meyers pushed me to my absolute limit?

It was certainly possible.

It would be better for everyone involved if they didn't.

CHAPTER 11

'D JUST STEPPED OFF the elevator on the second floor and was on my way down to Connie's office in public relations. She was the third candidate who had applied for the HR manager's position that Jim had mysteriously placed on hold last Friday, and now that we'd entered a new week, I'd decided to go ask her a few questions. I'd phoned her a half hour ago, and she'd told me to come right up whenever I was ready.

Connie's door was open, so I walked right in.

"Hey, Anise," she said, smiling.

"How are you, Connie?" I was just as cordial.

"So we're going for the same position I heard."

"Yeah, I guess so, except now that it's on hold, neither one of us may have a chance of getting it."

She frowned. "What do you mean, 'on hold'?"

"I mean 'on hold.' Didn't Jim tell you that last week?"

"No. He didn't. As a matter of fact, I was planning to call him if I didn't hear something by tomorrow, because I was just starting to wonder why it's taking them so long to make a decision."

"I don't believe this," I said, shaking my head in disgust. "He just told me on Friday that since he now has two managerial positions vacant, he was going to place the recruiting one on hold until he did some restructuring of the department."

"What other position is open?" Connie asked.

"Benefits manager. Elizabeth is leaving to go work for a company in Wisconsin." I'd finally had a conversation with Elizabeth this morning. She'd seemed happy about leaving, but I think it was mostly because her parents lived there, and now that they were dealing with some illnesses, she wanted to move closer to them.

"Really? When is she leaving?"

"Next Friday."

"Well, I didn't know anything about that or the recruiting manager's position being on hold."

"Actually, Connie, I'm not surprised, because this company doesn't do anything consistently. They handle every situation differently and that's what burns me about them."

"I agree, but I don't see how he could place a job on hold and not tell each person who applied for it. Although, maybe he didn't tell me because I'm not one of the people he's considering," she said.

As much as I hated to admit it, she was probably right. Not because she wasn't intelligent or couldn't perform the job duties, but it was highly unlikely that Jim would promote her into an HR managerial position with her background being in public relations. It was my understanding from Lorna that Connie had never worked in an HR department before, so even I could understand why he wasn't considering her. Although when they'd given the position to Jason six months ago, he hadn't worked in HR either. But since he was a man, his work history probably wasn't a factor.

I didn't stress my take on it, though.

"Who knows" was all I said.

"Are you thinking about applying for Elizabeth's job?" she asked. "Especially since you already work in the department."

"No," I answered, but didn't discuss the fact that Jim had already suggested the same thing. I liked Connie a lot, but I'd learned the day I was hired that you had to be careful about who you confided in here at the company. There were so many cliques and gossip columnists, and the last thing I needed was to have someone twisting something I said into a lie.

"Well, if you're not, then maybe I'll think about applying for it myself," she said and I could tell that she didn't care what job she was given so long as she could leave public relations. I'd heard a few rumors here and there about her and her supervisor not getting along.

"Yeah, you should if it's something you're really interested in doing."

"As long as it's a promotion and it gets me out of this department, I'll be happy regardless."

I knew I had been right about her.

"Well, I won't keep you any longer, but thanks for chatting with me about this," I said.

"No problem, and if you don't mind, can you put in a good word for me with Elizabeth? Because maybe she'll recommend me to Jim before she leaves."

"I'll see what I can do" was all I could think to say, because I knew Elizabeth didn't know Connie all that well. They might have seen each other in passing or at company events, but that was probably it.

I stopped by our department's interoffice mail area and pulled a stack from my open slot. I glanced through the pile, but most of it was information on HR seminars, a few gold interoffice envelopes and a couple of announcements.

I walked in my office and did what had become routine for me as of late. I closed the door. Then I sat down and read the first memo, which was informing all employees that flex hours would be in effect until the Tuesday after Labor Day. We'd already discussed it at a staff meeting last month, but as usual, memos didn't always go out in a timely fashion.

The next one described the latest job vacancy, manufacturing HR manager, and I wondered why Bob was leaving that one. People were dropping out of here like an epidemic had struck, and having so many key supervisory positions open wasn't a good thing. Those were the people who kept the departments running smoothly, so I didn't know how Jim was planning to handle losing three managers all at once. Even more interesting was how he thought he could keep that recruiting position on hold when they needed to recruit managers and fill other vacancies that had been posted for quite some time.

I picked up the phone and called Lorna.

"Hey, are you busy?" I asked.

"No. Why, what's up?"

"Did you see this latest job vacancy?"

"No, but Bob just told me himself over at the coffee machine that he's going to be taking Elizabeth's job."

"How? I mean, I'm not saying he's not qualified, because I know he is, but how can he already know he's getting the job if it was never even posted?"

Lorna laughed. "Anise, you and I both know that Jim and Lyle do whatever they want."

"What a joke. If you remember, I was just telling you over the weekend how Jim tried to convince me to take it."

"I know, but I guess Bob went and spoke with him as soon as he got wind that Elizabeth was leaving."

"Unbelievable. Everything is so freakin' unbelievable around here. Some jobs get posted, some don't. Some people need to have a certain number of years of experience or a certain degree and others are exceptions to the rule."

"This is the same old crap we've been talking about all along, and if you don't do what I keep telling you, they're going to continue getting away with it."

"I know, but I have to admit I'm wondering if maybe I should bite the bullet and go for this manufacturing position. Because at least I'd still be able to recruit people into the company, and I'd be promoted to management," I said, and realized I was sounding somewhat like Connie. Although, it wasn't as if I was applying for just anything so I could leave my current responsibilities, because I still felt passionate about recruiting employees. I'd hoped I would have a chance to recruit for corporate positions, but maybe this would be a stepping-stone the next time the corporate position was open. At least I tried to convince myself that it was.

"I don't think your chances are going to be any better than they were for the corporate position."

"I think they would be, because unfortunately, I don't think Jim would have a problem with me recruiting factory employees. He doesn't see that as a problem, because he's reiterated a thousand times that I work so well with the shop people."

"And that's pathetic, too," Lorna said. "Who is he to decide what people you work better with? You work well with everyone I've seen you come in contact with, so piss on him."

"I hear what you're saying, and I agree, but I'd hate to miss out on this position and the one on hold," I said, weighing everything back and forth as I spoke.

"I don't know, Anise. I don't know if you should just give up like this and do what they want. Hell, I wouldn't doubt if they'd purposely offered Elizabeth's job to Bob so you would be tempted to apply for his. They've done underhanded shit like that before, so it's not beneath them."

Lorna did have a point, so who was I fooling? I'd suspected the same thing as soon as I saw the memo, and if it hadn't been for the argument I'd had with David last week, I probably wouldn't be thinking about trying for any job I didn't really want. But he'd made me rethink my whole situation, and as much as I wanted to stay hopeful, I knew I had to be realistic. I had to keep in mind that maybe he'd been right about all the hurtful things he said to me. I'd never struggled with my self-esteem, but over the last few days he'd forced me to look in the mirror more times in one day than I usually did in a month. It was almost as if I needed to evaluate my appearance. I'd even thought about having cosmetic surgery in order to decrease the size of my nose and lips. Then I'd thought about having my hair stylist weave some silky straight hair into my own, just past my shoulders. It was such insane thinking, but I was starting to feel more desperate by the minute.

"This is all so crazy," I finally said.

"You deserve to have that corporate recruiting manager's position, and I can't see you taking anything less than that."

"But the manufacturing manager position would still be management, too."

"Okay, Anise. You do whatever it is you feel you have to do," she said, and I could hear how irritated she was.

"Why are you getting so upset?"

"Because you're actually going to keep quiet and let them get away with doing this to you."

"You mean like how you let Jim get away with sexually harassing you?"

Lorna was silent.

So was I, and I hated that we were talking this way to each other.

"Okay. I deserved that," she admitted.

"I didn't mean to offend you, but it's just that I'm in a bind here."

"I know, I know. And I guess I'm just being selfish about all of this, because if you get that manufacturing position, you'll be fine, and then Jim will never be stopped. And neither will Lyle or the company altogether."

"I hear what you're saying, Lorna, but I just don't know what I'm going to do."

"It'll come to you. Maybe we should talk later when you've had more time to think about all of this."

"Yeah, maybe so. I won't do anything without letting you know, and, hey, I really appreciate you listening to me. If I didn't have you, I wouldn't have anyone here at work to talk to."

"I feel the same way about you."

There was a short yet sentimental silence between us.

"I'd better get back down to the corporate conference room," she said. "I'm trying to reorganize the main training manual, and I've got stuff spread out all over the table. I don't think any meetings are scheduled in there for today, but there are tomorrow, and that means I need to finish up and clear it out before I leave this evening."

"I need to wind up a couple of things before lunch myself, so I'll talk to ya."

"See ya later," she said, and hung up.

I felt bad for her and me, but I didn't know how I could simply ignore this newest opportunity. I wanted the corporate position. Actually, I longed for it. But I couldn't take the chance of missing out on both. I knew if they denied me each of them, I'd have grounds to sue the hell out of them. But deep down, I really didn't want to go through all of that. This separation between David and me looked like a future divorce, so the idea of having to deal with another legal mess wasn't too desirable. Plus, I needed at least one area of my life to settle down. I was a Taurus and needed to have a certain amount of stability at all times. I was sure I could learn to love the manufacturing position, so maybe it wasn't such a bad idea to go for it. Maybe this was a blessing in disguise, and I just didn't know it.

At eleven o'clock, although I never drank coffee, I decided to walk over to the small break room to have a croissant. One of the secretaries was celebrating a birthday and had brought in a couple of trays of them. Lunchtime was only an hour away, but since I was planning to work right through it and leave an hour early, I decided I would grab something quick to tide me over.

But when I entered the room, I regretted making that decision. Frank turned and smiled as soon as he heard me walk in.

"Hey, beautiful," he said.

I couldn't believe he was calling me that.

"How are you, Frank?" I acknowledged. Then I looked around, wishing another employee would join us. Having lunch with him was one thing, but standing in a room all alone with him was another. I didn't trust what else he might say or do, but worse, I didn't trust my own feelings.

"I'm fine, now that I've seen you," he said.

"You shouldn't say things like that."

"Why? You're not going to file a sexual harassment claim against me, are you?" he asked, smiling.

"I don't know. I might." There was no humor in my tone.

"You're not serious," he said, and I laughed, because I could tell he was slightly worried that he'd crossed the line with the wrong person.

"Jeez. You scared me for a minute."

I reached for a napkin and grabbed a croissant.

"So then when are you going to let me take you out?"

"Frank, we've already been through this before, so why are you asking me that?" I said, but didn't turn to face him. I pretended I was concentrating on the croissant I was eating.

"Why can't you look at me?" he asked.

I didn't want to believe he was being so personal, but what was more unbelievable was that my heart was beating much too rapidly. He had an effect on me that I didn't like, and I wasn't sure how I was going to handle it. All I could think to do was to leave the room. But that was too easy, of course.

"I *can* look at you. But you're always making me feel so uncomfortable."

"I make you feel uncomfortable because you really do want to go out with me."

He was right, but I didn't admit it.

"Just give it a chance, Anise. All I'm asking is for us to go to dinner. You can even drive your own car if you want to."

"I'm married, Frank, and I've told you that before."

"I know, and I'm real sorry that you are, but I can't help how attracted I am to you or how much I like you."

"I have to go," I said for lack of anything to say. Then I turned and walked away.

"It's going to be hard for me to leave you alone, because I've seen the way you look at me. That is, unless you stop right now and tell me that you're not attracted to me, that you're going to try and work things out with your husband and that I'm the last person on this earth you want to be with."

I stood still, tried to repeat what he'd just said, but the next thing I knew, I was on my way back to my office. I hadn't looked at him, I'd just walked out of there in a hurry. I'd wanted to tell him to leave me alone, but like him, I knew I didn't want that. Deep down inside I wanted to be with him as much as he wanted to be with me, and I didn't know how much longer I was going to be able to prevent it from happening. I felt like a hypocrite, because part of the reason I was so angry with David was that he'd left me for a white woman. But here I was trying to settle my racing heart because of how emotional I became when I was near Frank.

What was a woman to do in a situation like this? I was married, and I'd never dated outside my race. But on the other hand, my husband was sleeping with another woman. I needed to be careful with any decision I made, though, because with everything I was going through, I was much too vulnerable. I was too eager to find happiness of any kind, and I had to make sure that I thought long and hard before making an irreparable mistake. I had to concentrate on my job predicament first, and then I'd deal with Frank later—if I was going to deal with him at all.

CHAPTER 12

DROVE into the health club's parking lot and waited for the downpour to cease. The rain pounded so hard that I couldn't see a thing through my windshield. I sat back and relaxed, though, because I knew it wouldn't last more than a few minutes since the sun was still shining. I wondered if the devil really was beating his wife like my grandparents used to claim. I'd always laughed when they discussed superstitious beliefs such as that. But deep down I knew the devil wasn't abusing his wife any more than people were receiving seven years of bad luck for breaking a mirror. Actually, my grandmother had quite a few things you couldn't and shouldn't do for one reason or another. You couldn't split a post if you were walking side by side with someone; instead you both had to pass it on the same side. You couldn't brush the top of anyone's feet with a broom. You couldn't bring eggs inside the house after sundown. No female of any kind could enter your house on New Year's Day until a man had visited first.

I, of course, had done all of the above. I'd broken quite a few mirrors during my adult life, I didn't always walk on the same side of a post as the person I was with—especially if it wasn't convenient—and I couldn't count the number of times I'd gone shopping at the market well after dark, purchased eggs and brought them inside the house with the rest of my groceries. I didn't abide by any of those rules, but Mom still took Grandma's superstitions quite seriously and never tried to resist them.

Monica pulled up next to me in her black Navigator and waved. We both sat patiently for another ten minutes, and when the showers finally cleared, we stepped out of our vehicles.

"Where did that come from?" Monica asked.

"I don't know, but I guess we needed it, since it's been so dry."

"You're right about that. Marc was just complaining yesterday about all the brown patches spread across our lawn."

"We have the same problem. You'd think the in-ground sprinklers would make a difference, but they haven't kept the lawn as green as they usually do. Well, I guess I shouldn't say that, though, because if we didn't have them, the grass would actually look worse."

"There's no doubt about it. And, hey, did you remember to bring your towel and toiletries so we can sit in the sauna for a while?" Monica asked.

"I have them right here." I raised my duffel bag to show her. I knew she was asking because I almost always forgot to bring what I needed whenever we met to work out. So much so that I eventually packed my bag with a beach towel, shower gel, deodorant and lotion and kept it in my SUV at all times.

We went inside, showed our ID tags and headed for the locker room. We were both already dressed in shorts and T-shirts, but needed to change into our socks and gym shoes.

"So how'd everything go at work today?" she asked, tying one of her shoelaces.

"So-so. I found out that Jim didn't tell the third candidate that the job was on hold. And I'm willing to bet that he didn't tell Kelli Jacobson either. That 'hold' situation is primarily being done because of me. But the one good thing, or at least I think it could be a good thing, is that they've posted another managerial job opening."

"Oh really? Doing what?"

"The person in this position would oversee the manufacturing portion of human resources—things like recruiting hourly employees and supervising the HR specialists who work with those employees. You know, that kind of stuff."

"So it is management then?" Monica asked.

"Yeah," I said, pulling on my other shoe. "But it wouldn't allow me to work with corporate employees. Which means I wouldn't be involved with recruiting any professional staff or any executives."

"Yeah, but maybe this job would be your foot in the door when the one on hold is finally released."

"That's my thinking exactly. I don't think they'll necessarily give it to me as soon as it's off hold, but I'm hoping they would the next time it's vacant."

"Well, maybe this is your answer. Maybe this will mean you won't have to file a complaint against them."

"That's what I'm hoping. Because, Monica, I'd really prefer not to, if at all possible. I just don't feel like going through any legal battles. But Lorna, my friend at work, doesn't think I should apply for the manufacturing position because I deserve the corporate one."

"I agree that you deserve it, too, but since they're fighting you so hard, and it's causing so much animosity, maybe this is a better choice. I don't want to see you backing down to a bunch of racist white men, but the bottom line is that, right or wrong, they still run things."

I didn't like the sound of that. It was something about the way Monica said, "They still run things." It made me cringe. I knew she was right, and that's why none of this sat well with me. They had every right to "run things" because of the positions they held at the company, but they didn't have the right to be unfair, break the law and say, "Black girl, take what we're giving you, and shut the hell up." Which is exactly what I would be allowing them to say if I gave in and took that manufacturing position.

"They do run things, but that doesn't give them the right to abuse their power at the expense of other people and their careers," I said.

"No, it doesn't, but maybe if you take this job, things will be different next time. I'm not saying that the way they've treated you is right, but I don't want to see you keep going through all of this madness either. You're upset about both your marriage and Reed Meyers, and I can tell that it's wearing you down. That's why I called you this morning to see if you wanted to come work out this evening."

"I know, and I'm glad you did," I said, and stood up when two other members walked into the locker room, sat their things down on the bench next to us and started removing their clothing. Unlike us, they hadn't gone home to change, and still had on business suits.

We shoved our belongings into our assigned lockers, removed the keys and went out to the area where the aerobic machines were located. Our ritual was to walk thirty minutes on the treadmill and then do upper- and lower-body weights. There were television screens lined across the wall, so I went and picked up the remote control and selected my favorite channel, Lifetime. Monica chose BET like she always did, because she preferred walking to music.

I straddled the center of the treadmill, entered my age and weight and then selected the fat-burning program. I waited for the machine to pick up speed, pulled on my headphones and then stepped onto the belt. Monica did the same and was already bobbing her head to one of Janet Jackson's latest videos. I laughed when I saw Sophia of *The Golden Girls* wearing a robe and carrying her handbag into the kitchen. She never left it anywhere, and I laughed even louder when she suddenly called Blanche a slut.

We walked, and before I knew it, the treadmill switched into the cooldown mode. That meant I only had five more minutes before going to lift weights. I'd thought about this job dilemma on and off the whole thirty minutes, but I'd pretty much decided that I was going to call Jim as soon as I arrived at work tomorrow to express my interest in the manufacturing position. I didn't know what his response was going to be, but I had a feeling he wouldn't have a problem with it. I knew Lorna wasn't going to be happy with my decision, but I had to go with my gut feeling. I had to at least try to make things work out while I was still working for the company. There weren't a lot of large corporations in the city, and Reed Meyers was truly where I wanted to keep working if I could. Especially since the pay was decent and it allowed me to live near my mother. Not to mention the fact that I had already invested several years with them and it wouldn't be good to give up my seniority and start somewhere else. Again.

We finished the cooldown, wiped perspiration from our foreheads and made our way over to the Lifecycle machines. Monica started, and I followed behind her with us each doing two sets of twelve reps on every machine. I loved doing weights, and although a lot of women worried about buffing up too much, all weights actually did was tone your muscles. That is, as long as you weren't overdoing it by lifting way too much, because then you could start looking pretty thick.

When we finished with the last piece of equipment, we returned to the locker room, removed our clothing and entered the sauna. It was already set to Monica's liking, which was still too hot for me, but I tolerated it. I enjoyed it, because the heat always relaxed me and opened my pores, and I felt so refreshed when I took a cool shower right after.

"So have you heard from David?" Monica asked with her eyes closed.

"No, not since Friday. But I told you about that craziness already."

"Hmmph. I still can't believe he called you a bitch and then had the nerve to trip about the color of your skin."

"I couldn't either, but I should have known with the way he always made comments about other dark-skinned people. It was the same old thing all the time. Somebody was beautiful, but they were dark. Somebody could be beautiful if they weren't so dark. Somebody needed to go lace some chemicals around their edges. Somebody needed some plastic surgery to tone down their facial features."

"But that's not even logical, because I know a number of attractive dark-skinned women like you, and at the same time I know light-skinned women who aren't attractive at all," Monica said. "Hell, I'm light-skinned myself, but we both know Marc is as dark as a brother can be."

"And he's as fine as they come, too," I added, and we both laughed.

"That he is." Monica beamed.

"But, girl, David has a problem with being black in general. He wasn't like that when I met him—well, maybe just a little, but not nearly the way he is now. He almost hates the fact that he's black, because he really thinks life would be so much better for him if he was white. He won't even hire any black employees unless he absolutely has to. He speaks about black people in a derogatory way all the time and doesn't see a thing wrong with it."

"That's too bad, because one day he's going to wake up and realize he doesn't fit in with black people or white."

"If you notice, you never hear me talking about my in-laws."

"No, actually, I don't."

"I always call them on their birthdays and send them gifts, and I do the same on Mother's Day and Father's Day. But David usually makes excuses about why he didn't get around to it. And there have been so many times when I've told him I'm getting ready to call them, and he'll tell me to wait until he leaves. Or I've even mentioned a few times that we should drive down to Peoria to visit them, and he always pretends it's not a good time."

"What?" Monica said, and opened her eyes.

"You hear me. He's ashamed of them because his father is darker than I am. The only reason David is so light is because his mother is part white and part Native American."

"Wait a minute. I can't believe you've never told me any of this."

"I was ashamed. I've always been ashamed of the way David treated his parents and how he criticizes certain black people. Normally I tell you everything, so you know I had to be really embarrassed about this," I said, and thought about the fact that I was keeping something else from her. I hadn't told her about my attraction to Frank. I couldn't. Not today, anyway.

"I can't believe David has gone off the deep end like this. I mean, who is he to think he's better than the rest of us? He may be high yellow, but in every white person's eyes, he's as black as the hair on my head. I don't care if you only have one ounce of black in you, you're black, and that's all there is to it."

"But he doesn't see it that way. About ninety-five percent of his friends and acquaintances are white. He doesn't even want to go to our church anymore, because he says it has too many ignorant black people who migrated from Mississippi and Arkansas. Can you believe that?" I said, and uncrossed my legs. The sauna was becoming hotter and hotter, and I didn't know how much longer I'd be able to sit in this wooden furnace.

"What a jerk. My parents migrated from Mississippi, and they're far from being ignorant."

"Mine did too, but of course when I mention that, he tries to play it off by saying he isn't talking about my parents. But I know he is. Because the thing with David is that you're nobody if you don't have a college degree and you don't speak properly with every word that comes out of your mouth."

"But isn't it so ironic, though?"

"What's that?"

"We go on and on about white people discriminating against us for no reason, but the truth is, there are a lot of black people who do the same thing to their own people. My girlfriend in Atlanta was telling me last year that working in Atlanta can be both good and bad, because even though there are lots of jobs for black people, it's tough when you work for certain black women. She was saying how she's had at least three supervisors who treated her like she was nothing, but couldn't wait to smile in every white employee's face all day long. It's almost like those black people believe white people will see them as equals if they separate themselves from other blacks. It just doesn't make sense."

"No, it doesn't, but that's why David is the way he is. He's extremely successful. Not just from the standpoint of being a black man, but he earns more money than most white people who work in his field."

"Well, let me ask you this. Did he act like he preferred dating white women when you first met him?"

"I've thought about that very thing ever since he left, and unfortunately, I have to say no. He seemed like he was interested in just me, but maybe I was blind to how he really felt. Sometimes I think we see what we want to see, depending on what the situation is."

"I guess so."

The door to the sauna room opened and two beautiful white women entered.

"Hello," they both spoke at the same time.

"Hello," Monica said.

"How are you ladies?" I asked.

"Exhausted," the shorter one said, "but this will make me feel much better."

"I know what you mean," I said, standing up. This was our cue to leave. Not because we didn't want to sit with them, but because I was really starting to swelter, and Monica and I certainly wouldn't be able to continue the discussion we were having in their presence.

Black people did this all the time and so did white people. We never said what we were thinking in front of each other, and our conversations were totally different when we were among our own people inside our own households. I knew that was how it was with my family and friends, and Lorna had told me it was no different with hers. It wasn't about being racist. This was simply the way it was. The way it had always been. The way it was always going to be.

The cool showers we stood in felt as good as we expected, and as soon as we finished drying off, we dressed and walked outside. The sun was just beginning to set, but the drenching rain that had fallen earlier had left the air uncomfortably muggy.

"So what are you going to do about David?" Monica asked.

"Nothing. If he wants a divorce, I will gladly give it to him."

"Man. I can't believe all this is happening, but I do understand why you feel the way you do about him. At first I was thinking you should try to work things out with him, but David really does have a lot of issues. I mean, don't get me wrong, I'm not telling you to divorce him, but what I *am* saying is that I understand why you don't love him the way you used to."

"It's definitely over, but now we'll have to deal with our property. The vehicles will be easy, but the house will have to be sold. I can't afford to buy him out of it or live in it by myself, and I know for a fact that he's going to make his permanent home in the Chicago area. You know he never wanted to come here anyway."

"It will be hard, but you'll get through it, because I did," Monica said, hugging me.

"I know," I said, and felt my eyes misting. I didn't want to be married to David any longer, but the idea saddened me nonetheless.

"I'm here for you, girl, any hour of the day. Okay?"

I nodded and sniffled a couple of times.

"But now I'd better get going, because Marc is planning to grill some burgers for us. I told him I'd be home by eight, and it's almost that now."

"I'll see ya later," I said, hating to see her go.

"I'll give you a call in the morning when I get to work," she said.

Monica backed out of her parking stall, and I did the same. Then I made a left turn out of the lot, drove a few feet and stopped when I saw traffic at a standstill. There were three cars in front of me, and I could tell that the lead car was waiting to make a left turn. So I waited. But when I glanced in my rearview mirror, I saw a car zooming toward me at full speed. I panicked, because there was nowhere I could go. I pressed on my brake as hard as I could, squeezed the steering wheel tight with both hands and heard tires screeching against the pavement.

The car behind crashed into me so hard that my SUV jerked forward. I looked around to make sure I hadn't been forced into another car or object. Fortunately, I hadn't. The woman who'd hit me drove to the right and beckoned for me to pull into the Mobil gas station. I drove behind her gray Honda Accord, placed my gear in park and tried to regain my composure. My hands shook the way they did whenever I drank too much caffeine. I took deep breaths and finally unbuckled my seat belt. Then I stepped out of the vehicle and walked around to the back to see how much damage was done. Thank God, there wasn't much I could see, except thick scratches on the bumper and paint from the other vehicle.

"I am so sorry," the woman said. "Are you okay?"

"I think so. What about you?" I asked.

"I'm okay. Is there any major damage to your vehicle?" she asked, walking around to see for herself.

"No, it doesn't look like it, but my exhaust system must have been jarred, because it sounded louder than usual when I pressed on the accelerator. It looks like your car slid under my bumper."

"Maybe so. I looked in my rearview mirror, and the next thing I knew, I saw a line of cars, but it was too late for me to stop. I am so sorry," she apologized again.

I didn't say anything, because a woman who looked to be in her forties walked up.

"Do you want me to call the police?" she asked, going up to the woman who hit me.

"Yes, if you don't mind," she said.

The forty-something woman never looked at me directly, but started dialing her cell phone.

"Hello," she said. "I'm at the corner of Rogers and Wilmington, and I'm calling to report an accident." She paused for a few seconds, I assumed listening to what the police had to say.

"I'm not sure," she said, and then looked at the woman who hit me. "What's your name?"

"Margaret Wilinski."

"Her name is Margaret Wilinski."

She paused again.

"Uh, no. I'm not sure what the other driver's name is," she said, looking toward the gas station.

What? I couldn't believe she was standing all of three feet away from me and wouldn't ask me my name the same as she had Margaret. Hell, I was the one who was rear-ended, so it seemed logical that she'd be concerned about me as well, and that she'd want to give my name to the police.

She said a few more words and dropped her cell phone in her purse. "They're sending an officer out right now to take care of you," she said to Margaret.

"Thank you so much for calling," Margaret said.

"No problem," she responded. "I was glad to do it for you—"

By now, I'd had enough of this racist bullshit.

"What I sincerely hope is that you were glad to do it for both of us," I interrupted. "Because in case you don't know the rules of the road, I'm the innocent party here."

She looked at me and then at Margaret.

"Do you need me to stay until they get here?" she asked Margaret. "I heard the crash, but I really didn't see anything. So I really can't say whose fault it was."

I didn't even give Margaret a chance to speak. I spoke instead.

"I was sitting in traffic on my brakes. You were sitting in front of me doing the same thing, so how on earth can you pretend like you don't know who's at fault? Especially since I was rear-ended and wasn't moving when it happened."

"Like I said, Margaret, do you need me to stay?" she repeated.

"No, I'll be fine."

"Bitch" was all I could think to say.

The woman got into her vehicle and drove away.

I was so humiliated. That woman knew she wouldn't have dared leave the scene until the police arrived if I had been the one at fault. As a matter of fact, she would have admitted to seeing everything that happened and then some. Now, though, because I was black, she'd hightailed it out of here like there was no accident at all. These bigoted tendencies brought out the worst in me, and I was so tired of dealing with one incident after another.

It didn't take long for the officer to arrive. He asked both of us if we were okay and then requested our driver's licenses and something to verify our insurance coverage. He was white also, and I feared almost immediately that he wasn't going to treat me with any respect. My mom had been questioned in the late seventies by two officers about the brand-new Lincoln Continental she and my father had purchased, and she'd never felt the same about the Mitchell police department ever since. She'd dropped me off at high school one morning on her way to work and was pulled over for no apparent reason. They'd asked her whose vehicle she was driving, she'd told them it was hers, but one of them yanked her keys out of the ignition. They asked for her license and told her to wait until they ran a check on her and "her new Lincoln."

She'd waited for twenty minutes, and when they'd discovered she was telling the truth, they returned to her window and threw her keys inside the car, along with her driver's license. Both items landed on the floor of the passenger side, and after she leaned over to pick them up, she saw them walking back to their vehicle. They never said one word, and sped off like they were on a high-speed chase. I could still remember Mom telling us that evening how she'd driven to work in tears, I will never forget how she cried like a child all over again when she verbally reenacted the story.

That happened in 1979, and now here I was wondering if I was about to deal with the same situation twenty-two years later. I loved my Lexus 470 SUV, but today, it was probably part of the reason that woman at the scene hadn't been so happy with me. I'd encountered a number of white people in the past who hated seeing a black person driving something more expensive than what they owned, and I'm sure that the beat-up Horizon the woman with the cell phone was driving—something Chrysler hadn't made in years—hadn't helped her attitude toward me.

Margaret's Accord was banged up pretty badly and the officer told her it would probably be a good idea to have it towed. She agreed and we waited for the officer to fill out the accident report and issue Margaret a citation. He smiled, asked me if I was okay again and handed back my information. Then he explained that I needed to complete the bottom portion of the report and send it to Springfield within ten days. I told him I would and drove away.

I drove away feeling uneasy. Partly because I was still shaken from the accident, but mostly because that woman who'd called the police had managed to degrade me. She'd managed to do what Jim and David had done, but on a different level.

What hurt was that there wasn't anything I could do about it. But I had to admit I thanked God for sending a police officer who hadn't cared what color I was. Or at least, from what I could tell, he didn't act like it.

CHAPTER 13

J IM, AS MUCH as I really want that corporate recruiting manager position, I'm seriously thinking about applying for the one in manufacturing instead."

I'd just sat down in front of Jim in his office for a meeting I'd initiated.

"Actually, Anise, I think it's a good fit for you, and I'm glad you came to see me about it."

I thought I'd be elated to hear him say those exact words, but for some reason, I didn't feel so great. Maybe it had to do with the fact that I knew I was allowing them to bamboozle me the way they'd planned from the beginning.

"I guess I'm verbally applying for it, but only if you know for sure that you're not going to fill the corporate position anytime soon."

"Well, not only am I not going to fill it soon, but I can't even say when."

I didn't believe him, but it wasn't as if I could force him to be honest with me.

"Then I guess I'd like to apply for it."

"Sounds good. This should all move along pretty quickly, because it's not as though I have to interview you again. I know you're qualified for the job and that you'd be perfect for it, but I do want you to interview with Mike, the plant manager. The person who gets this job will be working pretty closely with him, so Lyle and I think it's a good idea to have his input regarding each candidate."

"That's fine. So how soon do you think we can set something up with him?"

"I'm thinking this afternoon, because I'd really like to get this process rolling."

Boy, wasn't he the sweetest, most helpful man in America? I couldn't believe his change in attitude toward me or how caring and cooperative he'd suddenly become. It was amazing what people were willing to do in order to make others do what they wanted.

"I have a meeting with Elizabeth this afternoon right at one, but I'm free anytime after two," I said.

"I'll have my secretary call him to see when he wants to get together with you."

"Just let me know," I said, and stood.

"And Anise?" he said as I turned to leave his office.

"Yes?"

"I'm really glad you're interested in this newest management opening, and I hope you don't have any animosity toward me because we had to put the other job on hold."

I smiled and said, "Things happen."

"Unfortunately they do. But I can almost guarantee that this is going to make everyone happy. Including Lyle. So I think you'll be pleased with our selection," he said, smiling.

A naïve person would have believed he was actually fond of me.

"I'll wait to hear from your secretary about my interview with Mike," I said, and walked out, hoping I'd made the right decision.

I figured I'd better stop by Lorna's office again. I'd dropped in on her just before going to meet with Jim, and she hadn't been too thrilled about my decision to forget about the corporate position so I could concentrate on the one in manufacturing. I'd explained to her that I wasn't giving up like she kept insisting, and that the bottom line was that I had to do what was best for me.

I stuck my head inside her office, preparing to speak, but she beat me to it.

"So you finally sold your soul to that bastard Jim."

"Lorna, don't start this all over again. I did what I felt I had to do, and I don't want to keep explaining it to you or anybody else."

"Okay, okay. I'm sorry. I promise not to bring it up again."

"Good," I said, and we both smiled. A truce was a good thing.

I understood where Lorna was coming from, and right or wrong, I needed her to support me on this. I needed her to sit in my corner the way she always did when I dealt with anything work-related.

"You're not feeling any whiplash symptoms, are you?" Lorna asked, because I'd told her about my unfortunate fender bender last evening.

"No. I feel just fine."

"Well, if it were me, I would have gone straight to the hospital and gotten checked out, because these car injuries don't always show up until later."

"I'm telling you I'm fine. And I don't have time to go sit in some emergency room for hours, go through physical therapy or deal with the other driver's insurance company, trying to get my medical bills paid."

"Maybe. But I would make time. If you want to know the truth, I'd probably have on a neck brace right now."

I laughed. "No you wouldn't. And why is it that people always talk that way when someone else is in an accident?"

"Because they want to get paid."

"Yeah, right. Well, I'm not about to pretend like I'm injured just so I can sue some insurance company for no reason. I have better morals than that."

"Maybe you do, but some people would get paid and laugh all the way to the bank."

"No good will come to them either. Because bad things always happen to people who scheme."

"Well, first of all, not every human being is a Goody Two-shoes like you, Anise."

"I don't believe you said that. Just because I don't condone trying to get over on people doesn't mean I'm some saint."

"Whatever you say," she said, still joking around.

"Good-bye, Lorna. See you in another life."

"Bye, Anise."

I smiled as I walked away because Lorna really was a good friend. She was upset about my newest job venture, but I knew she was only looking out for my best interests.

As I strolled through the department, I saw Frank turning to leave my office. I considered heading in another direction until he was gone, but he spied me before I could make a quick detour. I walked toward him nervously, and the closer I approached, the more he grinned from ear to ear. I wished wholeheartedly that he wouldn't do that, because it would only be a matter of time before some nosy coworker discovered this attraction we were sharing—an attraction he obviously didn't mind proclaiming to the world, but which I wanted to disguise.

"What are you doing here, Frank?" I said, slightly brushing past him and entering my office.

"I'm here because whenever I see you, it makes my day run smoother," he said, following me.

"You know," I said, leaning against the edge of my desk, "you don't act much like the director of a department."

"I know. I'm acting more like a schoolboy who's having his first crush, don't I?"

I smiled, but I could tell this was going too far. It was a good thing I had a corner office, but I knew there were people walking by and others who had probably seen him come into my office. He'd been making a daily habit of it, and it was making me self-conscious.

He noticed my discomfort but didn't help the situation. "Just admit it, you're attracted to me, too."

I raised up from my desk and walked around it. Then I sat down in my chair. "I don't know about that, but what I do know is that I have a lot of work to do before my meeting with Elizabeth."

"Changing the subject isn't going to change the way you feel about me. You do know that, don't you?"

"Frank, I really do have to get to work."

"Okay, I'll leave, but just remember, tomorrow's a new day," he said matter-of-factly, and winked at me.

I was glad he was gone, but my heart was turning somersaults. He wasn't going to let up, and I knew it was just a matter of time before he persuaded me to see him outside of work. I was fighting this growing desire to be with him with powerful determination, but even the strongest person sometimes becomes too weak to win the battle. Truth was, I didn't know if I wanted to win the battle, anyway.

I looked at Elizabeth and was embarrassed, because I realized she'd said something to me.

"I'm sorry, what was that?" I asked.

"Must have been one serious daydream," she said.

We laughed.

"I was just asking if it was okay for us to meet at one-thirty instead of one," she said.

"Oh. Yes, that should be fine. I just came back from meeting with Jim and he's going to see if his secretary can schedule an interview for me with Mike this afternoon, but hopefully it won't be until sometime after three."

"Well, just let me know, because your interview is more important. I was so happy when you told me this morning that you were going to apply for it, and I want you to know that I'll keep my fingers crossed for you."

"Thanks. I really appreciate that."

An hour later, Jim's secretary called to tell me that I could meet with Mike at 3:00 P.M. in the HR conference room on my end of the building. Mike was intelligent and professional but very laid-back, so I wasn't worried about interviewing with him. Everyone in the plant loved him, and I'd known as soon as I met him that he was a respectable guy.

I met with Elizabeth and discussed what she wanted me to help her complete before she left next week, and what she would be doing at her new company. She'd told me bits and pieces over the last few days, but what I didn't know was that she was taking a cut in pay. She would still have a manager's title, but the company was smaller and didn't pay nearly as much as Reed Meyers. I didn't understand how that could be with the Milwaukee area being so much larger than Mitchell, but she explained to me that while her parents lived in Milwaukee, she would be working in a smaller city close by. It was unfortunate that she'd had to struggle all these years trying to make a good life for herself and then give it all up. She said she hadn't thought twice about it, though, because her parents meant everything to her. She told me how they weren't doing very well, and that the last thing she wanted was for one of them to suffer or pass away without her being there. She said she'd never be able to live with herself, and I understood without reservation. I realized I was no different from Elizabeth, because here I was living in Mitchell when I could easily have moved to Chicago, Atlanta or New York and gotten paid so much more. But I knew I was never leaving, not as long as Mom lived here.

After the meeting with Elizabeth, I entered the conference room five minutes early and Mike walked in five minutes late.

"I'm sorry for the short delay, but we had a situation out in the plant with one of the foreman and one of the machine operators," he said.

"That's not a problem. I haven't been in here for very long."

"So it looks like we might be working together," Mike said, clos-ing the door.

Another attractive white man. I didn't know why I hadn't noticed his looks before, but maybe it was because I'd never had too many one-on-one conversations with him. His shoulders were cut like a football player's, his skin was tanned Florida-style and his clothing fit him perfectly.

"Yes, I guess it does," I answered.

I was flattered that he was so optimistic about me having the job.

"Jim thought it would be a good idea for us to get together, but it's not like I have all that much to ask you, because I already know how sharp you are. I've also seen how great you are with the kids out in the plant, and I admire the way you treat them. From blacks to Mexicans to hillbillies like me, you treat everyone the same, and they love you for it," he joked.

He always referred to his employees as kids because he'd discov-ered sometime ago that they called him Daddy behind his back. They didn't do it because they disliked him, but said it in a teasing way, because when he gave an order, he didn't play. He was easy to get along with and would stand up for his employees when neces-sary, but wasn't one to deal with when production slowed down due to carelessness or absenteeism.

"Well, thank you," I said.

"I'm serious, because you and I both know that some of these corporate assholes around here treat the factory employees like shit, and I'm tellin' you, that crap burns my butt like jalapeño peppers."

That was Mike for you. What came up came out without any tact. But I liked him, because Mike was just Mike at all times and didn't have a hidden agenda.

"You're right."

"So like I said, I really don't have any questions for you."

"Well, if it's okay then, I have a couple for you."

"Shoot," he said, and rested his back against the chair.

"When you have job openings that need to be filled, do you get involved with the interviewing process, or do you leave the decision up to your area foremen and supervisors?"

"It all depends on the position. If it's strictly a line position like an assembler, drill operator or shipping and receiving personnel, I leave the entire hiring process up to the person who they'll be reporting to. If it's a lead person or skilled tradesman we're looking for, then I like to sit in on the interviews myself. I don't always, but I try to whenever I can."

"Either way is fine, but I just want to know how many people I'd be dealing with when there's a job opening that needs to be filled."

"We're all pretty flexible, and I can tell you right now that color and gender don't exist out in our environment."

"I'm glad to hear it."

"I know all about what's been going on with that other job you applied for, and don't think for one minute that I agree with how they've been handling it."

"Goodness. It sounds like my little ordeal is common knowledge around here."

"As a matter of fact, it is. Word travels quickly out in the shop, and even though I report to Lyle, I don't agree with a lot of his tactics. Just between you and me, I don't care for Jim or Lyle and the only reason I put up with it is because they pay me a damn good salary to be here. But that's where it ends with me. They're some dirty sons of bitches, and everybody around here knows it."

I was shocked. Not because Mike didn't care for them, but because he was giving me his honest opinion. I appreciated that, and now I knew that Mike had every bit of the integrity I'd always thought he had.

"I'll admit, my time here hasn't been all that wonderful," I said. "And I've been more frustrated in the last six months than I have in my entire life. At first I thought Lyle was different from Jim, but now I'm starting to think otherwise. They've made things as difficult for me as they could every time I've tried to move higher, so I figured I'd rather take this promotion instead of not getting one at all. But I have to be honest with you: if I had my choice between getting the corporate recruiting manager position versus this manufacturing one, I would have chosen the corporate one in a heartbeat."

"I figured as much, but that's not a problem for me. I hope you don't leave anytime soon, though, because we'd love to have you around for as long as we can. But if something better does come along, I won't be upset with you in the least. Hell, I'd do the same thing, so there's no way I would ever hold anything against you for trying to better your career."

"I appreciate hearing you say that, and that answered my other question."

"Well, now that we've got all the cow manure out of the way, are you going to take the job?"

"If you guys offer it to me, I suppose I will."

"Glad to hear it. And if you don't have anything else you want to ask me, I need to get back out to the plant for a meeting with two of my foremen."

"I don't, and thanks so much for meeting with me."

"No. *Thank you.* Because I know this isn't the job you really wanted, but on the other hand, I'll be able to sleep better knowing that you're going to be taking over this part of human resources."

"I'll do my best."

"I know you will," he said, smiling as he left the room.

Maybe this really was the right thing for me to do, because Mike genuinely wanted me in the position. Jim did too, but for different reasons. Maybe the corporate job wasn't meant to be. Maybe it was time for me to move on and try to find contentment. If nothing else, I could work in this position for a while and apply for a different job at another company, because now my résumé would show managerial experience.

Walking back to my office, I heard the phone ringing, so I rushed to answer it.

"Anise Miller."

"Hi, beautiful."

It was Frank.

"What do you want?" I said in a cheerful tone.

"Don't you sound like a happy camper this afternoon!"

"I am. At least I guess I am anyway."

"Why? What happened?"

"I decided to apply for the manufacturing position."

"Oh? And you didn't tell me?"

"No. I didn't tell anyone except Lorna and Elizabeth."

"Well, at least I know where I stand, in terms of how important I am to you."

"Don't take it personally."

"But I am."

"You shouldn't."

"I can't help it."

"Will you stop it?" I said, laughing because we sounded like two small children trying to outwit each other. Or worse, like two people who were beginning to fall in love.

The latter is what worried me the most.

"Will I stop what?" he asked.

"Being so argumentative."

"Okay. I'm sorry."

"That's better."

"So when will you know whether you got the job or not?"

"It sounds like pretty soon. I met with Jim this morning to tell him that I was interested, and I just finished meeting with Mike."

"Mike is a good guy."

"Yeah, I know, and I like him even more now that I've had a chance to speak with him."

"Better than me?"

"Better than you, what?" I asked.

"Do you like him better than me?"

"What kind of silly comment is that?"

"It's silly to you maybe, but I want to know."

"There's something wrong with you."

He laughed. "I'm only joking with you because whenever I try to be serious, you shy away from me. So if this is the only way I can get you to talk to me, then so be it."

"Frank, you know full well that I can't be serious with you because I'm married."

"I know. But just tell me this. If you weren't married, would you go out with me then?"

"I don't know."

"You don't know because I'm white."

"I didn't say that."

"You didn't have to."

I kept quiet.

"What difference should it make if a black woman and a white man want to go out together?"

"I guess it shouldn't make any difference at all, but society has decided that it does."

"And that's ridiculous, too."

"Maybe it is, but it's still reality."

"Well, I don't agree, and all I'm asking is that you give me a chance to show you that I'm no different from any other man who's attracted to you."

"You still keep forgetting the fact that I'm married."

"But you're not *happily* married, and I know you're attracted to me."

"Some attractions can get you into a lot of trouble," I admitted.

"Not the one we have for each other."

"Look, Frank. You're a nice guy. I like you a lot. But the timing isn't right for you and me. Maybe if this was a different time in my life and I was single, things would be different."

"There's never a right time for anything. You have to make time conform to your own wants and needs."

"You're just not hearing me at all, are you?"

"No, actually I'm not. And it's like I told you earlier, I'm not giving up unless you tell me to. I've dated black women and white women over the years, but I've never been so attracted to any woman the way I am to you. And regardless of what you say, I think that means something."

I was speechless again, something that was becoming quite common whenever I had conversations with Frank. If he only knew, I wanted to be with him almost as badly as he wanted to be with me. But I could never let on that this was true.

"Hey," he said. "I've got a dentist appointment I need to get to. But, Anise, please think about what I'm saying, okay? Promise me you won't throw our relationship away before we even have one."

"Maybe we'll talk tomorrow."

"Don't worry. If I have anything to do with it, we will."

"I'll see you later."

"I hope so," he said.

"Good-bye, Frank."

Happiness wasn't something I'd felt for quite some time, but I really was feeling rather optimistic about my meeting with Mike and the fact that I would finally get the promotion I deserved. Maybe not the one I wanted, but a promotion nonetheless.

I decided that if they offered it to me I would take it and try to feel satisfied afterward.

CHAPTER 14

S HE TOOK the bait a lot quicker than I expected," Jim said.
"Well, I'll tell you one thing, I never thought she'd go for
it at all," Lyle said, puffing his pipe.

"But you know this only happened by luck, though,
because if Elizabeth hadn't given us her two-week notice, we never
would've been able to move Bob into her position so quickly.
Which means we would have had to go forward with my plan of
forcing someone else out of another management position to make
it available."

"I know. It was a very close call."

"And if we hadn't been able to convince Bob to make the move,
we'd still be up shit creek."

"But ten more thousand dollars a year is pretty convincing."

"That it is," Jim said. "That it is."

"Actually, Anise seems like she's been pretty happy ever since
you told her the job was hers."

"She has, and that's why I wanted to tell her last week before I went out of town, even though we couldn't make it official until today."

"You did good, Jim, and I appreciate you putting in so much time with this. Now all we have to do is bide our time, and then we can fill that corporate position with Kelli. Although, just to be safe, I think we need to find some way to pacify Anise, just in case she starts screaming discrimination. I know Kelli has more seniority than Anise, but her lack of comparable education could shake things up a bit. I'm really hoping it doesn't come to that, but we need to be prepared just the same."

"I agree. And what about Frank? Is Tom still talking about making him an officer?"

"No, not after I told him what you'd heard," Lyle said. "He was mortified at the thought of Frank dating black women."

"Did he want proof of it?"

"No. Said a rumor like that was just as bad as having it happen, and that having someone like him in such a high position could mean trouble. So I'm afraid good old Frank is going to be the director of training until he decides to leave the company."

"Too bad," Jim added.

"Where is it that they're having Elizabeth's good-bye party?"

"Ricardo's. You know. Downtown."

"Oh yeah," Lyle remembered. "That new place."

"I'm planning on leaving here in about a hour. What about you?"

"I'll do the same and ride with you, if you don't mind. I can pick my car up when we come back by here."

"Not a problem."

"Finally, everything is settling down around here the way it should, so maybe now we can start back concentrating on something more important."

"That's for sure. We never used to have to work this hard in the past to keep things the way we want them, but it was worth every man-hour we dedicated to it."

"I told you it's those damn laws," Lyle reiterated.

"But what these lawmakers don't know is that they haven't stopped a thing here at Reed Meyers. And if I have anything to do with it, they never will," Jim said.

Lyle agreed with him and they moved on to another order of business.

I couldn't believe the salary grade for the manufacturing HR manager's position was one grade lower than the one for corporate recruiting manager. Jim had given me an official offer letter this morning, but I hadn't paid much attention to the grade level. They'd given me a twenty-six percent raise, and I'd signed the bottom of the letter almost immediately. I hadn't expected them to throw me for a loop at the last minute, so I was completely caught off guard. I'd expressed my concerns about it to Jim, but he insisted it didn't mean anything. I told him I was under the impression that the manufacturing position was equal to the corporate one, but he claimed they'd always been different. He didn't seem to understand what difference it made, because I would have gotten the same pay increase either way. But what I tried to make him realize was that the corporate position topped out five thousand dollars more than the one in manufacturing, and that meant I would have had more room to grow with the corporate one. He told me that I shouldn't worry, because by the time I topped out, I'd be promoted to something else. I knew that was a fat chance, but once again, I decided to grin and bear the situation.

I scanned the room at Ricardo's where we were having Elizabeth's going-away party. Everyone from each division of human resources was here to celebrate, along with quite a few other employees she was close to. The music was a bit louder than I preferred, and since I didn't drink, I had to find other ways to entertain myself. If it hadn't been for my relationship with Elizabeth, I probably wouldn't have been here. But sometimes we do things we don't want to because it's right.

"I hear congratulations are in order," Connie from public relations yelled over Mariah Carey's voice, and then sat down at my table for two.

"Thank you," I yelled just as loudly.

"I still haven't heard anything about the corporate recruiting position, so I assume they're not going to fill it. I heard through the grapevine, though, that a management position is going to open up in purchasing pretty soon, and if it does, I'm going to apply for it," she said.

I almost cracked up in her face. What did Connie possibly know about purchasing? First, it was recruiting, then it was benefits and now she was dying to get into purchasing? I didn't know how she thought she could simply leave public relations and go manage a department she knew nothing about. It just didn't make any sense. She seemed so excited and confident about it, too. But she would soon find out that Jim and Lyle were never going to promote her into any of those positions.

"Go for it, girl," I said, feeling guilty because I knew I wasn't being honest about the way I felt.

"I am. I'm going to get out of public relations yet."

"I hear you."

"Well, I'd better get over there and have another daiquiri before Lyle and Jim stop buying."

"I don't blame you."

"Hey, girl," Lorna said, taking a seat.

Kelli Jacobson walked up at the same time as Lorna.

"Congratulations on the promotion, Anise," Kelli said, smiling.

I couldn't tell whether her well-wishes were genuine or synthetic.

"Thank you," I acknowledged.

"Maybe I should have applied for that position, too, because it looks like the recruiting one is on hold indefinitely."

"Maybe you should have," I said, wondering why she'd come over here.

"It wouldn't have mattered, though, because everyone knew you were the best person for the job. Jim is always talking about how well you fit in with the factory employees, and really, I wouldn't know where to begin when it comes to those people."

"What do you mean, 'those people'?" I asked defensively.

"You know. The people who work out in the shop."

"Well, first of all, Kelli, I believe I'm qualified to work with *all* people at Reed Meyers. Factory, clerical, corporate—"

"She's even qualified to work with poor white trash like you," Lorna interrupted.

Lorna and I turned and looked at each other, laughing hysterically. It wasn't funny, but we knew our amusement would annoy our uninvited visitor.

"This is a conversation between Anise and me, Lorna, so I think you'd better mind your own business," Kelli said.

"Anise *is* my business, and if you don't step away from this table, you're going to get your little ass kicked."

"How unprofessional," Kelli said, pursing her lips, and walked away.

"What a stupid, ignorant, whorish bitch," Lorna said.

"I can't believe she even had the audacity to bring her butt over here."

"She's an idiot!" Lorna exclaimed. "And this is the type of thing I would expect from someone like her."

"Well, I don't care what she is, but I know she had better make that her last time approaching me with those crazy comments."

"They're giving her that job. I could tell by the smug look on her face, and even though I didn't think Jim would stoop low enough to screw trash like her, I'm starting to think I was wrong. Just look," she said, gazing in the direction Kelli had gone in. "Just look how giggly and close up on him she is. And look at the way Jim keeps smiling at her. It's almost like they've forgotten who and where they are. Liquor will bring out the darkest of secrets if you listen and watch close enough. I know about this type of thing all too well, because I spill my own guts to anyone who will listen every time I get drunk myself."

"If they give her that job, she'll be at a higher level than me, because I found out today that the corporate management position is one level higher than the manufacturing one."

"I thought you knew that."

"I didn't, because they conveniently left it off the job posting. Usually they always list the grade of pay, and I didn't even think to ask because I assumed both jobs were the same in terms of grade."

"We'll see what happens, but if they give Kelli that job, I don't see how you can just sit back and be happy."

"Oh, don't think I will for one minute."

"Damn, Anise. When I first came over here, I was planning to ask you how it feels to be promoted, but stupid Kelli ruined the whole vibe."

"I really don't know how it feels. I'm happy on the one hand and discontented on another. Maybe I'll feel fine once I've actually started the job. And when I've seen that first paycheck."

"That's the best part of all. And, hey, I know I gave you a hard time about applying for this, but I want you to know that I really am happy for you. I still don't trust those bastards, but I'm glad you finally moved into management. That's a major accomplishment, and I'm proud of you."

"Thanks."

"I hate Kelli for coming over here." Lorna frowned. "I was feeling like I could dance the whole night away, but not anymore."

"Yeah, you looked like you were having a pretty good time out there."

"I was. But there still aren't any decent men in here."

"Is there ever a time when you're not looking for a man," I said, sipping on my virgin raspberry margarita.

"No. Not really," she said, sipping from a beer mug and smiling. "You know, this music is a little loud even for me."

"I was thinking the same thing earlier."

"Elizabeth looks so happy, doesn't she?"

"Yes, she does. She really wants to be with her parents, and I have the utmost respect for what she is doing."

"So do I, but I would never do it," Lorna said. "My parents treated my brother and me like shit. We always felt like we were in their way, and I think they regretted having both of us. So when it comes time for them to be taken care of, I hope they die instantly, because otherwise I don't know who's going to do it."

"That's a terrible thing to say," I said.

"Maybe it is, but if you knew what I went through as a child, you wouldn't question me."

"I guess."

We sat and listened to the music for a few minutes, but I soon became tired of competing with it.

"I'm going to say good-bye to Elizabeth and head home," I said.

"Not me. I'm here until everyone else leaves."

"Figures," I said, smiling and hugging Lorna.

"You take care, and congratulations again on the promotion."

"Thanks."

I walked over to the crowd standing around Elizabeth. Half my coworkers needed designated drivers, which I thought was unfortunate on a weeknight. But who was I to say one way or the other. These were grown people.

"Anise!" Elizabeth beamed. She'd fallen into the drunken category as well. "You're not getting ready to go, are you?"

"Yeah, unfortunately I am. But I wanted to come tell you how much I've enjoyed working for you, and that I wish you all the best in Wisconsin."

"Thank you and congrats again on getting that promotion. Nobody deserves it more than you. I mean that."

"Thanks. Well, I guess I'm out of here."

"Okay," she said, and we embraced.

I really was going to miss her, and we were both experiencing a sentimental moment.

"You take care of yourself," she said, releasing me.

"I will, and you do the same," I said, and saw Frank staring at me from across the room.

I was congratulated five additional times on my way out the door. The night air felt exhilarating, and the stars shone for miles. I walked slowly, because I was tired, but partly because I was sure Frank would follow behind me. It probably wasn't such a good idea to be seen with him with so many Reed Meyers employees on the premises, but Frank usually didn't care about that. I took a few more steps and turned around, but he was still nowhere in sight. I even sat inside my SUV longer than necessary before starting the engine. But he never showed. I waited a while longer and drove off in disappointment. I'd resisted him for the longest time, and maybe he'd decided that it wasn't worth all the begging he was doing and that he wasn't going to bother me any longer. I hoped I was wrong about all of this. Because deep down, I had to admit to myself that I needed the attention he was giving me.

I drove into Greenwood Estates, circled around to the cul-de-sac and pulled into my driveway. Multiple lights beamed from each of the twelve houses in our subdivision, but the area was still darker than I liked.

I continued into the garage and then into the house, but like every other time I didn't come straight home from work, I forgot about the mail. I took off my blazer and laid it at the bottom of the staircase. Then I opened the front door, preparing to walk out to the mailbox, but stopped when I saw a huge bouquet of red roses right by the door.

I didn't bother going to get the mail, but brought the flowers inside. I opened the tiny envelope and pulled out the card, which said: "Congratulations on your promotion. We're all so proud of you. The training department at Reed Meyers."

What a nice gesture, I thought to myself, smiling.

But I was a bit confused, because I still didn't know who'd sent them. Lorna would have signed her own name and probably would have sent them during the day so I could enjoy them at work. No, without a doubt, this was something a man would do. Which meant it had to be Frank. Although, it didn't make a whole lot of sense for him to send me flowers and then keep his distance at the club. However, if it was him, I was glad he hadn't signed his name on the card. I couldn't help but wonder what David would have said had he been here to receive these. I mean, what if he'd casually dropped by for some reason? I knew that wasn't the case, but I had always been a what-if kind of person. I always worried about what might or could be, because it was better to be too cautious rather than terribly sorry.

I took the flowers into the kitchen, removed the wrapping, put them in a vase and set them on the island. They were absolutely beautiful, and I was glad the heat hadn't wilted them. Maybe they hadn't been delivered until late, because I didn't see how they could look so bright and alive when they'd been left outside.

I walked through the bedroom and into the master bath and filled the double Jacuzzi with bubbles and hot water. When it was ready, I undressed, stepped in, turned the jets on medium, closed my eyes and sighed with relief. This almost felt better than sex. Almost. Well, maybe not almost, but it would suffice for tonight, because there was nothing else. With the exception of the last time David and I had made love, which was now weeks ago, I couldn't remember how long it had been or when I'd actually wanted to. We'd never been all that compatible, and he wasn't the most attentive lover. I'd tried to have an orgasm while we had intercourse, but it never worked. Fifty percent of the problem had to do with him coming too quickly and the other fifty percent had to do with the same reason. He wasn't fond of foreplay, and when I suggested the idea of oral sex, he'd told me to forget it. He'd said it was filthy and unnatural, and that as much as he loved me, he would never be able to do it. I'd been disappointed, because I still remembered how good it felt with my boyfriend from college. Lorna had told me that every white man she'd been with had taken care of her without any instructions, and I'd heard the same thing before from another white girlfriend of mine. Black men were funny about things like that, though. Not all of them, because some of them knew how to sex you up so well that you thought you were floating on Mars. But there were those few who basically got what they wanted and rolled over in a coma.

I leaned back in the tub and thought about Frank. I wondered if he was still at the club and why he hadn't tried to communicate with me. Maybe I wondered about these things because I felt so alone. The house was too quiet, and even though David and I hadn't been all that happy, it still felt good knowing someone else lived here. I tried not to think about Frank—I even tried not to *want* to think about him. But I just couldn't help it. I wanted to talk to him. I wanted to be with him. I wanted to know what it was like to be held by him. I wanted to know what it was like to be with someone who seemed to really care for me. I didn't know if his obsession was a good thing or not, because sometimes he came on a bit too strong, but I loved the way he gazed at me. I loved the attention he showered on me. I was beginning to realize how much I wanted him to drop by my office. I even looked forward to seeing him in the break room, and almost enjoyed hearing him beg me out to dinner. But the way he'd acted at the party was so unlike him, almost as if he'd given up, and now I was feeling anxious.

I tried to relax my muscles, nerves and mind for a half hour longer, and then I drained the Jacuzzi, dried myself off and did all the other things I did after taking a nice long bath. I removed one of my short silk gowns from the dresser, pulled it over my head, folded back the comforter on the bed and fluffed two pillows, one after the other. I turned on the television and satellite and did my usual scanning, but when I didn't see anything, I searched for the continuous jazz channel and left it there. I lay in bed staring at the ceiling, and as much as I tried not to, I thought about Frank. I knew he'd been the one to send me those flowers, and I had a mind to call him. I didn't know if he was listed, but I knew directory assistance could tell me one way or the other. Which they did.

"Hello, Frank? It's Anise."

"I know."

"I hope it's okay that I'm calling."

"It's fine. Did you get the flowers?"

"Yes. And that's why I'm calling, to thank you."

"You're quite welcome. And I hope you don't mind that I sent them to your home."

"No, not at all."

"I figured you might get too many questions if I'd sent them to you at work."

"I'm sure I would have."

I waited for him to say something else, but he didn't.

"Well, I guess I'll let you go, but thanks again for the roses" was all I could say, because he sounded so distant. I was starting to feel nervous.

"You took the time to find my number, and now you're already going to hang up?"

"Well, yeah. Because you don't sound like you're in the mood for talking."

"It's not that, but I began wondering today if I was bothering you so much that you were getting irritated with me. So when I saw you at the club, I figured I would leave you alone."

"It's not that you're bothering me, it's just that this whole thing is awkward considering the circumstances."

"I know. You're married."

"Yes, I am. But I admit, it really is over between my husband and me. As a matter of fact, he's probably going to file for a divorce."

"I'm sorry to hear that. I know none of this is easy."

"No, it's not, and it's just a matter of time before people at work find out about it. Which is why I haven't even told Lorna about my separation."

"Lorna thinks the world of you, and she makes such a huge difference in my department," he said.

"She's good, and she's got a lot of personality."

"Yeah, she does have that."

"Were you busy?" I asked, because I was at a loss for words again.

"No, actually, I just walked in maybe ten minutes before you called."

"Were people from work still hanging out at Ricardo's?"

"Yep. There were a few people who left when I did, but the rest of them were still getting ripped."

"I can only take so much of that happy hour atmosphere, and then I have to go. It's not that much fun when you don't drink."

"I know what you mean. I don't mind drinking a beer or two every now and then, but getting sloppy drunk isn't my thing."

"Were Jim and Lyle still there when you left?"

"No, they walked out right after me, and the funny thing is, they don't talk to me as much as they used to. Not long ago they were pumping me for an officer position, but I haven't heard one thing about it in weeks. First Jim trusted me enough to try and talk you into taking my job if it opened up, and now he barely speaks to me."

"Why do you think that is?"

"I don't know. It's really strange."

"Who knows with them. They're both so unpredictable."

"This is true. So," he said, changing the subject, "did the flower shop do a good job with the arrangement?"

"Yes, it was beautiful. And just so you know, I was really happy when I read the card, too. It really made my day."

"I'm glad I sent them then. I had Rose Blossoms deliver them as close to dusk as they could. They don't close until seven, and the owner agreed to deliver them herself on her way home."

We were both silent again, and I felt uneasy.

"So tell me Anise, why did you really call?"

"To thank you for the roses."

"But you could have done that at work tomorrow morning, right?"

"Well, yeah. I guess," I stumbled.

I wished he wouldn't force me to the wire like this.

"Then tell me why you called. It's not going to hurt anything."

"Okay," I said, breathing deeply. "I called because it really bothered me when you didn't say anything to me the whole time we were at Ricardo's."

"You're serious?"

"I am."

"I wanted to. You know I did. But it's like I told you, I didn't wanna keep harassing you."

"And there's something else I need to confess. I hope I don't regret it, but I want to be honest with you."

"Okay."

"You were right when you said part of the reason I don't want to go out with you is because you're white. I mean, my marriage is part of the reason, too, but the other definitely has to do with you being white. It's not because I'm a racist, but it's just that I've been treated so horribly by some of the white men I've worked for, and I don't know if I could handle being stared at by every black and white person who sees us together in public. And the reason I know we'd be scrutinized is because I always take a double look myself whenever I see an interracial couple."

"Really? Why do you think you do that?"

"I don't know. I guess because it looks out of the ordinary. But don't get me wrong; even though I've never dated a white person, I've never had a problem with anyone else doing it. I think two people have every right to see each other if they want to."

"I agree with that."

"So if you want to know why I'm so hesitant, those are the reasons," I said.

"Well, at least you finally opened up to me. So I guess that's a start."

"I'm not promising anything, but I will say that I'm open to going out with you. I can't say when, and it will make things a lot easier for me if you let me work toward this in my own time."

"Say no more. I'll back off until you feel more comfortable with it."

"I'm not asking you to stop talking to me or to stop coming by my office. I'm just saying you've got to give me some time to work through some things emotionally."

"That's all I've ever asked, and I don't expect anything more. I know this is bad timing like you said, but I can't help the way I feel."

"I can appreciate that, and I'm glad I finally got the chance to express what I've been thinking. I've been fighting with this on and off ever since we had lunch that day."

"I sort of figured you were."

I yawned. Not because he was boring me, but because I was two steps from nodding off.

"Am I that dull?"

"No," I said, laughing. "Not at all. But I do have to get up early because I'm planning on taking my car by the body shop tomorrow morning before work, to get an estimate."

"Why, what happened?"

"Someone rear-ended me the other night. There isn't a lot of damage, but I still need to get it fixed."

"You weren't hurt, were you?"

"No, I'm fine. But it did scare me when I looked in my mirror and saw that the woman behind me wasn't going to be able to stop."

"Accidents are no fun."

"No, but I did learn something. I'm never owning a car again. Because if it had been the other way around, with me driving her little Honda and her driving my SUV, I probably would have been killed."

"You're probably right."

"Her front end was crushed to the point where she had to have her car towed, but my Lexus only has scratches."

"You were lucky."

"Actually, God was looking out for me."

"That He was."

We paused again.

"Well, Frank, I really enjoyed talking to you, but—"

"I know, you have to go."

"Unfortunately I do."

"Well, I hope you won't take too long calling me again."

"See you tomorrow."

"Sweet dreams," he said.

I laid the black cordless phone on its base and blushed like ten people were watching me. I felt like I'd just finished speaking to the man of my dreams. I wasn't sure where my relationship with Frank was headed or how it would turn out in the long run, but I was starting to think that maybe it was worth finding out.

I couldn't forget about David, because, like it or not, he was still my husband. But I wasn't going to shut out Frank anymore either. I wasn't going to stay miserable while David did whatever he wanted to.

That much I was sure of.

CHAPTER 15

EVERYONE GATHERED around the conference room table and waited for me to begin the meeting. Three weeks had passed since I'd accepted the promotion, and today was my first official day in my new office. I already knew Karla, my secretary; Jamie, my HR coordinator; and Mary, my HR specialist, but I figured it was a good idea to meet with them as a group, making our new working relationship somewhat easier. Although I wasn't sure how this first day was going to play out, because I didn't know if my staff was going to be receptive. Especially since Mary had applied for the job as well. But Lorna had heard that Jim didn't care for Mary and hadn't even bothered to consider her interest in the position. I wondered what that was all about, but hadn't asked Lorna to elaborate. Now, though, I wondered how Mary felt about reporting to me when she'd wanted the job herself.

"Since this is my first day, I thought it would be a good idea for us to meet for a few minutes," I began. "From everything I've reviewed this morning, it looks like Bob has done an excellent job running this side of HR."

Mary raised her eyebrows.

"Did I say something wrong?" I asked her.

"No, but I wouldn't say he did an excellent job."

"Really? And is there a reason why you feel that way?"

"Because the whole two years I've been here, I've worked my butt off trying to make him and this department look good."

My question had been answered. Mary was disgruntled about not getting my position, and I didn't know what to say to her.

So I made things up as I went along.

"I've always heard how great of an employee you are, and please know that I have nothing but the highest respect for your dedication to human resources."

Her face started to brighten.

So I continued.

"I wouldn't normally say this unless we were alone, but since it's sort of out in the open, and because I want all four of us to work as a team, I will. I'm sorry that you didn't get Bob's position, because, believe me, I know what it's like when you don't get promoted into a position that you really want. I'm sure you know that I applied for the corporate manager's position, but didn't get it because they placed it on hold. I know that saying I'm sorry doesn't help a whole lot, but I'm hoping none of this will cause a strain between the two of us."

"I don't have a problem with you, Anise, because this was Jim's decision. But I *am* upset with him for giving the position to someone else, even though I'm the one who did most of Bob's work whenever he wasn't here or needed help. It's not fair how they pick and choose certain people for certain jobs with no standard criteria. They do whatever they want, and couldn't care less about who they hurt in the process."

I didn't know what to say, because I agreed with her completely. I knew exactly how she felt, and I had to admit that Jim should have at least considered the fact that Mary already worked in this area. Which made me somewhat suspicious, because it was hard to believe that they'd given me any position over a qualified white employee. I'd been there maybe seven months longer than Mary, and while I wasn't sure what her educational background was, it still was pretty unusual for them to give the job to a minority. Jim had told me I was perfect for Elizabeth's job because I reported to her and had shared some of her responsibilities, so why wasn't Mary the perfect person for Bob's position when she'd done the same thing for him?

"I hear everything you're saying. Believe me, I do. But what we have to do now is move on. I know that's easier said than done, but I promise you, I'll help groom you for management as much as I can, starting today."

Karla and Jamie sat quietly, and I didn't blame them. This was a touchy subject, and had Mary not brought it up, I never would have discussed this in front of them. But I had to try and place Mary at ease before her resentment blew out of proportion.

"I appreciate that, and I'm still going to perform the same way for you that I did for Bob. It's just that I hate how Jim and Lyle handle things around here," Mary said.

I wanted to tell her ditto, but it wasn't the professional thing to do, now that I was a manager.

"So, Karla and Jamie, I've heard wonderful things about the both of you as well."

"Glad to hear it," Karla said.

"So am I," Jamie added. "We've heard great things about you, too, and we're happy that we'll be working with you."

"I appreciate that, and the main thing I want you to know is that my office is always open to you. So if you have any questions or concerns about anything, I want you to feel free to come see me. I know I've been given the responsibility of managing this department, but like I said before, I want us to work as a team."

"Are you planning on making any changes?" Mary asked.

"I'm sure I will. Not because things aren't already running the way they should, but I do have some ideas that might make our jobs a little easier and will improve certain aspects of what we do."

"There's definitely room for improvement," Mary said. "Bob was good at what he did, and we liked him, but we all know a woman can do better."

We all laughed at her comment.

"Mary, you think like my mom," I said.

"Really?"

"Yes, because she always says, 'Lord, I know I'm not supposed to question You, and believe me, Father, I never want to do that. But why oh why did You make man head of the household?'"

We laughed, and I felt good about the rapport we were already building with each other.

"Well, I'm not going to keep you any longer, but for the most part, I wanted us to get more acquainted and to say I'm really looking forward to working with all three of you."

They each smiled.

"So if you don't have any other questions, I guess that's it."

"I don't have a question, but I did want to let you know that I'll be on vacation all next week," Jamie said.

"Not a problem. Is there anything I need to know or do you and Mary already have a system worked out for when one of you is gone?"

"We do. We always cover each other's workload and Karla helps out as well when one of us is absent."

"Sounds good. I'll be spending the next two weeks or so familiarizing myself with everything, and I'll also still be helping the benefits section until they find a replacement for my old job. But, Mary, you let me know if you need help with anything."

"I will," she said, and I was glad to see her face soften more noticeably.

We left the conference room, and I sat down in my new office, which was much larger than my old one. I loved the contemporary gray ergonomic-styled desk and plush carpet that was mixed with hues of gray and tan. The walls were bare, but I had the perfect La Shun Beal painting I was going to bring in and hang. I already had two of his pieces hanging above two of our fireplaces at home, and had been keeping this latest one I'd purchased under wraps until I finally received my promotion.

I sat behind my desk feeling like I'd finally arrived. As late as yesterday, I still hadn't been sure whether this was the right thing to do, but now I was happy I'd swallowed my pride and taken this promotion. It was a good thing, and while I'd been worried about them giving the corporate position to Kelli, it didn't seem like Jim was ever going to release it from hold. I didn't know how I was going to feel when he did, but at least he must have realized Kelli wasn't the most qualified person for it. If he hired someone from the outside or transferred another manager into it, I could live with that a lot better.

My phone rang five times in thirty minutes, and each time it was the benefits secretary asking me to walk her through certain procedures. I'd even come in an hour early every day last week to spend time training her. I didn't mind helping out, but I hoped they'd find someone to hire fairly soon so I could concentrate on my new responsibilities.

When I finished accessing the manufacturing program on the computer, I lifted a stack of memos I'd retrieved from my mailbox right after lunch. I read the first one, which mostly discussed safety issues in the shop, but the next one was from Jim.

EFFECTIVE IMMEDIATELY, Kelli Jacobson is being promoted to the position of corporate HR recruiting manager, reporting to me. Kelli has held three positions in human resources since starting with the company four years ago and is knowledgeable in all aspects of the department. Kelli will now be responsible for recruiting all salaried positions, including those at the executive level. Please join me in congratulating Kelli as she settles into her new position.

I wondered if I was dreaming. I guess, more than anything, I hoped I was. Because I didn't want to believe that they'd hemmed and hawed all this time, waiting to drop this grenade on me. I knew they'd sent this memo to everyone in the company, but I was taking this personally for obvious reasons. I was so appalled, I couldn't think. I took deep breaths trying to lower my blood pressure, which I knew had skyrocketed instantly.

I needed someone to tell me why the position suddenly was no longer on hold, because I hadn't seen any of the "major reconstructing" Jim claimed he wanted to do. Which meant he'd lied the same as he did about everything else.

My underarms flooded with perspiration, and my body felt numb. I didn't know what I should do first. Storm into Jim's office or call EEOC in Chicago to find out what their business hours were.

I walked around my desk and slammed my door closed. I didn't care who saw or heard it, and I dared someone to question me about it. When I sat back down, I did what I always do when Reed Meyers messes over me: call Lorna. But all I heard was her outgoing voice-mail message. I pressed the button and dialed Monica at her office, but when she didn't answer I called Mom instead.

"Hello?" she answered, and I thanked God she'd gone straight home from work.

"Hi, Mom."

"Hey. You must have seen me walking through the door."

"I guess so. And I don't know what I would have done if you hadn't been there. Mom, do you know that they gave that first job I applied for to someone else?"

"You mean the one that you said was on hold?"

"Yes. That one."

"Who did they give it to?"

"Kelli. The girl I told you about who wasn't as qualified as I was. So what they did was wait until I was all situated in this one and then they gave it to her," I said, holding back tears.

"Baby, I am so sorry. I can't believe they've done this."

"Neither can I, but they're going to pay. I am not going to let them get away with this. Not by far."

"I don't blame you, honey. Because if you keep putting up with this at every company you work for, nothing is ever going to change. Somebody's got to stand up for what they believe in, and if it has to be you, then that's just the way it is."

I sniffled and swallowed hard.

"Honey, I know you're hurting over this, but you've got to be strong. Because if you're not, you won't be able to do your job, and then they'll really have a reason to discredit or try to fire you."

"I know, Mom, but I'm so tired of having to go through this. I'm so tired of having to fight for what's right and then not getting anywhere."

"I hate to see you going through this, too, but now you only have two choices. You can either sit back and be happy in that job they just donated to you and let them get away with blatant discrimination, or you can fight back. It's not going to be easy accusing two white VPs of discrimination and then still having to work for them. They're going to take you through hell, and it's going to take everything in you not to quit. But once you start this, you're going to have to stick with it until the end."

"I know, but it's going to be so hard for me, trying to keep quiet until I have everything in place legally."

"But you can do it. With prayer and all the confidence I tried to instill in you, you'll make it."

"First David and now this. It seems like everything is crashing down around me all at once."

"God never places any more on us than we can bear. It may seem like it from time to time, but He never does."

I held the phone with my shoulder and blew my nose with a tissue.

"I'm going to try and call Monica again, okay, Mom?"

"Tell her I said hello, and if you want to talk, I'm here. I have a couple of errands to run this evening, but I'll be back by seven or so."

"Thanks, Mom. I love you so much."

"I love you too, honey, and you hang in there. Everything'll work itself out."

"I hope so, Mom."

"Bye, sweetie," she said, and I hung up.

I'd changed my mind about calling Monica again, because it would be better to call her when I was in the privacy of my own home. That way, I wouldn't have to worry about what I was saying, how I was saying it, and I'd be able to scream as loud as I wanted.

I thought about calling Frank. I'd only seen him once this morning, but not this afternoon. He was the person I wanted to console me. I needed someone to tell me that things were going to be okay the same as Mom just had, but I wanted to hear it from the man who'd made it clear that I was important to him. I wanted to lean into his arms, cry on his shoulder and feel safe. I wanted to feel safe the way I used to before all these problems with David and me began, and before I realized Reed Meyers wasn't going to treat me like a human being. But I decided that maybe I would call him later.

The next couple of hours passed slowly, but I didn't leave my office until it was time to go home. When the clock struck five, I rushed out of the building, wishing I never had to return.

David was just full of surprises. I was on the phone with him right now, and couldn't believe he'd had the nerve to ask me if I was thinking of seeing someone else. I almost hung up, but decided I would hear him out just for the hell of it.

"Well, are you?" he asked when I didn't answer him.

"It's really none of your business. I don't ask you about your life with Christina, and I would appreciate it if you wouldn't ask me about anything I'm doing."

"It's no big deal. If you're planning to see someone else, just say it."

"Why are you so worried about it, David?"

"I'm not. I'm just asking."

"Well, don't ask me anymore."

"Fine. Whatever. Anyway, the real reason I'm calling is because I think it's time for us to talk about getting divorced."

I'd been wondering when he would finally drop the D word, but with everything I was feeling toward Reed Meyers, I didn't have any anger left to dedicate to this. Giving him a divorce didn't bother me, and the more I thought about it, the more I wanted us to hurry to get it over with.

"Have your attorney draw up the papers and send them to mine," I said. "I'll be using Ray Stevens."

"I don't believe you. With all that we've been through and with all the years we've been together, that's all you have to say?"

"What is it you want me to say, David? Because right now I can't think of anything."

"For the life of me, Anise, I don't know why I ever married you."

"I don't know either. Especially since my skin is much too dark and my hair is too buckshot nappy."

I couldn't wait for his comeback, but he fooled me and threw the phone on the hook. Which didn't bother me, because no matter how I looked at our situation, I couldn't forget that he was seeing another woman.

The clock on the VCR showed 9:00 P.M. I'd driven straight home from work, warmed up some leftover chicken and turned on some jazz down in the lower level. I'd fallen asleep for maybe an hour on the oversize black leather chair and matching ottoman, but now I was wide awake thanks to David.

I was tired of thinking about Jim, Lyle, Kelli, Reed Meyers and all this racial madness, but I couldn't seem to think about much else.

I remembered things I hadn't thought about in years. Like when I was five and Mom told me that the reason she and my grandmother had taught me so much was that from the time I entered kindergarten, I would have to be more knowledgeable than white children. Back then I didn't understand why, but now I knew what she meant. Or when I was sixteen, and my then best friend, who was white, invited me over for dinner without telling her parents and was told it was okay to be friends with me at school, but that under no circumstances was she to bring me to their home again. I remembered the day I entered college, was assigned a white roommate, and she acted as though the world was coming to an end. So much so, that she threatened to drop out if her parents didn't lease her an apartment, because all the other dorm rooms were full. I remembered the time when David and I traveled to New Orleans by car, saw a vacancy sign at a hotel in Cape Girardeau, Missouri, but had to keep driving because the clerk told me they had no rooms and never looked up at me again, once she saw that I was black. I remembered how we hadn't had the courage to try another hotel even though we could barely keep our eyes open. I remembered having my first interview at Reed Meyers, going to a top department store in Mitchell looking for a new suit and having the same thing happen that happened to Mom and me at that store in Woodfield. But with this humiliating incident, it was a weeknight, I was the only person shopping in better sportswear and still the salesperson never acknowledged my presence. I remembered my recent car accident all over again, and how the woman who'd called the police hated me for no reason. I even thought about being the only black household in our subdivision and how certain neighbors made it a point not to speak to David or me. But I did thank God for the neighbors who had embraced us from the very beginning.

I replayed every racial slur or action I'd ever experienced or witnessed. I knew what it felt like to want sweet revenge against the people who had wronged you. I knew what it was like to be consumed with anger. But deep down I knew this way of thinking wasn't going to help me. I knew my fury was causing more harm to myself than anyone else. I knew now that, instead of burdening myself with hostility, it was time I utilized the legal system. It was time to research the laws that had been created to protect someone like me—someone who was being wronged for no justifiable reason.

I closed my eyes and listened to the soothing music.

I prayed for God to bring me through these unbearable circumstances.

CHAPTER 16

I T WAS SEVEN FORTY-FIVE, but I sat in my car ten more minutes. I'd played hooky from work yesterday, but still dreaded going inside Reed Meyers the way a convict dreaded the death penalty.

I dragged myself up the sidewalk, swiped my ID card through the reader, and entered the brick building.

The department seemed rather quiet for a Thursday morning, but that suited me just fine because I didn't want to be bothered by anyone who worked here anyway. The reason: I had personal business that needed taking care of.

I closed myself off from the rest of the world, kicked my shoes under my desk, dialed Frank's extension and hoped he was in.

He didn't disappoint me.

"Frank Colletti," he answered.

"Hi" was all I said.

"So I see you made it in today?"

"Yeah, but I didn't want to," I admitted.

"Your secretary told me you were out yesterday, and I was a little worried."

"I'm fine. Well, not fine, but I'm here."

"You weren't sick, were you?"

"Depends on how you define being sick."

"Meaning?"

"Meaning, I'm sick of this job and this place we work for."

"Doesn't have anything to do with that memo Jim circulated two days ago about Kelli, does it?"

"That's exactly what the problem is, along with a ton of other complaints I could whine about. But that's not why I'm calling."

"Oh?"

"I'm calling because I'm ready to take you up on your dinner offer."

"You're kidding?"

"No. I'm dead serious."

"And what may I ask led you to this decision?"

"A number of things. Too many to go into."

"Your reasons don't matter to me anyway, and all you have to do is tell me when and name the place."

"I was thinking about tonight."

"Tonight is fine. What about Morton's Steakhouse in Schaumburg?"

"Sounds okay to me. Anything is good as long as it's not in Mitchell, where we can be seen by people we know."

"I'll call to see if we can still get a last-minute reservation, and if you don't hear back from me, then we're set."

"All right."

"Will you be ready after work?"

"Yes."

"Do you wanna meet somewhere and leave your car?"

"What about the truck stop near Marengo?"

"I'll meet you there just before six."

"I'll see you then."

"Anise?"

"Yes."

"You're not going to change your mind at the last minute, are you?"

"No, I'll be there."

"I'm looking forward to it."

"So am I," I said, feeling somewhat strange.

"You know I've waited a long time for this."

"I know. See you soon."

Last night had brought on a whole new way of thinking for me. My anger was starting to build, and for the first time, I realized it was time for me to take a stand. It was time for me to get some of the things I wanted personally and professionally. I knew Frank could help me with both.

Lorna came into my office an hour later, expressed how pissed off she was over Kelli getting that promotion and then stormed back out right after I received a phone call I had to take. She'd phoned me at home yesterday in an outrage but was still ranting and raving about it the same way today. She'd insisted for the trillionth time that I had to sue the company or else. I agreed with her, but didn't let her know that I had everything all figured out. I didn't think it was wise to share my game plan with anyone except Frank. Something told me it was better to keep my newfound strategy to myself.

I lifted the phone to call Monica, because I still hadn't had a chance to tell her what was going on. I'd called her the night I was so depressed over Kelli's great accomplishment, but remembered she'd gone away with Marc the day before on one of his business trips. I didn't know how I could forget something like that, but I knew it had a lot to do with how riled up I was. They were supposed to return late last night, so I doubted she'd gone to work this morning.

I reached to dial her number, but someone knocked on my door and I laid the phone back down.

"Come in," I said.

"Excuse me, Anise, but I have a job requisition for a forklift driver," the only black foreman at the company said, entering and passing me the official document. "Vivian has given her two weeks' notice, so we'll need to fill the position pretty quickly."

"I'll get on it right away."

"I appreciate it, and call me if you have any questions."

"I sure will," I said, smiling.

"So is everything going okay with you?"

"Yeah, still have a few things to learn, but it's coming. And it didn't help that I missed yesterday, since it was only my second day being a manager."

"Some things you can't control, and what's important is that you're here now."

"Yeah, I guess so."

"Well, like I said, call me if you have questions."

"Sounds good," I said, and he left.

I so wanted to be enthusiastic about my new responsibilities, because I didn't want to disappoint Mike or any of the shop employees. But I couldn't. It wasn't fair to them, but emotionally I wasn't able to function the way I used to. I'd been fine the day I started, but I hadn't been the same ever since reading that announcement about Kelli. My mind was fixed on other things. I concentrated on how I was going to snatch Jim and Lyle away from their mighty thrones. Right now, that was my priority.

I lifted the phone again and called Monica.

"It's about time," I said when she answered.

She laughed. "I know. I don't think we've gone two full days without talking since high school."

"And you claimed you'd always be there for me when I needed you. Some friend you are."

"I couldn't help it. The whole first day we were gone, I shopped, and then I found out that Marc didn't have any business the second day or yesterday. So we locked ourselves in the room until it was time to go to the airport last night. I was so surprised, because we haven't gotten away all summer."

"I guess I know what you were doing while you were so holed up in that hotel. I bet all of Nashville could hear you."

"They probably could."

Monica was my girl, and I was so happy to hear her voice. I needed to hear it more than I realized.

"Well, while you and Marc were making love two days straight, I found out that they gave the corporate position to that Kelli chick I told you about."

"What? How?"

"They wanted her to have it, and they gave it to her. Simple as that."

"I don't believe you're telling me this."

"And the best part is that they had the nerve to send out the memo the same day I started my new position."

"Well, that was pretty deceitful."

"Yeah, but what they don't know is that I've taken as much as I'm going to take from them.

"I don't blame you, because it sounds like they've completely broken the law."

"There's no doubt about it. Kelli is clearly not qualified for the position based on the requirements they posted, and that means they've totally violated my rights. Let alone the fact that they've disregarded both state and federal equal employment opportunity laws."

"I still don't want to believe they could be so blatant."

"Well, believe it. And if you want to know the truth, I've had it with these racist people here at Reed Meyers *and* this situation with David."

"Have you heard from him?"

"Unfortunately I have. First he wanted to know if I was planning to see other people, and when I wouldn't answer him, he told me that he was filing for a divorce."

"Oh no," she said. "I know things haven't been good, but I still hate hearing that."

"Don't. It was bound to happen with the way things have been going, and I think it's better for both of us. The quicker we get this over with, the quicker we can both move on with our lives without each other."

"You're so calm about this. I would be hysterical, the same way I was when Xavier and I split up."

"I think it's different when your marriage has experienced a slow death. We've basically just been sleeping in the same bed, but you know that this marriage has been over for a very long time."

"I still hate hearing this."

"I'll be fine, Monica. I know you're worried about me being alone, but I'll get through this the same way I've gotten through every other problem in my life. And with all that I'm going through here at work, I've decided that I'm not going to spend any time worrying about David, too. I can't deal with both, and right now this Reed Meyers thing has to be my priority."

"What are you planning on doing?"

"I'm still thinking everything through. I thought about it a lot last night, and I've got some ideas that I think will bring everything they've done out in the open."

"Just be careful."

"You know I always am."

"Yeah, but just be extra careful with this, because no white executive is going to roll over and play dead after some black woman goes out of her way to expose him."

"I don't expect any of them to play dead, I just want them to stop breaking the law and give me what I deserve."

"I understand what you're saying, but like I said, Anise, be careful."

"You're worrying for nothing," I said.

"Maybe I am, so let's change the subject. What are you doing after work?"

Why did she have to ask me that? Because there was no way I could tell her the truth about where I was going and who I was going with. I didn't want to lie, but how was I going tell her that I was having dinner with another man, and that this other man was white? She was so dead set against this kind of relationship, so it was better to keep my dinner date private.

"Not much," I said. I didn't sleep too well the last couple of nights, so I'll probably get to bed early."

"Well, I'll give you a call at work tomorrow then."

"I'll be here."

Grand Central Station had absolutely nothing on me and all the phone calls I'd received this afternoon. First there were the calls from the benefits secretary, who was still pulling her hair out trying to handle my old responsibilities, and now some of Kelli's. Then I'd handled two additional job requisitions for another foreman and another call from the temp agency who filled our temporary job openings.

I stood so I could take a few items that needed typing out to Karla, but Jim entered my office before I made it to the doorway.

"So how's everything going?" he asked.

I wondered if I would actually be arrested if I caused him bodily harm.

"Okay" was all I could force between my lips.

"I understand you weren't feeling too well yesterday?"

"No, I wasn't. But I'm better now."

I could feel my heart racing like a roller coaster.

"So are things going okay with Karla, Jamie and Mary?" he asked.

"I couldn't ask for better employees. Each of them is a very hard worker, and they've helped make my transition to this area a whole lot easier than it could have been."

"Glad to hear it," he said, folding his arms. "Well, I just wanted to stop by to see if you needed anything or had any questions."

What I needed was for him to drop dead. But I regretted thinking in such a harsh manner.

"So far I don't have any major questions. I have a couple of things I may need to ask you about early next week, but nothing crucial."

"Well, my door is always open, and I hope you will come talk to me whenever you need to," he said.

I nodded in agreement, but I wanted him out of my office.

"I'm glad we were finally able to get you into management, because you really do deserve it," he said. "Oh, and Lyle wanted me to tell you that he's extremely proud of you, and that he'll be stopping by later to see how you're doing."

I feigned a smile, he did the same and I exhaled deeply when he left.

My hatred toward Jim was stronger than I thought, and I didn't like it. It wasn't healthy to have these sorts of feelings, and the level of anger he caused me was frightening. I didn't think I was capable of hurting him physically, but for the first time, I realized just how much all of this was affecting me. I didn't want to believe that one man could cause so much unrest inside me, but Jim had proven exactly that. This whole incident was taking its toll on me, and I wanted it to be over with. I wanted to take care of this once and for all and get on with my life. I wanted the same thing every other human being aimed toward: living a comfortable life and being happy. I didn't want to be rich, but I wanted a fulfilling career. I didn't want a perfect relationship, but I wanted to know what it was like to love my husband unconditionally and have him feel the same way in return. I didn't think I was asking too much. Although

I had to admit that I was partly responsible for the flaws in my marriage. I had to admit that my strong determination and ultimate focus on having a career hadn't helped the situation. I had to admit that my priorities weren't completely centered around David. But when I thought of Monica and her husband, I knew that being happily married really was possible. Although maybe I was still searching for something I was never going to discover. Maybe true happiness really didn't exist, and all a person could strive for was something average. Maybe all I could expect was to be happy every now and then.

But this was an extremely sad thought, and I refused to buy into it until someone proved that mediocrity was the most I could hope for.

CHAPTER 17

PARKING WAS SCARCE when I arrived at the truck stop, but I eventually found a stall after circling the parking lot a few times. I hadn't noticed so many cars when I'd come here before, but maybe it was the time of evening that made the difference.

We were having another ninety-degree day, so I sat with the air conditioner running and waited for Frank to show up. It was only twenty minutes till six, so he still had a few more minutes to arrive. I leaned back in my seat and relaxed. The afternoon had been rather busy, but I'd cleared my desk and walked out of the building right at five like I'd told him. There was a time when I never thought twice about working late, but I decided I wasn't doing that anymore unless it couldn't be helped.

V103 was playing one of Anita Baker's old cuts, "Caught Up in the Rapture," and I hummed along with her. She was still one of my favorite singers, and I lived for the day when she released a new CD. She'd decided some time ago to take a break from entertainment so she could spend quality time with her husband and children, but I didn't blame her. A small part of me still wondered if maybe I'd given up my own career, David and I would have turned out differently. But who was to say, one way or the other?

I sat five more minutes, and smiled when I heard Whitney singing "My Love Is Your Love," because she was both mine and Mom's favorite female singer of all time. Monica and I would sometimes laugh at Mom because she'd played that cassette with Whitney singing the national anthem at the 1991 Super Bowl every single time she drove her yellow Cadillac. As far as she was concerned, there was no one like Whitney or Luther Vandross, and I had to agree with her. Although she did grow just as fond of Babyface when I turned her on to his top-selling single "Whip Appeal" back in 1989. She even watched the video on BET and couldn't stop saying what a "cute little thing" he was.

Frank finally pulled up behind me, so I turned off the radio and opened the door to get out. First I set the alarm, locked the doors and walked toward his SUV, which was the same as mine except it was black.

"Sorry I'm a little late," he said when I sat inside next to him.

"No problem."

"I wasn't able to leave as early as I thought, but I made it."

He drove around to the exit and then onto the ramp leading back to I-90 East.

"So was the traffic still okay coming from Mitchell?" I asked, making small talk.

"It wasn't bad at all considering it's prime time for rush hour."

"Well, the parking lot at that truck stop was packed."

"I noticed that, but maybe it's because so many people are traveling on vacation."

"Yeah, that's probably true."

We drove in silence for a whole sixty seconds, which felt more like an hour.

"Believe it or not, I'm a little nervous," he said, keeping his eyes on the road.

"So am I."

"I feel like a big kid, because I've spent all this time trying to take you out, and now I'm acting like a coward."

"This is a little awkward for both of us, so don't feel bad."

"Well, I guess we can start with you telling me why you said yes in the first place. I'm still a little surprised about that."

"David asked me for a divorce, and after finding out about Kelli getting that job, I decided it was time for me to do something for me."

"And that's it? That's the only reason?"

"No, that's not the only reason. I really wanted to go out with you."

"So it doesn't have anything to do with the fact that you're attracted to me."

"Yeah, it has something to do with that, too."

I couldn't believe I was finally admitting that to him.

He looked at me and smiled. "I knew you were all along."

I smiled, too, when he looked back at the highway and felt a warm feeling disseminate over me.

"Some things take a little longer to evolve than others."

"This is true, but I'm just glad it finally happened."

Traffic slowed as we traveled closer to Elgin. Every lane was lined with cars and semitrucks, and it wasn't long before we rolled to a complete stop.

"Now, why don't you tell me something about you," I said, because even though I'd told him quite a bit about myself, I didn't know all that much about him.

"I've been at Reed Meyers for five years, worked for a company in Chicago for two years prior to that, was married once, which is a long story, and don't have any children . . . oh, and I love beautiful black women like you."

I smiled looking straight ahead, and while the comment about beautiful black women was flattering, I wanted to know more about this previous marriage.

"But I guess you already knew that part, huh?" he asked.

"What part is that?"

"About my weakness for beautiful black women?"

"I don't know about the beautiful part, but I had a pretty good idea that you preferred dating black women," I said, thinking how ironic all of this was since David preferred dating white women.

"Oh, so you're trying to be modest, right?"

"No. I'm not."

"Well, whether you realize it or not, you are beautiful."

"Is that so?" I asked, trying to disguise how happy he was making me feel.

"Yes. It is."

I smiled but didn't respond.

So he continued. "And let's see what else? Oh. I was born in Evanston, but my parents moved to Mitchell when they opened up their Lexus dealership."

"Really? The one on North State?"

"Yep."

"That's where I leased mine a few months ago."

"Really now? I wish I'd known, because I would have gotten my dad to give you a better deal than you probably ended up with. And if you'd gone to dinner with me before now, I would have known you were in the market for a new vehicle and could have put in a good word for you."

"I got it over a year ago when David and I were a lot happier, so I wouldn't have been able to go to dinner with you back then, anyway."

"Oh well, I guess not."

"Do you have any brothers and sisters?" I probed a little further.

"One brother who's two years older than me," he said, and changed to the middle lane, which was moving faster than the others.

"How old are you?" I wanted to know.

"Thirty-eight."

"What about you?"

"I'm thirty-six."

"I was thinking you were more like thirty-two," he added.

"Yeah, right," I said.

"I was. You look a lot younger than thirty-six."

"I don't think so, but thanks for the compliment."

"You're very welcome, Anise Miller."

"Does your brother live in Mitchell?"

"Yeah, he does. He's a State Farm agent."

"Sounds to me like your whole family is successful."

"Maybe, but we've got our problems like everyone else."

"I was thinking earlier how none of us can probably get around that."

"One thing that's going on with us is that my brother did the unthinkable, and my parents aren't too happy about it."

"What was that?"

"He married a woman who'd already had two children out of wedlock."

"Are they happy?"

"Who? My brother and his wife?"

"Yes."

"Extremely."

"Then, no offense to your parents, but why should it matter that his wife had children?"

"It shouldn't, but they don't treat her the way they should. They've treated previous girlfriends of mine better than they treat their only daughter-in-law, and my brother is constantly battling with them about it."

"That's too bad," I said, wondering which girlfriends Frank had taken to meet his parents.

"It really is," he said.

"So have they met all of your female friends or just the white ones?"

I hoped my question hadn't sounded rude, but I felt this was something I should know.

"They haven't met all of them, but they've met both black and white friends of mine, if that's what you mean. And they don't have a problem with me dating whomever I want to."

"That's good to know, because if they weren't okay with it, holidays would be pretty uncomfortable for all of you if you married a black woman."

He looked at me, and I wished I could take back what I'd said. I'd left the conversation wide open for any comment he wanted to make.

"Maybe you'll end up being that woman."

"Have you forgotten that I already have a husband?"

"But it doesn't sound like you will for long."

"I think we'd better change the subject," I said.

He chortled under his breath.

His remark made me feel special, but I didn't let on.

We discussed our college years, my childhood, my parents, their divorce, and now he wanted to know about David.

"So what do you think happened between the two of you?" he asked, tossing fifteen cents into the 290 East toll basket, preparing to drive into Schaumburg.

"It's a long story, but basically we grew apart. I think we really did love each other, but we were never passionately in love with each other like I thought in the beginning. And he's sort of forgotten who he is and where he came from."

"Meaning?"

"He hates the fact that he's black and refuses to interact with other black people unless he absolutely has to."

"I knew someone like that at Drake. This guy made more racial jokes about blacks than any white students I knew."

"Then you know what I mean."

"Yeah, unfortunately I do."

"He even thinks the reason I'm not being treated fairly by Jim is because I'm too dark."

"Unbelievable. Even I know the saying, The darker the berry, the sweeter the juice. For me, the darker the skin, the more beautiful it is."

"Well, David doesn't see it that way. He sees it as something to be ashamed of."

"That's too bad. And if that's why he's not happy with you, then it's his loss."

"He's probably happy now, though, because he's seeing someone else—who isn't black."

"Oh."

We pulled into Morton's parking lot, which was full, and valet-parked. Frank walked around to where I was standing and rested his hand on my back as we entered the restaurant.

"Hello," the hostess said. "Do you have a reservation with us this evening?"

"Yes. Two for Colletti."

The woman with long dark hair scanned the book and crossed out Frank's last name when she found it.

A sandy-brown-haired woman gathered two menus and showed us to our table. Which happened much sooner than the first time David had brought me here, because on that particular evening, there were at least a couple dozen people sitting in the bar waiting to be seated. But that was on a Saturday night around seven, the peak dining hour.

Our waiter was standing at the candlelit, linen-covered table and pulled a chair back for me to sit down. Frank sat across from me. The waiter asked what we wanted to drink. I told him water and Frank requested a glass of red wine.

I'd purposely not made eye contact with any other customers as we wove through various tables. But now I couldn't help but look around to see who was looking back. I glanced to the right and saw a black couple staring at me. Then I looked to the left and saw a white woman doing the same, but she quickly switched her eyes back to the man she was having dinner with when she realized I'd seen her. But everyone else I scanned wasn't paying Frank and me any attention.

I was embarrassed, however, when Frank noticed what I was doing.

"Does it bother you that much?" he asked.

"What?" I said.

"Does it bother you that some people are staring?"

"Actually, it does."

"We don't have to stay if you don't want to."

Now I felt bad.

"No, I'll be fine. I'm just not used to this. Well, actually I am used to going into nice restaurants with David and being stared at because we were the only blacks in there, but for some reason this feels different."

"I understand, and that's why we don't have to stay. It won't get dark for a couple of hours, so we could pick up something on the run and go sit in a park if you want."

"No, this is just fine."

"You're sure?" he asked, smiling, and I appreciated how considerate he was.

"I'm sure."

"I always get the filet whenever I come. But if you want to see what else they have, we can wait for them to bring out that huge table of raw meat, trying to impress us with the large cuts they offer," Frank said, smiling and skimming his menu.

I did the same and said, "The filet is fine for me as well."

"Do you wanna share some sides?"

"Asparagus and garlic potatoes would be good."

"I see we have something else in common."

"You like those, too?"

"Love them. Could eat asparagus seven days a week if someone prepared it for me."

"I know what you mean."

The waiter brought our drinks, and Frank told him what we wanted to order, including two salads with French dressing.

Frank rested his elbows on the table, locked his fingers together, leaned his chin on the back of his hands and gazed at me in silence. I looked away from him as if I was searching the restaurant for someone in particular, but when I looked back at him, his eyes were still fixed on me.

He was making me nervous, the same way he had on other occasions.

"What's wrong?" I asked.

"I love watching you."

I beamed, took a sip of water and sat my glass back on the table.

"I know I'm embarrassing you, but I can't help it. You are so beautiful, and I can't believe I'm actually sitting here with you having dinner."

"Well, believe it."

"You are everything I want in a woman."

"But you really don't know me that well."

"But I know what I like. I love the way you look. I love your smile. And I love your personality. So what else is there?"

"I don't know."

"Well, I guess there is one problem. You don't feel the same way about me."

The conversation was dipping a little deeper than I wanted it to.

"I wouldn't say that."

"Then are you saying you do feel the same way?"

I didn't answer. Instead I looked around to see if anyone could hear what we were discussing, but no one was even glancing in our direction. I was self-conscious, and I was starting to realize that I was feeling uncomfortable on my own and not because of what these strangers were thinking.

I looked at the waiter as he approached our table and set our salads in front of us. He also put down a basket of dinner rolls.

"Look, Anise. I know you probably feel like I'm coming on too strong, but it's hard not to. Being here with you is the highlight of my week. Hell, my year if you want to know the truth."

I was still speechless.

He continued.

"But if you don't like me speaking to you this way, just tell me."

"It's not that. It's just that it's hard for me to believe that you feel so strongly about us being together. I'm attracted to you too, but this is all a little scary for me. I've got a lot going on in my life right now, and I don't want either of us to get hurt. I still have to deal with my divorce, and now this new problem at work."

"What new problem?" he asked.

"This thing with Kelli getting that position."

"I know, but why do you say it's a new problem."

"Because I've decided that I'm not going to let them get away with it. I found out that Kelli's job is a level higher than mine, even though she's not more qualified than I am. I've taken enough from Jim and Lyle, and I'm not going to do that anymore."

"I don't blame you. I didn't realize that there was a difference in the pay grade. So what exactly are you planning to do?"

"First I want to gather as much information as I can about all Reed Meyers employees, so I can make comparisons of salaries, raises and promotions for women and minorities versus those of white employees," I said, wondering if he was offended.

"Are you able to get that from the system?"

"No. That's part of my problem. I have access to the manufacturing side of the system, but not corporate. So all I'm able to pull up is information on factory employees."

Frank didn't say anything, but I knew he was best friends with the director of management information systems and could get me whatever I needed. I didn't know if he'd be willing to put his job on the line for me or not, but that's what I was counting on. There was a ton of other items and documents I needed to pull together, and access to the corporate system would help me more than anything else.

"If you can get the information, what are you planning to do after that?" he asked.

"I haven't figured everything out, but I'm thinking I'll compile a report with my findings and make certain demands. And if they don't do what they're supposed to, then I'm driving over to Chicago to file a complaint with EEOC. Then, if nothing happens with that, I'm going all the way with hiring an attorney to file a lawsuit."

"It's too bad that you're going to have to resort to all of this, but they deserve whatever they get, because they never should have discriminated against you. It makes me sick to my stomach to know that some white people believe it's okay to act this way. The thing is, I know you were the most qualified person for that job they gave Kelli, and that your skin color is the only thing that prevented you from getting it. I'm embarrassed to admit it, but my gut feeling tells me that you were passed over twice on purpose."

"I know this isn't going to be easy, but you do understand why I can't just let them get away with what they've done to me?"

"I understand clearly."   .

The waiter brought out our dinner and told us to enjoy. I scooped out a helping of potatoes and placed it on a small plate, then lifted some asparagus onto it.

"So that's where I stand with Reed Meyers," I said.

"And what about David? Do you really think it's over for good?"

"Actually, I do. It's been over for longer than I care to remember."

"And you don't think there's any chance that you might reconcile?"

"No, it's definitely over, but I'm hoping the legal part of this won't take forever because of property."

"Hopefully it won't."

Our conversation turned to his position at Reed Meyers and how Lyle and Jim were no longer discussing the idea of Frank being promoted to VP. I wondered why, the same as he, but there was no telling what the reason was. There was no way to tell why Lyle and

Jim did any of the things they did on any day of the week. They basically did what was convenient for them, and everyone else had to live with it.

After dinner, Frank drove back to Marengo in record time, because the traffic had returned to normal. This time the parking lot at the truck stop wasn't too full, so he pulled next to my SUV and shut his off. I opened the door, but he told me to wait. He came around to open the door the rest of the way and helped me step out.

"So did you have a good time?" he asked, facing me as we stood between cars.

"I really did. It was wonderful, and I'm glad we were finally able to do it."

"So am I, and I hope we can do this again."

"I'm sure we will."

"You're not just saying that?" he asked.

"No. I'm serious. I don't know when, but soon."

"What about tomorrow?"

"I don't know about that. We'll see," I said, but I knew I really wanted to. At the beginning of the evening I'd thought my main reason for going out with him was so he could help me obtain the confidential information I needed, but now I knew it didn't matter whether he did or not. There was something very real going on between us, and it was time for me to admit that I hadn't felt this strongly about any man, not even David.

"Just let me know tomorrow. That is, unless you want to call me tonight when you get home."

"I think I'd better go before it gets too late," I said, ignoring his suggestion about phoning him.

"So is it okay for me to kiss you good night?"

I felt awkward again. It was like we were sharing illegal chemistry. No matter how I tried to forget about David, I couldn't forget about the vows we'd taken before God six years ago.

"I'm sorry, but I don't think so," I said regretfully. I wanted to oblige his request, but I couldn't will myself to do it.

"I understand, but you can't blame me for trying."

"I'll see you tomorrow," I said, and sat inside my vehicle.

He closed the door. I started my engine, threw my gear in reverse and drove away.

I watched him through my rearview mirror and saw him still standing there in the dark. My heart ached, because I'd passed up the opportunity of being held by a man who wanted me.

I drove all the way back to Mitchell imagining how his lips would have felt against my own.

CHAPTER 18

O F ALL THE APPOINTMENTS in the world, I don't
know how I could have forgotten my annual pap
smear. I hadn't remembered until I woke up this
morning, and although I wanted to cancel, I knew it
would take three months to get in if I rescheduled. My gynecologist
was always booked three to four months out for yearly exams, and
the only way a patient could see her sooner was if they had an
urgent situation that needed immediate attention.

I arrived at her office just before 9:15 A.M. and made it to work
by 10:30. Now it was 11:00, and I'd decided to go see if I could find
Lorna in one of the training rooms.

I walked toward the corporate HR section and saw Jim and
Kelli laughing with each other in a way that implied intimacy. They
stopped when they saw me passing, but I didn't bother speaking to
either one of them. I didn't even offer them the phony smile I
would have given them before today. I wasn't in the mood for any
insincere conversations, so I kept the pep in my step and pretended
I didn't see them.

I entered the training room and saw the class participants gathering their belongings and making preparations to leave. I was glad the class was over, because I needed to speak with Lorna in private. I'd thought about waiting until later, but there was something I needed to know before I came straight out and asked Frank to help me with what I was planning to do. I needed to know if Lorna had any additional information that could help prove that Reed Meyers had practically made discrimination part of the company's mission statement. We'd had conversations regarding this in the past, but now I needed her to tell me everything she knew to increase my ammunition.

"Looks like I caught you just in time," I said.

"Yeah, I guess," she said, but didn't stop what she was writing to look at me.

"How many more classes do you have to teach today?"

"I have no idea. I haven't even looked at my afternoon schedule."

I started replaying the last few days in my mind, trying quickly to figure out why Lorna was treating me so coldly. She'd never done this before, and for the life of me, I couldn't guess what was going on now.

I looked around the room and saw the last employee walking toward the door.

"Excuse me, Clifford. Would you please close the door on your way out?"

"Sure," he agreed.

"Thanks," I said, and turned back toward the person who was my only true female friend here at the company.

"Lorna, what's wrong with you?"

"What's wrong with *me*? No, the question is, what's wrong with *you*?"

"What are you talking about?"

"I'm talking about the fact that you've been keeping things from me."

"Keeping things from you like what?"

"You know what I'm talking about, Anise."

"No, I don't."

My defense mechanisms were kicking in, and I was growing angrier by the minute.

"Yeah, I think you do," she said.

"If I had something to tell you, then I would."

"Then why didn't you tell me that you've been fucking my boss?"

I was mortified.

I couldn't believe what I was hearing, although I knew I'd heard her loud and clear.

"Where did you get an idea like that?"

"If you're going to meet Frank undercover, I suggest you do it somewhere a lot farther away than the Marengo truck stop."

My heart must have stopped for a few seconds because I felt like I couldn't breathe.

"I left right after work driving over to Spring Hill Mall in Dundee and stopped at the truck stop to get some gas and cigarettes on the way," she continued. "And who did I see pulling up? Frank. And then I saw you step out of your truck and get into his."

"I don't know what to say, Lorna. It wasn't planned before yesterday morning. And all we did was go to dinner in Schaumburg. But under no circumstances did we sleep together."

"Well, actually, it's none of my business if you did or didn't, is it?"

"You know what, Lorna? You're right. It's not your business. And I resent your attitude, because my personal life doesn't have a damn thing to do with you."

I left the table where Lorna was sitting and headed toward the door.

"My feelings were hurt, Anise," she blurted out.

"Hurt why?" I asked, turning to look at her.

"Because I thought you and I were such close friends. I thought we told each other everything. I've told you things about my life that I've never told another living soul, and I guess I expected the same from you."

She was right in one respect. She did tell me everything except what color panties she had on. She'd probably even tell me that too, if I wanted to know, but that's just how open she was. I, on the other hand, wasn't. Even Monica and my mother didn't know about my dinner with Frank. Sometimes certain things needed to be kept private, and I didn't see anything wrong with it.

"We *are* good friends, Lorna, but given my marital situation and the fact that Frank is a director here at the company, I thought it was best to keep our relationship between the two of us. Because you know most people around here wouldn't be too thrilled if they found out that he's interested in me."

"That doesn't bother me, and you know it. But what hurt is that you've been so busy with your new job, we haven't really been able to talk hardly at all."

"We've seen each other every day," I said, trying to figure out where all this was coming from.

"Yeah, but it's not the same. I've come into your office a couple of times, but you always get a phone call while I'm in there, and I end up having to leave while you're still talking. And I don't think you spoke to me yesterday at all, so when I saw you with Frank, it really hurt me."

"But why?"

"Because I felt excluded. I'm the one who's been here for you through all of this Jim-and-Lyle bullshit, and now you're ditching me to be with Frank."

"My friendship with you hasn't changed, and it's completely different from my relationship with Frank, anyway. And I guess I'm a little confused too, because I'm not understanding why this is bothering you so much."

"Did you ever once stop to think that maybe I might be interested in Frank?"

"No, because you've never told me anything like that before."

"You've heard me talk about how good he looks."

"Yeah, but you say that about a lot of men, so how was I supposed to know that you were interested in Frank? And even when we've discussed him casually, you've never said one word."

"I know. Shoot me for not telling you. But I've always been interested in him, and I guess I'm a little envious because he wants you."

"Well, I'm sorry, Lorna. I didn't know."

"I know you didn't, but it just seems like I'm the only one who doesn't have a serious relationship with anyone. Because here you are married, and still you've got someone else who wants to be with you."

I didn't know whether I should tell her that David and I were getting a divorce or not. Maybe it would make her feel better. But I couldn't be sure. She seemed so irrational, and while we were supposed to be friends, I was terrified that she might blab this thing between Frank and me to someone else. Maybe if I told her, she would find some confidence in our friendship again.

"David and I are separated, and we're getting divorced."

"Oh no."

"I didn't tell you because this has been too hard for me to talk about with anyone."

I was only being partly truthful, but I hoped the reason I gave her would suffice.

"I didn't know, and I'm really sorry to hear that. And I'm sorry for saying what I said about you and Frank earlier. I was completely out of line."

"I'm sorry, too," I added.

I didn't know why I was apologizing, but something told me I'd better handle Lorna like expensive crystal. She seemed like a time bomb waiting to explode and the funny thing was, I didn't know why. She seemed different, twisted even, but maybe it really was because she'd wanted Frank for herself. Now, though, I knew our friendship was never going to be the same, and that I had to make sure to tell Frank that she'd seen us in Marengo. She was the last person I would have ever worried about, but now she had the potential of being the top whistle-blower. She'd told me why she was so upset, but it didn't make any sense. It was almost as if she'd turned into someone I didn't know in a matter of minutes, and I didn't understand it.

"So what are you going to do about this Kelli situation?" she asked, changing the subject.

"I haven't quite decided, but I will very soon."

The whole reason I'd come in there was to ask her about some of the things that had happened with certain employees before I came to work at Reed Meyers. But now I wasn't going to question her about anything. I just didn't trust her, so it was better to leave well enough alone.

"I still say you should go to EEOC first thing next week."

"We'll see. I want to think everything through before going forward with anything."

"It's your call, but if it were me, I wouldn't let them get away with it."

She kept saying that, but she'd allowed Jim to get away with sexually harassing her. I wasn't going to dare contradict what she was suggesting, though.

"Hey, I hate to run," I said, "but I've got to get back to work."

"Maybe I'll see you later?"

"I'm sure you will."

I made it back to my office and closed the door behind me. I saw my message-waiting light blinking and dialed into the voice-mail system to listen to my messages. The first was from Monica, wanting to know where I was last night and why I hadn't called her when I got in. The second was from Mom, saying she was planning to call me last night but didn't get home from summer revival until after ten.

I was happy she hadn't called, because I would have felt guilty about not telling her where I'd been. I wasn't going to call Monica either, because it was better to tell her about Frank in person. I'd tell her and Mom both face-to-face, but on different days because I knew they didn't agree on the subject. Mom wouldn't care that Frank was white, but she would care about the fact that I wasn't divorced from David.

So when I listened to my third message and heard that it was from Frank, I decided to call him instead.

"Good morning, Frank Colletti's office," his secretary answered.

"Good morning. Is he in?"

"Sure, may I tell him who's calling?"

"Yes, this is Anise Miller."

"Oh, hi, Anise. I'll put you right through."

"Thanks."

"Hi, beautiful," he said.

"Why is your secretary answering your phone? Not that a director shouldn't have someone answering his phone, but you've always answered your own calls in the past."

"I know. I hate that formal garbage these other managers try to pull, but today I'm working on an important project and don't want to be disturbed unless I have to."

"Well, then how did I get through?"

"Because I told her that I was waiting on you to call me about some new training ideas you had for some of the factory employees."

I wondered how many more lies Frank and I were going to have to tell. I'd been taught at an early age that it was always better to tell the truth because when you told one lie, you would certainly have to tell another in the future.

I was lying to people left and right, both directly and indirectly, and I didn't like it. Now, Frank was lying to his secretary because he didn't want her thinking I was calling for personal reasons.

"So did you sleep well last night?" I asked.

"Very well. Better than I have in a long time. I really had a good time with you, and the reason I left you a message is because I hope you're free again this evening."

"I don't know, Frank. Lorna was upset with me a little while ago because, believe it or not, she saw me get into your SUV at the truck stop."

"She what?"

"Yes, you heard me. She said she was on her way to Dundee to the mall and stopped to get some gas and cigarettes. So I don't know if she's telling the truth or whether she simply followed one of us."

"Even if she did see us, why was she upset?"

"I'll talk to you about that in person."

"Tonight?"

"I don't know. I don't think that's a good idea."

"I think it's a great idea. And I'll tell you what. Instead of going out, why don't you come to my house? I'll rent a couple of DVDs and order a pizza."

"To your house? I don't think so."

"Why? Don't you trust me? Or is it that you don't trust yourself?"

"Both."

I was being honest.

"Oh come on. It'll be fun. You can dress casual, and we'll have a good time."

"I'm telling you, I don't think it's a good idea."

"And I'm begging you to please come. Unless you have something else better to do."

"No, actually I don't have anything to do."

"Well, I think it would be a shame for you to sit home alone on a warm Friday night."

"Okay. What time?"

"Say around eight?"

"That works for me, because I need to run a couple of errands and make a few phone calls after work."

"Then I'll see you at eight. Oh, and what do you like on your pizza?"

"Double cheese, sausage and green peppers."

"That's pretty boring," he said.

"Sorry, but you asked."

"I'll get it half and half, because I like just about everything they can put on it."

"That's a man thing."

"You're probably right."

"I'll see you tonight, okay?"

"I look forward to it."

I knew I was getting myself into something that I wouldn't be able to get out of, but I had to see him. I needed his help in terms of obtaining additional HR information, but I also wanted to see him for just him. Which is why I knew there was a chance our intimacy would go further than the kiss I wouldn't provide him with last evening. I wondered how I'd arrived at this point in my life. But I didn't dwell on it for too long because none of that mattered. What was important was how I was going to rise to the next level in life without looking back. It was hard not looking back at any mistakes, but I knew it was better to move forward.

My phone rang again, and this time I debated whether I should answer it or not because I didn't want any questions from Monica or my mother. But at the same time, I knew it could be Lorna, whom I didn't want to ignore, or it could be one of the shop foremen. Or it could be Frank calling back. So I picked it up.

"Anise Miller," I said.

"Hi, it's me."

Hearing from David was all I needed.

"So how are you?" I asked, trying to force a cordial tone.

"I'm fine. And you?"

"I'm good."

"I thought I'd give you a call to see if you're planning to buy me out of the house or if you want to place it on the market," he said without hesitation.

"Well, I think you know that there's no way I can afford a three-thousand-dollar mortgage on my own. So I guess we don't have a choice but to sell it."

"Do you have a Realtor in mind?" he asked.

"Not really, but I'm sure I can find one."

"I think we should get the ball rolling on this as soon as possible before the divorce proceedings begin. I would do it myself, but it'll be kind of hard meeting with them since I'm in Chicago most of the time."

"That's fine. I probably won't get to it today, but I'll do it first thing on Monday."

"Then I guess the other thing we need to do is decide how we're going to split up the bank accounts and the furniture," he said.

I'd already thought about the money, but I figured I'd wait to see what he had to say about it.

"How are you wanting to handle it?" I asked.

"Well, I think it's only fair that we split up our savings accounts based on how much we've deposited into them."

"Which means?" I asked, hoping he wasn't saying what I thought he was.

"Meaning that whatever I've put in over the last few years, that's what I expect to get back out, plus interest."

"You do realize that by law, whatever we've accumulated together belongs to both of us."

"No, I don't realize anything. I earn five times what you do, and it's only right that I get every bit of what I've worked so hard to save."

"Well, I'm not going for that. We're splitting any money that we have fifty-fifty, and I'm not budging."

"Anise, do you think I'm going to let you take fifty percent of everything, when you've probably only contributed a small percentage of the total balance?"

"No, I don't expect you to *let* me do anything, but I'm sure the judge will see things a lot differently when he finds out you deserted me for another woman."

"This is bullshit. And I guess you want fifty percent of my 401(k) as well, too?"

"No, actually I don't. Because I don't agree that any working person should collect fifty percent of an ex-spouse's retirement plan. Maybe if I didn't work and had children to take care of, it would be different. But I work every single day, and I save money toward my own retirement. So all I'm talking about are the checking, savings, and CD accounts we have."

"We're still talking about at least a hundred thousand dollars, and a lot of that came from my yearly bonuses."

"Regardless. We're splitting that money fifty-fifty, David, and if you try to take any more than that, then I'll change my mind about not wanting part of your 401(k)."

"Why are you doing this?"

He sounded like a child throwing a temper tantrum, and what he didn't know was that I wasn't doing it because I wanted a ton of money. I was doing it because of how he'd betrayed me.

"You asked for all of this, not me," I said. "We're both at fault to a certain extent, but I know you don't expect to walk away with everything and leave me nothing. Because it's not going to happen."

"What about the furniture, then?" he asked, raising his voice.

"We need to figure it out."

"I'm taking everything that I brought when we first got married."

"I expect you to."

"And I'm also taking our master bedroom set and the furniture in the great room."

"You know, David, I can see right now that we're going to have to let our attorneys deal with this."

"Why, Anise? Why can't we work this out on our own instead of running up legal bills?"

"Because you don't want to be fair, that's why."

"Like I said, this is bullshit."

"No, it's not. It's what you asked for when you went out and screwed some bitch," I said, and hated that he could still agitate me.

"I screwed someone else because I was tired of looking at you."

"And if you keep talking, you'll be lucky if you leave the court-house with ten pennies."

"You know, those petty threats really don't become you."

"Call them petty if you want, but I'm not playing with you. Because even though I'm more than willing to give you a divorce, I'm not about to be left high and dry financially."

"You know what? This conversation is going nowhere, so I'm out of here," he said, and clicked the phone in my ear.

Which was fine because I didn't have anything else civil to say, anyway. I knew divorce was the right way to proceed, but I wasn't going to walk away with nothing. I couldn't believe he'd suggested that I should. But I knew that splitting the money equally wasn't the problem, and that it had everything to do with my not begging him on hands and knees to come back to me. David thought quite highly of himself, and he was disappointed to hear that I, too, wanted to end this marriage. He didn't want any part of me, but he couldn't stand the idea of me successfully moving on without him. He couldn't stand the fact that I didn't need any man in my life or that I didn't mind being alone.

For that reason, I was glad he didn't know about Frank.

CHAPTER 19

RANK'S SUBDIVISION was more ritzy than I imagined. There were groups of evergreen trees at the entrance, and each house I passed must have averaged five to six thousand square feet. Some were brick, some were stucco, some had a mixture of both. Every lawn was beautifully landscaped with concrete or brick circle driveways. A few had exquisite-looking waterfalls or huge boulders in the middle.

I continued around the curve, searching for the address he'd given me right before leaving work. When I saw 12002 on one of the brick pillars, I drove into the driveway. His home was to die for. I lived in a forty-eight-hundred-square-foot house myself, but it seemed only a small guest house compared to his. The brick was light tan and the windows were bayed all the way across the front. It was every bit of five to six hundred thousand dollars, and I wondered how a director of training could afford all of this on his own.

I turned the ignition off and stepped out of my SUV. Then I walked up the sidewalk leading to Frank's front door and pushed the button on the intercom system. I waited to hear his voice, but he opened the door instead.

"So you made it?" he said.

"Yeah, I did."

He wore jean shorts and a black pullover and looked even more attractive than he did at work. I walked in and he reached to hug me before closing the door, which left me wondering what his wealthy neighbors would think if they caught him doing it.

"Come in and make yourself comfortable," he said, pointing to the sunken living room, which was decorated in light tans, blacks and blues. I slipped off my sandals, followed him, and took a seat on the sofa. Contemporary jazz played through the built-in sound system. He sat next to me, and for some reason I felt uncomfortable. Not because I didn't want him sitting so close, but I think it was because this whole thing between us was still so new. Time was passing, and I knew I had feelings for him, but I still wasn't used to the idea.

"About an hour ago, I started wondering if you were really going to come," he said.

"Why wouldn't I?"

"I don't know. I guess because you seemed so hesitant when I first invited you this morning."

"Well, I'm here now" was all I could say.

"That you are," he said, and stared at me the way he always did.

"Your home is beautiful."

"Thank you. Wanna see the rest of it?"

"I'd love to."

We stood and moved toward the dining room.

"I'm not so sure I would have chosen this particular dining room set, but it was a gift from my mom, and I didn't want to hurt her feelings," he said, referring to the cherry wood buffet and matching table. "I think I would have gone oak in color and probably would have bought a lighted china cabinet instead, but I can live with it."

"It's nice," I said, but I agreed with him about the china cabinet, because I loved those as well.

We strolled past the winding staircase, down a hall and into the kitchen. It was every woman's dream. Major cabinet space occupied each wall and a unique island created an elegant focal point. The marble countertops accented the entire room, and the glass breakfast table did the same.

"This is where we'll eat when the pizza gets here," he said, pointing toward the family room.

"Sounds good to me."

We walked up the second staircase and took a look inside two guest bedrooms and two full baths. Then we entered the master bedroom suite, which had a fireplace, sitting area, double walk-in closets and a bathroom large enough to do exercises in. There was even a custom vanity for the woman of the house.

Frank showed me his home office, which was also on the second floor, and then we went back down to the main level.

"Tell me something," I said. "How do you keep all of this so clean?"

"I don't. I pay someone else to."

"I have a cleaning service that comes every two weeks, but I would think you'd need someone much more often."

"I do. I have someone come in twice a week, but one of those days is for washing and ironing my clothes and to cook a meal that will last for two days."

"Must be nice."

"It is, but if I had a wife, maybe she'd be willing to cook for me herself every now and then."

He looked at me, waiting for a reaction, but I didn't offer one.

He led me toward the stairway leading to the lower level, which was another house in itself. There was another family room, an exercise room, a billiards room, an office, another bedroom, a kitchenette, and a sauna. I was in awe of how well the house had been constructed and how tastefully decorated it was. It looked like a woman had done it for him.

"You really do have a gorgeous home, and I love the decorating."

"Thank you. It's a lot of house for just me, but I'm hoping to change that one day. This bachelor lifestyle is not as appealing as it once was."

"I can understand that. Nobody wants to be alone for the rest of their lives."

Upstairs, we went out on the deck, which wrapped halfway around the back of the house, and came back inside. As soon as we sat down in the family room, the doorbell rang.

"That's probably the pizza," he said.

I positioned myself on the red leather sofa and scanned the modern artwork on the walls. I admired the six-foot artificial plant and thought about how I would love to have one exactly like it in my great room. I had one, but it couldn't compare to this.

"I'm going to set this on the table, and I'll be right back with the plates," he said, and walked into the kitchen.

It would have suited me just fine to eat at the breakfast table, because Frank's family room was a lot nicer than most I'd seen. But this was his domain, and his call, so I didn't suggest we do anything different.

"What do you want to drink?" he asked.

"Sprite, Sierra Mist. Something without caffeine, because I've had too much of it this week."

"What about ginger ale?"

"That'll work, too."

He made two trips between the kitchen and where we were sitting, bringing plates, a knife, glasses of ice and cans of ginger ale.

"I always sit on the floor when I eat in here, but you don't have to," he said resting on the carpet.

"Sitting on the floor is more comfortable to me, anyway."

I scooted down and sat adjacent to him.

"Is the music okay, or do you want to start one of the DVDs?"

"What do you have? *Jungle Fever?*"

"Funny," he said, and we laughed.

"No, actually, I picked up *Armageddon* because, believe it or not, I never saw it, and I also picked up *Pretty Woman* and *The Original Kings of Comedy.*"

"You're kidding?"

"About which one?"

"The Original Kings of Comedy."

"Why? Have you seen it already?"

"Yeah, and I loved it, but that's not what I mean."

"Then what?"

"I guess I'm just surprised that you would rent a DVD with all black comedians."

"I've seen all four of them on TV shows or in movies, and all of them are funny as hell. So it doesn't matter to me what color they are."

"I'm glad, but I'm still surprised."

"You'll get used to the way I am, eventually," he said, taking a bite of pizza.

"I guess so."

I bit into my piece and then drank some ginger ale.

"I was thinking you'd ask me why I rented *Pretty Woman* with it being so old, and because most men would never rent it because it's sometimes categorized as a chick flick," he said.

"It's one of my favorite movies, but why did you get it?" I asked.

"Because in the movie, Julia Roberts and Richard Gere come from very different walks of life, yet they are extremely attracted to each other, end up falling in love and live happily ever after."

"Oh, so you're wanting to make a point?"

"Exactly. You and I were born of different races, but that doesn't mean we aren't compatible in other ways."

"I agree. I never would have before, but I do now."

We finished our food, drank a little more.

"There's a couple of things I need to tell you before we go any further."

I knew it. I knew this was all too good to be true. Him *and* this mansion. His family was either dealing mega drugs, was very well connected with the mob, or Frank really didn't own this house. Because the more I thought about it, the more I realized I hadn't seen one photo of him, a family member or friend.

"Will I want to leave right after you do?" I asked.

"I don't think so, but I know what most people think when they come here and see how well I'm living on a seventy-thousand-dollar job."

"So how do you?"

There was no sense pretending I wasn't as curious as everyone else.

"My grandparents were very wealthy. My father inherited everything except a separate trust fund they willed to me, but I couldn't touch it until I graduated from college and grad school. The other stipulation was that I had to be married before the funds could be released."

His money was the least of my worries, so I asked, "What happened to your ex-wife?"

"She was black, I was white, and twelve years ago interracial marriages weren't so acceptable in Mitchell. And when she realized her family was never going to accept us as man and wife, she left. Didn't tell me she was gone, didn't want any money. Just up and left with the clothes on her back and a few things from her closet."

"I'm sorry to hear that, Frank. I had no idea."

"No, it's fine, but I have to admit I loved her more than life itself, and my heart was broken for years because of it."

"That's too bad that her family wouldn't support her."

"You'd think my folks would have been the ones who didn't want us together, because that's usually the case. But my parents loved Tracy."

"Wow."

"But I will say that even though I practically hated her family for ruining our marriage, I do understand why they despise white people so much. Tracy's grandfather was tied to a tree down in Mississippi and hanged by the Klan for no reason."

Frank was starting to depress me, and I wanted him to change the subject. I needed him to discuss something else or I wouldn't be able to stay here.

"So she filed for a divorce, I paid for it and I never heard from her again," he said.

I felt bad when I saw his eyes watering. "I'm sorry that you had to go through that. I really am."

"I didn't mean to weigh you down with all of this, but I don't want to keep any secrets from you, and I didn't want you thinking that I'm the son of some mob king."

We laughed. "A lot of thoughts did cross my mind, so I'm glad you explained everything."

"Now, on a different note, what's this about Lorna seeing us together last night?"

"To tell you the truth, Frank, I don't know what's wrong with her. I went into the training room to ask her something, and she was very distant. Then, when I asked her what was wrong, I couldn't believe what she said."

"What?"

"She asked me when I was going to tell her that I was fucking her boss."

Frank frowned. "You're kidding?"

"No, she was very straightforward with what she had to say."

"And where did she get an idea like that?"

"I told you earlier. She saw us at that truck stop. But the most interesting part is that she said she was interested in you herself."

"Lorna said that?"

I could tell he was just as surprised as I was.

"Yes."

"Well, that's something I didn't know about. Plus, she's not my type. Not by a long shot."

"Why?"

"Because she's too needy."

"Well, that's not a nice thing to say."

"Hey, I call 'em as I see 'em."

"I'm still bothered by the way she was acting, because Lorna and I have always been such good friends. And I don't know how to handle things between us anymore, because now I don't feel like I can trust her. I learned a long time ago that you can't trust anyone who envies you."

"This is so unlike her, though," he said. "I've worked with her the whole time I've been at the company, and she's always been a wonderful employee. She's always on time, she works overtime without being told and she's good at what she does."

"I know. But for some reason she was totally through with me for being with you."

"Well, that's not our worry, and if Lorna can't deal with what you and I have, then I'm very sorry for her."

"That's easy to say, but what if she becomes so irritated that she tells someone at work about us?"

"She'd never do that."

"How can you be so sure?"

"I'm not exactly, but I really doubt that she would do something like that. Maybe she's upset, but I'm sure it'll pass."

"I'm not as confident as you are, but I hope you're right."

Frank glanced toward the DVD player. "Enough about Lorna. Which movie do you want to see?"

"Whichever one you want. I've seen all three of them and don't mind seeing any of them again."

He picked up *Pretty Woman*, placed it inside the DVD player and turned off the stereo system. Then he sat on the sofa and motioned for me to sit next to him. I told him to give me a few minutes, and I excused myself and went to the powder room. When I closed the door, I leaned the back of my body against it with my eyes closed. I was so nervous I couldn't think straight. I'd agreed to come here knowing that one thing could lead to another, but now I wished I'd turned down his invitation. I wanted to be here, and at the same time I didn't. I was so wishy-washy about the way I felt, but I knew I couldn't hide in the rest room forever. He was waiting for me to come back out, and it was time for me to push whatever terror I had out of my mind and go face what I knew would happen. I'd told myself that this would be an innocent visit, and then I'd go home. But deep down I'd known better all along. I'd known that I was about to sleep with him, and I felt guilty about it.

I relieved my bladder, washed my hands and took one last look at a woman who'd never slept with anyone besides her husband since the day she married him. I walked slowly back into the family room, and Frank looked at me like he'd won some sort of prize.

I sat on the sofa next to him, but closer to the television. I left two feet between us on purpose.

"Is it too much to ask if I want you to move closer?"

"No, I guess not."

I moved over until I felt my hip rub against his.

He wrapped his arm around me and caressed my shoulder. A chill spiraled through my body. He caressed my shoulder continuously, and then I felt the warmth of his breath skim the back of my neck. He kissed me gently, over and over again, and I closed my eyes in enjoyment. He turned my face toward his and stared at me with passion. My heart pounded as I gazed back at him. He smoothed his hand across my face and then moved closer and kissed me softly on my lips. He kissed me a little harder. Then it became more passionate. We kissed for a long while, and finally he pulled my feet onto the sofa and stretched out on top of me. He pressed himself against me, and I felt him growing harder with every second. I wanted so desperately to feel him inside me, but I couldn't bring myself to make the first move. He pulled my sleeveless shirt out of my shorts and pushed it above my breasts. He pushed my bra in the same direction. He kissed my breasts and my stomach. I moaned when he took one of my nipples into his mouth and then the other. I held the top of his head and felt myself getting moist just beneath him. He slid my shorts and panties over my buttocks and down my legs. I closed my eyes when I saw him pulling them over my feet, and I was thankful that I had freshly manicured toes. He removed his shirt. I did the same with my shirt and bra. He pulled a condom from his pocket and asked me with his eyes if he had to use it. I nodded yes, and he slipped off his shorts and under-wear. I lay on the sofa, watched him tear open the wrapper and roll the rubber onto his well-endowed penis. I felt my heart flutter again when he kneeled to the floor and spread my legs wide open.

He rested his head between my thighs and his lips showered me with a level of love I didn't know existed. My pleasure was building.

"Frank," I called out to him. "Oh my goodness. Frank. Please. Oh my. Oh, Frank."

He quickened the stroke of his tongue and held the top of my thighs tightly. He stroked me with great intensity. I felt months of denied pleasure preparing to explode. He increased his speed, and I moved his head with my hand, aiding the process.

"Oh," I spoke deeply. "Oh. Oh. Oh . . . Frankkkkk!" I screamed in ecstasy. I continued screaming until the throbbing sensation subsided.

He stood to his feet and thrust himself inside me. He was so much bigger than David, and I loved every inch of him. I loved the way he felt inside me, and I felt my body heating up all over again. He moved in and out of me. In. Then out. He breathed heavily, and I felt him mushroom wide inside me. He breathed deeper and deeper. He yelled out to his higher power. I felt myself verging on eruption a second time around.

"Oh, Anise."

"Oh, Frank."

"Sweetheart."

"Baby."

"Oh, Anise. I'm coming."

"Come on, baby."

"Oh . . . oh . . . oh . . . Anise. Ohh myy goodness."

His body shook, and my system burst forth with satisfaction. He rested on top of me, and we held each other like our lives depended on it.

It was a good thing the central air was blasting, because our bodies were somewhat heated. I lay there wondering where Frank had been all my life, because no man had made me feel the way I was feeling currently. We were just getting to know each other, but this wasn't just sex. Frank had left me feeling so satisfied, I felt like I was betraying my own race.

He moved his head to the side of me and said, "You don't know how long I've dreamed about making love to you. It's been almost like a fantasy because somehow I knew you would feel even better than what I ever imagined."

"I haven't felt this way before either, and I'm not sure how to deal with what I'm feeling."

"Just enjoy it," he said. "Just be happy, and don't think about the life you had before this evening."

"You know it's not that simple."

"It can be, if you let it."

"You know my situation."

"But you won't have to deal with that for very long. I know I said I wouldn't pressure you, but, Anise, the truth is, I'm in love with you."

"Frank, please don't say that. We haven't even known each other for very long," I said, trying to dismiss what he was saying.

"I know what I feel and it's very real. At first I thought it was just an attraction I had for you, but when I watched you across the dinner table last night, I knew. I knew I was really in love with you. And after tonight I don't want to go another day without having you in my life."

"But now I'm feeling like my life is even more complicated than it already was."

"You only feel that way because you're in love with me and don't want to accept it. We didn't just have sex a few minutes ago. We made love to each other."

I sighed in frustration. I didn't want to accept what he was saying because I knew he might be telling the truth. I wasn't sure how this had all evolved and how these intimate feelings I had for him had crept up on me without any warning. I was dealing with so many problems, so I wasn't sure how I might be falling for someone so quickly.

"Tell me I'm wrong," he said. "Tell me that you absolutely don't love me."

I turned my back to his chest and curled into the fetal position.

"Tell me, Anise. Tell me that I'm just imagining all this, and that you don't have a feeling in the world for me."

I didn't say anything. I wanted to, but I couldn't. I didn't want to admit how strong my feelings were for him because I knew our lives would never be the same once I did. There was a fine line between doing what felt good and what was best for everyone involved. I'd acted hastily by accepting his dinner invitation yesterday morning, and then again when I agreed to come to his home this evening. I'd plunged into this situation with my eyes wide open, but I'd purposely ignored all the consequences. I was lonely and vulnerable, and it felt good having someone feel so attracted to me after David had made me feel so undesirable. But I didn't know how this was all going to play out, and it alarmed me.

"Anise, please tell me that I'm right about the way you feel."

"I do have strong feelings for you, but—"

"Don't say that you're not in love with me, because you are. I can tell by the way you look at me, and I could feel it when we were making love."

"We've only been together twice, so how could we possibly be in love?"

"I can't answer that, but I know we are."

"I think I'd better shower," I said, standing up and grabbing my clothing.

"Anise, please don't do this. Don't deny what we have together."

"I can't deal with this right now, Frank. I'm sorry, but I just can't, and if you care about me, you'll let me shower and go home."

He rubbed his hands through his hair, front to back, and I could tell he was hurt. I didn't want to hurt him, but I couldn't think of anything else to do except flee this accident we were now equal parties to.

"You can use the one upstairs in my bedroom. There're some towels in the closet right in front of it."

"I'm sorry, Frank. I know you don't understand, but this is all too much for me to handle."

He gazed at me with sadness. I expected him to say something, but he didn't. So I turned and went up to the bathroom and took my shower. When I was dressed, I came back downstairs, picked up my purse from the living room and walked into the family room. He'd thrown his clothing back on and was sitting on the sofa watching what was left of *Pretty Woman*.

"I'll walk you outside," he said, and waited for me to turn and go toward the door. When I did, he followed behind me. I slipped on my sandals, opened the door and walked out. I unlocked my car with the security remote on my key ring, and Frank pulled my door open. I sat down inside and turned the ignition. He shut the door, and I rolled down my window.

"Frank, I don't know what to say except I'm sorry."

"Why are you fighting against what we have?"

"Because if we take this any further, it will only mean trouble for both of us."

"What kind of trouble? Because if you're talking about racial trouble, we can deal with that. As long as we love each other, every-thing else will work out the way it should."

"I'm about to go through something major at work, and after speaking with David today, I can tell my divorce is going to get messy. I've got too much on my shoulders right now, and I can't afford to add anything else."

"But what about me? I can help you through all of that."

"If you support me at work and they find out that you and I are seeing each other, you'll lose your job."

"Take a look around, Anise. Do I look like I care about losing a job? If they fire me, I'll just go work somewhere else."

"My life is too complicated right now, and I don't want you to get hurt," I pleaded with him to understand.

"I'll be hurt if you push me away."

"I've gotta go, okay? I'm sorry."

He stepped away. I pulled my gear in reverse and looked behind me.

"Anise?"

"Yes?"

"I really do love you. I love you so much it hurts."

My heart crumbled into a thousand pieces, and deep down I hated leaving him. But I had to.

"I'm sorry. I really am," I said, and backed out of his driveway.

I left the subdivision in tears. I did love Frank, and I wanted nothing except to be with him. But all odds were against us. I knew it must be love, because I hadn't thought one time about asking him to help me obtain the evidence I needed at work. One day ago, my intention had been to use my relationship with him as a means to get what I wanted, but now I didn't feel comfortable doing it. I cared about him too much to take advantage of his love for me.

Tears streamed down my face, and I blinked, trying to focus on the road in front of me. My vision cleared up enough so that I wasn't forced to pull over, but I felt an emptiness I hadn't felt when we were making love. I hadn't thought about any of my dilemmas, and it felt good being free of them for at least a short while.

As I drove into my subdivision, I wondered why I'd left Frank standing alone in his driveway.

I wondered what he was thinking at this very moment.

I wondered how I was going to make it through the night without him holding me.

I wondered how I was going to face him on Monday.

CHAPTER 20

ETTING DIVORCED, suing Reed Meyers and falling in love with Frank was a tad more drama than I wanted to deal with. I tossed and turned all night, and no matter how hard I tried, I couldn't force Frank out of my mind. I tried to imagine how life would be for both of us if we entered an exclusive relationship. I wanted to believe that love really could conquer all, but I wasn't so sure in this situation. My family would be fine with whomever I dated, Frank claimed his parents loved his first black wife, but how would the rest of the world handle the love we'd be professing to each other? I wanted to believe we'd be able to ignore the rest of society, but logically, I knew we couldn't. This was a real problem in a real world, and there was no way of overlooking it.

I brewed a pot of vanilla coffee from Gloria Jean's and read the newspaper I'd just brought inside the house. I debated calling Monica, but realized she'd be even more suspicious if too much time passed without us communicating. So I dialed her number.

"It's about time you called back," she said after the second ring.

"Some people depend way too much on Caller ID," I said.

"Don't change the subject, missy. I called you at work yesterday and then again last night around ten. So where have you been? Are you and David trying to work things out after all?"

She couldn't have been more wrong if she tried to be, and I didn't want to think about what she would say if I told her the truth regarding my whereabouts.

"No, David and I are over for good."

"Well then, where were you?"

"I was out."

"Out where?" she insisted.

"Just out. I had some errands to run and a couple of other places to go."

"Like where?"

She wasn't going to ease up with this cross-examination, and now I wished I'd followed my better judgment and not called her until later.

"I was out, and I'll have to tell you about it in person."

"I know you're not seeing someone else?"

"What if I am?" I said, testing her reaction.

"Don't play with me like that, Anise. Were you out with someone else or not?"

"I was, but I'm not telling you anything about it until I see you in person."

"Well, I'm on my way over right now then."

"Hold on a minute," I said when I thought I heard the garage door opening.

"Anise, don't try to change the subject—"

"No, I'm serious. Hold on a minute," I said, and walked over to open the door leading to the garage.

A heat wave encased me when I saw David step out of his vehicle.

"Monica, let me call you back."

"Why?"

"Because David is here."

"Then I was right. You *are* trying to work things out with him."

"I'll call you back, okay," I spoke louder than before, because I could tell she wasn't about to say good-bye.

"Fine. I'll be waiting."

"Bye, girl," I said, and pressed the off button.

David walked in wearing a golf outfit I hadn't seen before. I tried not to say anything, but I couldn't resist starting an argument with him.

"So what dragged you here this morning?"

"I decided to come because we need to talk."

"About what? Because if money is the subject, I've already told you how I feel about that."

"But you're not being reasonable."

"I don't have to be. You messed around on me, remember?"

"Anise, please don't start that same old tired conversation again."

"If you don't want to hear what I have to say, then leave."

"Why can't we just try to stay cordial for a change?" he asked, and sat down at the island.

I leaned against the kitchen countertop, facing him.

"Cordial is fine, but don't expect me to budge on what I already told you yesterday. We're splitting the money in the bank fifty-fifty."

"But you didn't contribute fifty-fifty."

"Well, that's what I'm getting in return."

"Look, Anise, you're usually a fair person, so I know you want to do the right thing."

"Huh! Is that some kind of new psychology you're trying to use? Because if it is, it's not working on Anise Lynnette Miller. Not today. Not for as long as I'm alive."

"You're wrong, and you know it."

I folded my arms and positioned my neck the way I always did when I'd had enough foolishness. It was time to set him straight once and for all.

"No, you're the one who's wrong for pretending like you wanted to work things out when all along you knew you were screwing someone else. You didn't even have the decency to tell me that you wanted someone else. At least if you'd done that, I wouldn't feel so humiliated. And it pisses me off even more when I think about the fact that you'd still be sneaking around if I hadn't busted you on the phone with her. But the good news for you is that I don't care enough to make a scene about it. I've moved on, and you're going to have to deal with this divorce on my terms or not at all."

"Moved on how, Anise? Because if you've done so much moving on, then why are you still so angry with me? Why am I still able to push the wrong buttons and send you into a frenzy?"

"Whether you believe it or not, I have moved on," I said, and wanted desperately to tell him I'd made love with Frank, and that Frank had given me more pleasure in one night than he had the whole time we were married. If he kept pushing me, I would have no choice.

"Yeah, right. Whatever you say."

"I have."

"Yeah, right."

"You really think I'm joking, don't you?"

"I know you are," he said, pretending to ignore me by picking up the newspaper.

I was becoming a little annoyed. "You don't know anything. You haven't been here. So how could you possibly know what I've been doing?"

"Okay, then, if you *are* messing around, then who with?" he asked, looking straight at me.

"I wouldn't worry about it."

"That's what I thought. It's nobody, Anise. So why don't you stop playing these games?"

"I'm seeing a white guy I've known for quite some time," I said when I couldn't take his cockiness any longer.

"What? You really should stop this," he said, cracking up at what he truly thought was a joke.

"Whether you believe me or not, I am."

"Oh, so just because I'm seeing someone white, you think making up some lie about a white guy is going to make me jealous? Please, Anise. Even you can come up with a better story than that, can't you?"

"It's not a story. You may think it is, but I'm telling you the truth."

"And my name is Willy Wonka, too."

He shook his head in disbelief and turned a page of the newspaper.

It was obvious that he wasn't going to believe what I was confessing, and in all honesty, it was for the best. I didn't need him using my relationship with Frank against me in court, so I quickly changed the subject.

"So why are you here?"

"I told you, so we can talk. But I can see now we're not going to get anywhere."

"The reason we're not is because you want to call the shots on everything, and I'm not going for it."

"You can have that little money," he said.

"I already know that, and I don't need your permission either."

"Just be glad I didn't stop by the bank and withdraw every penny," he threatened.

"I hope you do, because I already told you yesterday what would happen if you did."

"More threats, I see," he said, standing up.

"No, these are promises I plan to keep."

"I don't know why I thought you were going to be more sensible about this, but I should have expected this all along from a black woman."

"And what is that supposed to mean?"

"Black women can never go along with the program. They always have to have a fucking opinion. Which is all the reason why I jumped ship and found me a beautiful, caring white woman. Just being with me makes Christina happy. And unlike you, she doesn't need to call the shots in the relationship."

"I'm happy for you. And she can have your sorry ass, because I don't want a man who expects me to agree with him even when he's wrong."

"That's why you'll always be alone, too, my dear."

He sounded sarcastic, and I wanted to bring him down a couple of notches.

"Being alone is much better than sharing my bed with you," I shot at him.

He glared at me in disgust.

"Just stop it, Anise. Because you know you loved this," he said, standing and pointing toward his crotch.

I could tell that he believed what he was saying.

"David. Honey. Listen to me," I said with a straight face. "Regardless of what Christina is telling you, you're horrible in bed. You always have been, you always will be. But it's not your fault, because I don't think you can help being a minute man."

"You know, I'm getting a little fed up with you criticizing my sexual ability."

"Then you should leave me alone, because I'm tired of hearing you criticize me for being a black woman."

"I criticize you because you always act so ignorant."

"Don't keep pushing me, David."

"More threats? Don't you ever get tired of that?"

"I think it's time for you to leave before somebody gets hurt."

"Oh, so now you're about to act ghetto and pull a knife on me again, I guess?"

I walked away from him and went into the great room. If I'd stayed where I was, it wouldn't be long before I did something foolish.

"What do you want to do about the furniture?"

I ignored him.

"Anise?" he said, walking in my direction.

"What?"

"Which pieces of furniture do you want?"

"All of it," I said without having to think about it.

"Now I know you've lost your mind," he said, looking confused.

"No, I'm fine. And since I'm so ignorant, now I want half of everything—including your 401(k)."

"Stupid bitch."

"Call me whatever you want, but it's not going to change anything."

"I'll die first, before I let you have all my money."

"It makes no difference to me what you do, so long as I get my half of it."

"People get killed for shit like this, Anise, so if you know what's good for you, you'll stop playing these silly little games with me."

"Whatever" was all I said, because for the first time since he'd arrived he looked dead serious.

He walked down into the basement, stayed there for maybe twenty minutes and then came back up carrying two boxes.

He stopped in front of me and said, "The next time we see each other, it'll be in court."

"I look forward to it," I tossed back at him, but knew deep down that I didn't want to enter this war we had officially declared. But there was no turning back for either one of us now. We'd have to fight this thing until the end, regardless of the consequences.

He left.

I sat in the great room wishing this nightmare would cease.

After David stormed out of the house, I washed two loads of clothing, spoke with Mom and told Monica that I would attend church services with her and Marc tomorrow morning. Mom had asked me if I was coming to my own church since I hadn't been there in a while, but I'd told her I didn't think so. I didn't dare tell her that I preferred the services at Monica's church over ours.

I walked down to the basement and scanned the bookshelf for something to read. I didn't see anything I hadn't already read, so I decided to watch a movie instead. I scanned all the pay channels and stopped when I saw *Sugar Hill* with Wesley Snipes and Theresa Randle. I hadn't seen this in a long while, but I remembered loving it when Mom and I saw it at the movie theater.

I watched it all the way to the end and tried to find something else to watch as soon as the credits began rolling. But what I really wanted to do was call Frank. I wanted to hear his voice. I wanted to feel his touch, but I knew I had to avoid being intimate with him again. I wondered if he was still upset about my leaving his house the way I did.

I sat for a while, trying to resist dialing his number, but eventually I couldn't help myself.

I no longer wanted to hear his voice, I *needed* to hear it. I needed him.

I pulled the phone from its base and dialed his number from memory. I'd only dialed it once before, but I still remembered it. Mom always said that even the most forgetful person could remember what they wanted to.

He answered on the first ring, which didn't give me much time to prepare my reason for calling.

"Hey, beautiful," he said the same as always.

"I see you've got Caller ID like everyone else in America."

"Are you saying you don't?"

"No. But I don't just start talking to people before saying hello."

"Oh well, can I help it if I'm so happy to hear from you?"

"No, I guess not."

"I've been thinking about you all day, and so many times I wanted to call you but didn't know if it was safe."

"Actually, David was here this morning, so it's probably good that you didn't."

"Are you okay?"

"I'm fine. We had another huge argument, but what else is new?"

"I'm sorry."

"It's not your fault, so don't be."

"I'm sorry that you have to go through this, because I know it's not easy."

"This won't go on forever, but until it's over, I'll just have to deal with it."

"I guess, but I still hate it."

"So what did you do today?" I asked, switching subjects.

"I told you. I thought about you."

"You didn't do anything else?"

"I went to the store, by the dealership to see my dad and by the house to see my mom. But I still thought about you the entire time."

"Well, I haven't been out of the house all day."

"I wish you had called me when you got home last night, so we could have discussed what happened."

"I don't think we *should* discuss it," I said, wondering how we ended up on this subject.

"Why not?" he asked.

"Because it shouldn't have happened."

"How can you say that when I know you enjoyed me as much as I enjoyed you."

He was right, but I hated that he knew the way I was feeling.

"Is my perception correct?" he continued.

"I'd rather not say."

"You don't want to say because you know I'm right."

"What we did last night was wrong, and me calling you on the phone is wrong."

"Then why did you?"

"Why did I call?"

"No, why did you make love to me the way you did last night?"

"I can't answer that."

"You did it because you couldn't help yourself. You did it because you're in love with me. And if you'd just admit that to yourself, things would be a lot easier for both of us."

I wanted to. I really did. But I couldn't. I didn't know what was wrong with me, because it wasn't even the fact that I was still married to David. It was something deeper than that. It was the color thing that I kept playing over and over like a tape recorder.

When I didn't respond, he said, "Anise, why don't you drive over here so we can talk about this in person?"

"You know I can't."

"You can if you want to. And I know you want to, so what else is stopping you?"

"I don't know," I said.

"Please, Anise. I need to see you. We don't have to do anything you don't want, but I really need to see you."

"I shouldn't have called."

"I'm sorry if I sound like a pest, but when a man loves a woman the way I love you, I don't see how he can help it."

I kept quiet.

"Anise, I love you so much," he said.

My heart raced, and I felt like melting.

"I need time to think things through," I tried to explain.

"Okay, but can I ask you something?"

"Go ahead."

"Have you ever felt with anyone else the way you felt last night with me?"

Why was he asking me the question I'd already answered in my mind as soon as we'd finished making love? But I didn't want to lie, so I didn't see any other choice except telling him the truth.

"No, I haven't."

"Then don't fight me on this. Get your keys, and drive over here. You're alone and so am I, but we don't have to be."

He did have a point.

"What if things don't work out between us?" I asked.

"They will."

"But what if they don't?"

"They will, but if for some reason they don't, then we accept it like we would any other problem."

I sighed, not knowing what to do.

"I won't pressure you about anything. All I want is to see you."

"I'm warning you, Frank, if you try to take things too far again, I'm leaving."

I tried to sound convincing, but I knew he didn't believe a word I said.

"Cross my heart and hope to die."

"I'll see you in an hour," I said.

"I'll be waiting."

I pressed the off button, sat the phone on the arm of the chair and wondered why I was so eager to make things hard on myself.

CHAPTER 21

KNOW you don't like it, but you wanted to know, so I told you," I said to Monica. We'd gone to church as planned, and Mom had met us afterward for dinner at Ledora's, the only soul food restaurant in Mitchell. I still hadn't told Mom about Frank, but when we were alone again I'd told Monica. Now she was out here on the patio firing rocket missiles at me. Which is what I had anticipated.

"A white man, Anise? Are you out of your doggoned mind?"

"No, I'm not. I know exactly what I'm doing. I had my reservations when I went to dinner with him, and then again on Friday at his house, but after last night, I know that I'm in love with him. I didn't plan for this to happen, but it did."

"I don't believe you."

"What's not to believe?"

"That you're actually seeing a white man. I mean, it's bad enough that you're seeing someone on the rebound, without being divorced, but this is the worst of all."

"Why should it matter what color he is? It's like Mom says, if a man treats you good, what difference does it make if he's white, red or blue?"

"So your mom already knows about all this?"

"No."

"Well, since she doesn't care about color, why haven't you told her?"

"Because I just haven't."

"You haven't told her because you don't know how she's going to react. It's one thing to say you don't mind interracial dating, but it's another when your own daughter is doing it."

"Mom isn't hypocritical like that. If she has an opinion, it stands for everything and everybody. And you know that."

"I still don't believe you're telling me this. I'm so glad Marc isn't here, because he has the same crazy idea that you do," she said, referring to her husband, who'd gone to visit one of his frat brothers since Monica and I had important issues to discuss. "For some strange reason, he believes that any two people of any race can live happily ever after."

"And he's right."

"But think of all the problems you're going to have to struggle with."

"Every couple has problems."

"But the problems that interracial couples have are much different."

"And we'll deal with them."

"Like I said, I can't believe you're telling me this."

"Well, it's true, and you may as well get used to it, Monica, because this is how it's going to be."

"I'm never going to get used to you messing around with a man whose ancestors raped our own."

"Monica, please. How many years ago was that? Huh?" I was becoming irritated. "And what does that have to do with Frank?"

"It has everything to do with him. You're just in denial about it."

"What is there to deny? His ancestors did some things he's not responsible for. Plain and simple."

"I just can't believe this."

"How many times are you gonna say that?"

"Until you stop seeing him."

"Well, that's not going to happen, and what I need is for you to support me on this. You and I have been like sisters since forever, so I know you're not going to turn your back on me now."

"I'm not turning my back on you, Anise. I'm just trying to get you to see what a huge mistake you're making."

"I can see right now that this conversation is going to be a no-win situation."

"I think you should tell your mom about this."

"I'll tell her when the time is right."

"Didn't she go to your aunt's after we left the restaurant?"

"Yeah. So?"

"I think you should call over there and talk to her. This is more serious than I think you realize."

"I'm not calling Mom about this because I've already decided that I'm not going to tell her until my divorce is final."

"You're making a big mistake."

"Well, if I am, then I'll be the one who suffers the consequences, won't I?"

I was furious and Monica noticed my tone.

"Look. I'm sorry. You do what you have to," she said, just as irritated. "It's your life."

"Exactly. Which is why I didn't come over here to ask your opinion. I came to share with you what's going on in my life. I know you don't agree with what I'm doing, but I still expected you to be here for me no matter what."

"Like I said, I'm sorry. But you've really caught me off guard with this."

"I realize that, but I can't help that I've fallen in love with some- one other than a black man. And I know it's wrong to see any man while I'm still married, but if David hadn't betrayed me, I never would have allowed myself to open up to anyone else. I was vulner- able, and to a certain extent, I was looking for anyone to fill the void I was feeling. David made me feel ugly, but Frank kept insisting I was beautiful. He calls me beautiful every time he greets me, and I feel like I'm on top of the world when he does that."

"So what does Frank look like?" Monica finally broke down and asked.

"He's Italian, and he's gorgeous."

"Really, now?"

"Yes. And, Monica, girl, he makes me feel like I've never been in love with anyone else. I thought I loved David, but now I know that what we had was so superficial. It was based on status and a lot of other stuff that has nothing to do with intimacy."

"That's too bad."

"It was, but now I'm feeling a lot better."

"You haven't slept with him yet, have you?"

I turned my head away from Monica and glanced across their backyard.

"Anise? Please don't make me have a heart attack out here."

"Okay. Then I won't answer your question."

"You didn't? Please don't tell me you slept with this man after only being with him a couple of times?"

"Well, I did."

"Not you? Not the person who criticized every girl in college who slept with someone she hardly knew?"

"Things change and so do people."

"I'll say they do. Because the Anise I've known most of my life is not the same one sitting next to me right now."

"I'm the same, just wiser."

"I hope so. Because you're going to need all the wisdom you can get to deal with this."

"I'm going to need it to deal with everything. My divorce, my relationship with Frank and my issues with Reed Meyers."

"And what exactly are you planning to do about Reed Meyers, anyway?" she asked in a less combative tone, and I could tell she was still concerned about my job situation.

"I'm planning to beat them at their own game without filing a claim with EEOC or filing a lawsuit in court. Actually, part of the reason I went to visit Frank was because I needed him to help me obtain some confidential information from the corporate system. But I wasn't planning on falling for him the way I did so quickly. So when that happened, I didn't have the heart to ask him to help me. He even offered when I was at his house on Friday, but I didn't feel comfortable. I love him, and I don't ever want to give him the impression that I'm using him."

"You are so caught up. I've never seen you like this with any man. Not even with David."

"I told you, no one can compare to Frank. He's one of a kind and in my heart I know we were meant to be together."

"What about his family? What do they have to say about all of this?"

"His parents don't care who he dates so long as he's happy. Thank you very much."

"Hey, I'm just asking, because I don't want to see you going through a lot of changes because of this decision you're making."

"The only person who can't accept it is you."

"It sounds like I don't have a choice *but* to accept it, but it doesn't mean I have to like it."

"That's all I'm asking. You're supposed to be my friend, and friends don't judge each other."

"I agree, but I don't want to see you get hurt either. You've already had to hear some derogatory comments from David, and those comments would be even more hurtful if they ever came from Frank. Because somehow being called a black bitch by a black man is not the same as when a white man does it."

"I don't think Frank would resort to something like that."

"If he became angry enough, you don't know what he might say or do. You haven't even known him long enough to know one way or the other."

"And I'm not going to worry about any of that either. I'm going to take my chances with him the same way I took them with David. End of story."

"Okay. You know what's best."

"I do, and I hope this doesn't come between you and me."

"Don't ever think that. I have my opinions, but that has nothing to do with our friendship. I love you the same as I always have, and I'm here for you."

"I'm not saying things will be easy, but being with Frank is what I want."

"And I respect that."

We chatted another hour about how she wanted to plan a surprise birthday party for Marc in a couple of months, and how she wanted to do the same thing for Tamia next year. Our lives were so different, yet we were as close as two women could be. We had our disagreements, but it never changed the way we felt about one another. Our friendship was bond, and no matter what, I knew Monica would be here to pick up the pieces if things didn't work out, as I'd been there for her. I didn't let on, but I knew she was right when she said I might get hurt. But there was also a chance that things would work out the way I wanted them to.

That, of course, is what I was counting on.

I didn't bother waiting until I got home to call Frank. I called him from my cell phone instead, as soon as I left Monica's subdivision.

"So did you sleep well after I left this morning?" I asked, and turned down my CeCe Winans CD so I could hear him.

"Yeah, I had to get at least *some* sleep, because you kept me up all night," he said.

"Look who's talking. I was the one who had to force myself to get dressed and then try to stay awake in church once I got there."

"So did you have a good time at dinner?"

"I did. And I'm just now leaving my friend Monica's now."

"Did you tell her about us?"

"Yes."

"What'd she say?"

"She wasn't too happy about it, but it's mostly because she thinks our relationship can't work, and that I'll end up hurt."

"But you won't. I promise you that."

"I hope not, because I don't think I could handle being treated the way David treated me all over again."

"Your husband is a jerk, if I must say so myself. And I would never treat any woman the way he's treated you."

I didn't comment, but I prayed he was telling the truth.

"So what are you getting ready to do now?" he asked.

"I'm on my way to pick up some office supplies and then home, so I can go over some of the documents I pulled from the manufacturing system, and so I can start drafting the memo I'm going to give to the Big Three."

"Who's that?"

"Jim, Lyle and the CEO, of course."

"You crack me up."

I was pleased that he enjoyed my sense of humor.

"You know, Anise. I've spent all day thinking about what you're up against, and I've decided that I'm going to help you in any way I can. Not just because I love you, but because it's flat out wrong the way they discriminate against certain people."

"I told you, you don't have to do that."

"I've already made up my mind. And it won't be that hard because you know I'm friends with Todd, the director of MIS, right? Actually, he's one of my best friends."

"Yeah, I've heard that before," I said, and felt a little guilty since that was one of the reasons I'd been so willing to go to dinner with him in Schaumburg.

"He's a good guy, and if I tell him what I need and why, he'll give it to me. No questions asked."

"Do you think?"

"I'm positive."

"But what if you get caught and you both lose your jobs over this?"

"I really doubt that that will happen, but I'll discuss everything with Todd to make sure all our ducks are in a row."

"Well, all I can say is that you really must care about me a whole lot to risk your job and your reputation like this."

"I'm in love with you, Anise, and I would do anything for you. And like I said earlier, I'm also doing it because the way they treat women and minorities is wrong. Enough is enough, and somebody has to stand up for what's right."

"I keep hearing you say that, but it's hard for me to believe that you feel the way you do about discrimination. And it's even harder for me to understand how you feel about me and how I fell for you so quickly."

"Some things are meant to be. It was love at first sight for me, but I had to grow on you."

"Still, it didn't take as long I would expect."

"I don't think you can put a time limit on love. It hits you when you least expect it, and even if the time isn't right, I think you have to go for it. I know you're still concerned because you're still married to David, but I think you have to keep in mind that he's seeing someone else, too."

"But no matter how I try to pretend like there's nothing wrong with what I'm doing, deep down I know it's completely wrong. It was also wrong when I made love with you practically all night and then came straight home this morning to get ready for church. I felt so guilty the whole time service was going on. My morals have always been so much better in the past, and I can't deny that I'm being a hypocrite. I'm committing one of the worst sins there is. It's one thing when you do wrong without knowing it, but I'm wholeheartedly aware of what I'm doing. I'm committing adultery, and I'm going to have to pay for it somewhere down the road."

"That's pretty deep. I didn't realize you were that religious," Frank said.

"I don't attend church as often as I should, but I've been going since I was a baby. Then, when I was five, I joined the Angelic Choir. When I was ten, I became a junior usher, and when I was thirteen I joined the young adult choir. I didn't just go to church every Sunday, I was really involved with it."

"Is that right? Well, my parents never spent much time in church, and I've only been maybe a couple of times in my life. Unless you count weddings and funerals."

"You do believe in God, don't you?" I wanted to know.

"Let's just say I don't disbelieve."

"Hmmm."

"Why do you say that?"

"It sounds like you don't know one way or the other."

"Sometimes I believe there's a higher power, but when I see children being abused, people living in the street, and innocent people being killed, it's hard for me to understand how a merciful God could allow such things to happen."

"I can understand that, because I've had my own questions from time to time. But I still believe in Him, and I try to keep my faith as strong as possible. Although I'll admit, it has been a little shaky lately, because I feel like everything is piling up on me all at once."

"Not every day can be the same with anything."

"This is true, but I have to ask this. Are you open to going to church with me in the future?"

"I don't have a problem with that."

"Are you sure?"

"Of course, because I can tell it's important to you, and I don't want you to stop doing something you believe in because of me."

I didn't know if this was going to cause an issue between us later on or not, but I knew that successful relationships required both giving and taking, so I didn't have a problem with working out our differences when they occurred.

I turned into Target's parking lot and pulled into a stall. Normally I would have gone to Office Depot, but they were already closed for the day.

"So what about you? What are you doing for the rest of the evening?" I asked, pushing my gear in park.

"Not much, since it doesn't sound like I'll be seeing you."

"I would come by, but I need to spend some time going over those documents I brought home so I can figure out how I'm going to go about writing my memo."

"I know. And I think I'll call Todd when I hang up with you to see what he can do for us."

"I really appreciate this. It's a major undertaking, and I'll owe you for the rest of my life."

"If you spend the rest of it with me, you won't owe me anything."

My heart did that fluttering thing again, and it was so good to feel this happy about at least something.

"We'll have to see about that," I said.

"You do know that before the ink is dry on your divorce papers, I'm going to ask you to marry me?"

My throat muscles contracted. Partly because I was shocked, but mostly because his promised proposal made me feel uncertain.

"You did hear me, didn't you?"

"Yes."

"I guess you're surprised about that, too?"

"Sort of."

"I'm in this for the long haul, and I hope you feel the same way."

"I don't know what to say."

"You do love me?" he asked.

"Yes. I do."

"Well then, why shouldn't we be married?"

"I didn't say we shouldn't, but there are still so many things we need to learn about each other before doing something like that."

"I agree, but I also think that with love, you just have to take a chance."

"We'll see," I said.

"I hope so."

"Well, as much as I hate to go, I need to go inside the store to pick up a few things. But I'll call you later, okay?"

"I'll be here. I might step out for a minute to get something to eat, but that's about it."

"Okay, then I'll talk to you soon."

"Bye, beautiful."

"Good-bye, Frank."

I shut off the air-conditioning and the ignition and stepped outside. I was starting toward the entrance of the store when I saw a black woman and white man walking out. They were laughing with each other like they'd just won the lottery. They looked so happy, and I wondered if Frank and I could really have a great life together. I hated worrying about what other people thought, but it was hard not to. I wanted to love him unconditionally and not care whether people approved of our relationship or not. I hoped I could move past these self-conscious tendencies once I was finally able to see him publicly. If I didn't, I knew our love for each other wouldn't be enough. We wouldn't stand a chance, and our relationship would be doomed immediately.

I saw people, both black and white, stare disapprovingly at the young couple, and it bothered me that they stood out like plaids and polka dots. I wondered if anyone noticed how happy they seemed with each other, rather than their difference in color.

What bothered me most, though, was that I, too, would have noticed color before happiness before I fell in love with Frank.

CHAPTER 22

ONDAY ARRIVED in record time. I'd spent most of the evening comparing salaries of manufacturing employees, but I hadn't found much to help me prove discriminatory practices. Mainly because it was hard for management to offer unequal pay to the factory employees, since the union implemented a set rate for everyone, depending on the person's job class. I'd started outlining the memo I was going to give my superiors, but I still needed additional information to back up what I was planning to accuse them of. So I was elated when Frank called, asking me to drive to his house right after work. At first I thought he wanted me to come for personal reasons, but then he told me in so many words that he'd taken care of everything.

I hoped this was true, because I didn't know how much longer I'd be able to deal with working under these conditions. My morale couldn't have been lower, and I knew I wasn't setting the best example for my staff. I was sure, by now, they knew something was wrong, but there was no way I could offer them any details.

I looked up from my desk when I heard Lorna knocking at my door.

"Hey, Lorna," I said. I didn't know whether she was the same friend I'd always known, or if she was still upset about Frank and me. She'd probably have ten cows if she knew we'd made love all weekend.

"What's shakin'?" She closed the door behind her, and I wondered why.

"Not much. Trying to get a few things done before lunch. What's going on with you?"

"Nothing new. But I wanted to come apologize to you because of the way I acted on Friday. I was completely out of line, and I haven't been able to think about anything else. I almost called you at home, but I was ashamed. I don't know what came over me when I saw you with Frank, except that it made me think about how alone I am. How no decent man ever gives me the time of day. I don't know what's wrong with me, and the reason this thing with you and Frank hurt me, is that I've worked with him side by side for four years and he's never asked me to go out one time. He's never even tried to flirt with me. So it's not that I envy you personally. I'm just upset because it seems like every man I'm interested in doesn't feel the same way about me."

I didn't know what she wanted me to say.

Lorna continued, "Do you know what I'm saying, Anise? And then there's this thing I told you about Jim. I keep wondering why he sexually harassed me the way he did. It was almost like he thought I couldn't do any better, and that I should just be happy a man of his authority would be interested in screwing me at all. You should have seen the way he looked at me whenever he spoke to me back then."

"But see, that's why I think you have to do something about this, or you'll never be able to rest," I finally said.

"You know I can't do that. I'll lose my job if I go this alone, and what will I do then? It has to be both of us if this is going to work."

I wanted to tell her that in a matter of days, I'd have the entire executive team scrambling like children, trying to find an alibi for their wrongdoings. I wanted to tell her that she'd finally be able to expose all she knew about Jim. But I still didn't know if I could trust her, so I didn't. She seemed very sincere, almost like the old Lorna, but I couldn't risk confiding my plan to her and then having her betray me in some weird fashion. For all I knew, she was working with Jim and Lyle to destroy me. I didn't really believe that, but I couldn't help being so suspicious, based on the way she'd turned on me three days ago.

"You won't lose your job, because once you file any charge of harassment or discrimination, the company can't touch you," I told her. "It will make them look too guilty if they do."

"But I told you before, I'm not as strong as you."

"Well, maybe something will work out in the long run. Everything done in darkness eventually becomes exposed."

"I hope you're right, because I'm so miserable. I'm depressed about my love life, which may as well be nonexistent, and I'm depressed about what Jim did to me. It's been a while ago since he tried to force himself on me, but every time he smiles at me, I feel like throwing up. He gawks at me like he has total control over me. And I guess, in a sense, he does."

"That's ridiculous, and you have to do something about it."

"I don't know how to," she said, bursting into tears.

"You're going to be fine," I told her, and reached for her hand.

"I'm so sorry for the way I treated you last week," she said.

I was starting to believe that maybe she really meant it.

"Just forget about that," I said.

"I can't. The way I spoke to you was uncalled for, and I'll never forgive myself for confronting you like that. I've always done stupid stuff like this with other friends of mine in the past. I get close to people, and then I do everything I can to push them away. It's hard for me to trust anybody, and even though your date with Frank was your business, I felt betrayed because you hadn't told me about it. I know it was wrong to jump to conclusions the way I did, but I couldn't help it. So please don't hold what I did against me," she said, drying her nose with a tissue from my desk.

"I'm not even thinking about that anymore."

"But are we still going to be as close as we always were?"

"I don't see why not," I told her.

But the reality was, I didn't know for sure. I supposed we could with time, but even though I'd agreed to forgive her, there was still that tiny piece of doubt in the back of my mind. But based on how broken up she was right now, maybe she was genuinely sorry.

"I think maybe my hormones had a little bit to do with my actions on Friday as well," she said, and closed her eyes. "Oh God, Anise, I don't know how to tell you this."

I didn't know what she was about to say, but I already sympathized with her. I could tell that her news wasn't going to be something to sing praises about.

She looked at me, shaking her head in shame. She hadn't said a word, but her eyes warned of trouble, the same way animals scattered when a storm was near.

"I'm pregnant."

It was inconsiderate of me to have such thoughts, but I wondered who she was dating seriously enough to have a baby with.

"Oh no," I said, holding her hand with both of mine.

"And I don't know what else to do except have an abortion."

"Are you sure about that?" I asked, because although I was undeniably pro-choice, I could never do something like that myself. I knew it was easy to say, but I really didn't think I could.

"What else can I do? I'm barely making ends meet now. I don't get help from my daughter's father, and it's not like I'm going to get child support for this baby either."

"I hear what you're saying, but I think you need to be sure about your decision. Once you go to that clinic, it'll be much harder to turn back."

"Even if I wanted this baby, I don't have a choice. I don't even know who the father is."

"Lorna?" I said in disappointment.

"I mean, I have an idea, but I really can't be sure. So how in the world could I face that child when he or she is old enough to ask questions about their father?"

"Gosh, Lorna. I hate that this is happening to you."

"I've known since the beginning of last week. At first I was too embarrassed to tell you, and then when I came into your office on Thursday, you were too busy to talk to me. So by the time I saw you getting into Frank's SUV, I was so angry at you for not being here for me."

"I don't know what else to say except I'm sorry."

"I know you are, and I never even made it to the mall after I saw you. I was only going over there because Zoe was at a sleepover with one of our neighbors, and I didn't feel like being at home all alone. But after I came out of the truck stop, I didn't have the energy or desire to go shopping anymore. I just feel so down."

"I'm so sorry," I said again, leaning back in my chair.

"I'm going to call the clinic this afternoon and make an appointment."

"I really wish you would think about this another couple of days."

"I've had a whole week to think about it, and I know what I have to do. If I was married, or maybe if I knew who the father was, I might handle this differently. But since I don't, having an abortion is my only option."

"Well, I'm here for you if you need me."

"I appreciate that," she said, sniffling. "And I guess I'd better get back to work."

"Are you going to be okay?"

"I'll be fine. I just needed to explain some things to you is all."

"I'm glad you did, and like I said, I'm here. And even if you need to call me in the middle of the night to talk, I hope you will."

"Thanks, Anise," she said, and we hugged.

"No problem."

"Maybe one day I'll have my life together the same way you do," she said, smiling.

"The grass always looks greener. Remember that."

"I'll see you later," she said, and stood up. Then she walked out.

I felt bad for her, and I wished there was something I could do to help. But there wasn't. I wondered if she'd be able to live with her decision once her pregnancy was terminated. Most of all, I wondered who the father of her baby was, because I had a feeling she knew more than she was telling me.

Frank smiled and kissed me on the lips as soon as I walked inside his foyer.

"Can I get you something to drink?" he asked.

"Some lemonade or tea would be fine."

I followed him into the family room, and he walked over to his kitchen and opened the refrigerator.

"I've got everything all spread out on the coffee table," he said. "And I think all the documents Todd printed for us will suffice for now."

I took a seat on the carpet and picked up the closest stack of papers near me.

"There's a lot of stuff here," he said, joining me on the floor.

"He wasn't sure exactly which pieces of information were more important than others, so he printed just about everything that looked suspicious. There are even a few printouts for some of the managers," he said, gazing in my direction. "Although there's not much to compare when it comes to upper management, because there aren't any minorities in those positions to begin with."

"I don't believe Todd did this for me, and I don't believe you took the chance on asking him."

"I'm glad I could do it, and when you analyze some of that paperwork, you're going to be even more angry with those bastards than you are now."

"Why?"

"Well, first of all, I went through and compared the salaries of women and men in similar positions, and in some cases, men started out with salaries four to eight thousand dollars a year higher than women. Even if they started in the same year. And when I looked at the clerical employees, I compared the two black secretaries and the one Hispanic secretary I know personally with other white secretaries." He set our tea down on two coasters and dropped down beside me.

"And?"

"And in one case, the white secretary started one year after the black secretary, but the white secretary started at $12.60 an hour. The kicker is that the black one started at $10.57."

"Maybe the white one had a lot more education."

"Anise, the white secretary is my own, and I know for a fact that she only took a couple of typing classes at the community college. The black secretary reports to Todd and has an associate degree in secretarial sciences."

I was astounded. I'd suspected all of what Frank was telling me, but it seemed a lot worse now that I could see it written in black and white. It was proof positive, and it sickened me.

"How can they keep getting away with all of this?"

"That's just the beginning of what I've learned, and you're going to need something much stronger than that tea you're drinking when I tell you the rest."

"I hope it's not about me."

"It is."

"It's bad enough that they kept passing me over for a promotion, so what else have they done?"

"You and Kelli were both benefits specialists, right?"

"Yeah."

"You were in that position for two and a half years, and she was just promoted one year ago, right?"

"And?"

"Well, before Kelli was promoted to manager, she earned just over thirty-eight thousand dollars, like you did."

"But how? I worked in that job for eighteen months longer than she did, and I have a graduate degree."

"There are no standards at Reed Meyers, Anise. Everything is determined by your gender or your race. And, of course, who you're screwing can weigh heavily in your favor."

"Why do you say that?"

"I always thought it, but Todd told me that Kelli has been sleeping with Jim for the longest."

"You know, I can't believe Elizabeth would allow Kelli to be paid more than me. We both reported to her, but she always said I was her best employee."

"I doubt that she had any say-so one way or the other, and I'll bet if you call her, that's what she'd say. Jim and Lyle are relentless. Lyle is a little more toned down, but what he does is wait for Jim to do his dirty work. Jim is his most loyal flunky, and it's been that way since Jim came to the company."

I sat there with no words to speak.

Frank continued. "I hate doing this, but there really is something else you should know."

"What?"

I could hear myself breathing out loud.

"Kelli got a higher raise percentage than you every single time your performance reviews were done. Her percentages were even higher than yours when she was in clerical."

"This is so disheartening, and I'm going to make them pay for all of this."

"You have to. They deserve what they get, and you've got to strike them where it hurts."

"At first I was only planning to make them give me that

corporate manager's position, but now I'm taking this to another level. I want them to pay dearly for what they've done to me, because they're committing crimes that would never be tolerated if they were made public."

"This is very true."

"And that's also why I wish I could use this information to bring a class action lawsuit against them. I've thought about it over and over and over again, but I don't know if I could spend years spearheading something like that."

"I don't think you can afford to, and I'll tell you why," Frank said, folding his arms. "When I worked in Chicago, there was a black woman who worked at one of our subsidiaries in Ohio, and she tried doing the very thing you're talking about. She decided to organize a group of employees who were being discriminated against, and they all filed a claim with EEOC. But then after a few months passed, every one of them took an out-of-court settlement from the company. Some kept their jobs and some resigned. But the bottom line is that the woman who initiated the whole lawsuit was left holding the bag all by herself. And the worst part of all was that she couldn't find a job anywhere else in the city because of all the publicity. And from what I hear, she ended up settling with the company for an undisclosed amount herself because EEOC was taking too long and she needed money to pay bills."

"That's really too bad," I said. "And actually it reminds me of a woman who used to work with my mom. She'd spent months trying to start a union, and at first everyone thought it was going to happen. But all I know is that the workers didn't get a union, and the woman was basically blackballed from that point on."

"That's pretty much the norm. Every now and then employees are successful when they go up against a company, but it's not common. I know you feel bad for the other employees, but the fact of the matter is you'll probably end up doing yourself a major injustice if you don't do this alone. If you were willing to stick it out and then move to another city, then I'd say maybe. But if you're planning on living here in Mitchell, you need to remember how small it is, and that it's only twelve percent black."

"I agree, but I can't help thinking about all the other women and minorities who are being treated the same way I am."

"Well, there might be something we can do without you having to place yourself in jeopardy."

"What's that?" I asked.

"We can have Todd print the salary information again after you confront them, so I can send copies to EEOC myself and then circulate them to every employee we believe is being discriminated against. That way, everyone has the information, and it will be up to them to do what they want with it."

"You amaze me," I said, smiling and feeling grateful that he would do this.

He smiled back.

"Also, there's a ton of other examples here, and I have a dummy ID and password for you to use if you need to print anything else. But you have to cut off the date, time and some other information that will print at the bottom of each page. I trimmed these before you got here. Todd doesn't think they'd be able to track anything, but he wanted you to get rid of the dates just in case. He even printed the documents on the same paper that you use in your office so it will look like you printed everything yourself if someone questions it."

"Tell Todd I owe him big-time."

"He was happy to do it, and wanted me to tell you to knock 'em dead."

"And thank *you*," I said, blinking to keep from crying.

"I told you I would do anything for you, sweetheart, and I meant that," he said, leaning his back against the love seat and pulling me into his arms. I love you, and it pains me to see someone treating you like this. I hate that they're doing this just because you're black."

"It's so humiliating. They really shook my confidence, but

having access to all of this is going to make me feel a lot better after this week."

"I can't wait to see their faces when they realize you have proof of their criminal behavior."

"Frank, I don't know how to say this, but I need to be honest with you about something."

"You're not going to break my heart, are you?"

"I don't know. It depends on how you take what I have to say."

"Okay," he said.

"When I called you last week and said I was ready to take you up on your dinner offer, one reason I did was because I knew you were good friends with Todd, and I needed you to help me get this salary information."

"Ouch," he said, and I felt horrible.

"I was attracted to you all along, but if I hadn't found out about Kelli getting that promotion and if David hadn't asked me for a divorce a few hours later, I don't think I would have called you. I'm not saying that I never would have, but I did have ulterior motives when I went out with you."

"But you don't feel that way now, do you?" he said, and I could hear the disappointment in his voice.

"No, I really do love you, and if you hadn't offered to ask Todd to get this information, I never would have asked you. Not after we made love the way we did on Friday."

"I won't tell you that I'm not hurt, because I am, but I'm glad you were honest with me. Honesty means a lot."

"I'm sorry for hurting you, but I wanted you to know."

"I'll get over it," he said, and turned toward me.

I was glad he understood, because I didn't want to lose him. I knew now that I needed him more than anything else in my life. I was glad that I'd finally found someone who loved me for me and someone who could accept my imperfections.

CHAPTER 23

T WAS 6:05 on a Tuesday evening, and Lorna and I were sitting in my office taking a break after all the hours we'd put in today. She'd been working down in the training room, binding together some training manuals for a class she was teaching tomorrow, and I was still printing and comparing salary differences. I'd spent the entire day not doing much of anything else, and for the first time in my career, I didn't feel bad about stealing company time. I'd found even more evidence than what Frank and Todd had gotten for me on Monday, and it was wearing me down emotionally. I'd gone from being disgusted to being angry to feeling sad, because I just didn't want to believe Jim and Lyle had made the art of discrimination normal policy and procedure. I knew this sort of thing went on throughout the country all the time, because I'd read a number of magazine articles and seen programs about various class action lawsuits, but still I was amazed at what I kept discovering.

I still hadn't informed Lorna about what I was doing, but I was hoping I'd be able to before the week ended. Now, though, we were discussing her personal dilemma—something I thanked God I wasn't going through myself.

"So you're sure this is what you want to do?" I asked, feeling a bit uneasy about her decision.

"An abortion is my only alternative. I can't take care of another baby, and if I have the baby with the intention of placing it for adoption, I'll want to keep it. So I really don't have any other choice."

"Then I guess that's what you have to do."

"You don't agree, do you?"

"I don't agree or disagree, because it's not my place to judge you or any other woman."

"What would you do if it were you?" she asked.

"I would hope that I would have the baby and keep it, but that doesn't mean I'm going to look down on you for doing just the opposite. This is your life, your body, and I'm still going to be your friend no matter what."

"I appreciate that so much, Anise. Especially after the way I treated you last week."

"And I keep telling you to forget that. Everyone has bad days, and every relationship has tension from time to time."

"I feel like such a failure, and I guess my biggest worry is that the decision to end this pregnancy is going to come back to haunt me someday."

I didn't know what to say. Normally I would have told a person to pray for guidance when trying to deal with something like this, but I'd never heard Lorna mention God or church since I met her. I wanted to bring it up, but I didn't want to sound preachy or like I was the perfect Christian, because I wasn't.

"I guess you just have to go with what you think is right, and you have to listen to your heart," I said.

"I don't know if having an abortion is right or wrong, but I don't see any other way around it."

"Maybe you should think about it some more, because yesterday you were pretty sure about getting it done, but maybe there's a reason you're sitting here now trying to weigh things out all over again."

"I don't know. I'm so confused."

"If I were you, I'd take some more time to think about it."

"I'm already three months, so I really need to make a decision now."

"One more day isn't going to hurt, so maybe you should sleep on it."

"I guess," she said, sighing.

"I think when it's all said and done, you'll do the right thing, whatever that is."

"We'll see. But I guess I'd better get back over to the training room and finish up these manuals. I need them first thing in the morning."

"I thought Frank's secretary handled that?"

"She does, but she was out sick today."

"Oh."

"So now I'll be stuck here for another two hours at least."

"I'll be here as long, if not longer."

"Lot of new responsibilities came with the new job, I see," she said.

I didn't bother telling her that I hadn't done more than thirty minutes of actual work today.

"Yeah, actually quite a few" was as far as I went.

"Let me know when you're ready to leave. Maybe we can walk out together."

"That's a good idea, and if you finish before I do, give me a quick ring and I'll wind things up."

"See ya in a little while," she said, and left.

I tried to imagine what Lorna must be going through, but I couldn't. I'd never been pregnant, and didn't have any idea how she was feeling about all of this. So the most I could do was listen and give her as much moral support as possible. But I still wondered for the life of me whose baby she was carrying.

I searched through one of the piles on my desk for my salary history and placed it on top of Kelli's. In my memo, I'd eventually bring up how unequal salaries were being paid to other women and minorities at the company, too, but my history versus Kelli's would be the first item discussed. I hadn't decided how I was going to approach my superiors, but I knew it had to be soon. My plan was to draft the memo, along with a detailed outline, finalize it, and mail copies to Jim, Lyle and Tom, the CEO. Then I would wait until I finally heard from one of them. I had a feeling, though, it wasn't going to take more than a couple of days once they realized their plot had been cracked wide open. It would clearly be in their best interest to take care of this as soon as possible.

Another hour passed before I realized how strained my eyes felt. I'd been working obsessively for ten hours straight, and I knew it was time to call it a night. So I packed up every document I didn't want to leave on my desk and lifted the phone to call Lorna's office. It rang six times before I remembered she was working in the training room.

I slipped on the pumps I'd kicked under my desk a few hours ago, stood and walked down the hallway. The training room entrance was only a few doors down, and it sounded like Lorna was talking to someone inside. I figured it was someone else working late like we were, or one of the shop foremen who worked second shift.

As I got closer to the training room, I wondered why the door was closed. I turned the knob and opened it.

"Please don't do this. I'm begging you, Jim," Lorna pleaded with tears pouring down her face.

Jim had his back to me.

"What in the world are you doing?" I yelled at him.

Jim quickly turned around and, when he saw me, hurried to force himself back inside his pants.

I frowned in disbelief. "*What* is going on?"

"None of your fucking business. This is between Lorna and me, and I'd appreciate it if you'd get the hell out of here!" he ordered while zipping his trousers and buckling his belt.

"No. I'm not going anywhere," I said, walking toward them. "Lorna, are you okay?"

She began crying again and didn't respond.

"She's fine!" Jim exclaimed. "So I suggest you go back to your office or wherever the hell you came from."

"I'm calling the police." I turned to walk back out of the room.

"Noooooo, Anise. Don't! Please don't!" Lorna screamed.

"Lorna, we have to. This bastard was sexually assaulting you, so why do you want to let him get away with it?"

"I'm okay," she said between breaths. "I'm okay."

"*Now* are you happy?" Jim asked.

"No. I'm not," I answered. "Lorna, what's wrong with you? What are you so afraid of?"

"Please, Anise. Just go."

"No. I'm not leaving until you walk out of here with me."

"I'm fine. Really."

"I don't believe you're allowing this, Lorna. I don't believe you're going to let this idiot walk all over you like this."

"Look, you nosy bitch!" Jim yelled. "I'm warning you. Either you get the hell out of here and mind your own damn business, or you can start looking for somewhere else to work. You and your boyfriend Frank."

"What?" I said, looking directly at Lorna.

"Anise, it's really best if you go."

They didn't have to tell me again. I hightailed it out of there in a hurry. I walked back to my office, picked up my overstuffed briefcase and headed out of the building. I strode hastily to my car and sat inside it. I was so baffled by what I'd just witnessed. I didn't know whether Lorna had been giving in to Jim's advances all along, or if she'd even told me the truth about what supposedly happened when he first came to the company. What was more perplexing was that she didn't want me calling the police. She seemed almost terrified when I suggested it.

I started the ignition, left the parking lot and drove straight to Frank's, stopping only for red lights. I'd thought about calling Mom on the way, but didn't want her to hear how upset I was.

I pulled into Frank's driveway like a madwoman, turned off my SUV, locked it and walked up to his door.

He opened it barely seconds after I rang the doorbell.

"Well, isn't this a pleasant surprise?"

I went inside without looking at him.

He closed the door and asked, "Are you okay?"

"No. I'm not."

"What happened?"

"I don't even know where to begin."

"Let's go in here," he said, placing his arm around me and leading me into the family room.

We sat down on the sofa, and I breathed deeply.

"Around six or so, Lorna took a break from doing her training manuals and came into my office. We talked for a short while, and then she went back. I worked for maybe another hour, but when my eyes started feeling tired, I decided to go down to the training room to see if she was ready to leave."

"And?"

"When I walked in, Jim was there with his pants unzipped."

Frank's eyes bugged in surprise.

"Yeah, you heard me right. Then he tried to force himself back inside his pants and told me to mind my own business."

"What was Lorna doing?"

"She was crying, and I heard her begging him to stop when I first came in. But the craziest part about all of this is that she didn't want me calling the police. When I told her I was going to, she pleaded with me not to. She kept insisting she was okay. Then that bastard Jim had the audacity to call me a bitch and you my boyfriend."

"Why would he say something like that? He doesn't even know about us."

"Apparently he does," I said.

"I don't understand how."

"Please tell me you haven't told anybody about us."

"How could you even think anything like that?"

He was irritated by my accusation, and I couldn't blame him. I didn't mean to suspect him, but I was so upset I didn't know what to think or who to trust.

"I'm sorry. I didn't mean that. Maybe Lorna told him, but I can't understand why she'd do something like that."

"Well, you said she was pissed when she saw us together."

"I know, but why would she tell Jim if he's sexually harassing her the way she said he was? It just doesn't make any sense."

"Damn," Frank said, leaning back on the sofa.

I could tell he was worried about his job and the fact that Jim knew about us. He'd claimed he didn't care whether he lost his job or not, but reality was forcing a different spin on this.

"You've got to get that memo sent to him and those other two SOBs he works for tomorrow."

"But I don't have it ready yet."

"Then you're going to have to work on it all day tomorrow. Because the longer you wait, the more time they'll have to build some illegitimate case against you and me for something we didn't do. I heard they framed someone else a few years ago when they wanted to get rid of them."

I wondered why he hadn't told me about that before. "Who was it?"

"Some innocent Hispanic guy in accounting whom they didn't want there."

"What kind of company do we work for, Frank? It's almost like we're twirling through the twilight zone."

"Believe it or not, they've done worse. Jim and Lyle are ruthless, and they learned everything they know from Tom. And when the

CEO is dirty, conniving ways are bound to trickle down to other employees."

"Well, if you think about it, the only way discrimination can truly work is when you have a group of people who feel the same way about it. There's no way one or two people could get away with doing something so systematic by themselves."

"Exactly," he said.

"I'm so tired of all of this."

"I know, but you've got to hang in there until you grab them by the balls and make them pay for what they've done to you."

I closed my eyes and laid my head against Frank's chest. I felt so out of sorts, and I wanted this whole fiasco to be over with. I wanted to get what Reed Meyers owed me and resign from the company effective immediately.

Frank and I held each other until my nerves finally settled. I really didn't want to leave, but decided it was best since I didn't have a change of clothing for work.

I drove in a daze, trying to figure out what could possibly happen next. At home, I didn't even bother taking a shower but pulled on a nightshirt instead. When I removed the pillows on the bed and pulled back the comforter, I noticed the Caller ID light blinking. I pressed the appropriate button to see who had called and saw Lorna's number displayed seven consecutive times. She'd called every ten to fifteen minutes, but her last attempt was over thirty minutes ago.

My first thought was to ignore her, but I truly wanted to know what was going on between her and Jim. I knew I was going to be livid if she confessed that she was the one who'd disclosed my relationship with Frank, but I needed some sort of explanation. Anything would do at this point.

I reached for the phone, but before I could pick it up, it rang. Lorna's name and number displayed on the screen again.

"Hello?"

"Anise, please don't hang up."

"Why would I hang up? Because you told Jim about Frank and me?"

"I didn't. I mean, I knew that he knew about you guys, but I wasn't the one who told him."

"Then who did, Lorna?"

"I don't know. All he said was that someone saw you leaving Frank's house on Friday."

"Wait a minute. I'm confused. He told you that, and you didn't let me know about it?"

"I wanted to, but he threatened me."

"Then why didn't you tell me that he was still harassing you? What about that?"

"Because I didn't want you to know that a few months ago, I'd started having an affair with Jim, until I found out about him sleeping with Kelli."

"But I thought you said you didn't know if they were messing around or not?"

"I know, and I'm sorry for lying to you."

"How could you sleep with someone like Jim, Lorna?"

"Because he promised me that he'd get me promoted and get me more money if I did. But then he didn't."

"Well, if you've been sleeping with him, then why were you begging him to stop what he was doing when I walked in? And why were you crying?"

"Because I didn't want him forcing his dick down my throat. He was angry because I told him I was never sleeping with him again, and he tried to make me give him oral sex right there in the training room. But I swear, Anise, I didn't even know he was still in the building."

"I don't understand. Because if you didn't want him doing that to you, why didn't you want me to call the police?"

"Because I knew I would lose my job, and because he knows that I'm pregnant by him."

"My God, Lorna. How many lies have you told me?"

"A lot. But you have to understand why I did it," she said.

"No, I don't understand anything. I befriended you as soon as I started working at Reed Meyers. Something I rarely do with anyone so quickly. And you've done nothing except lie and betray me. First you lied about Kelli and Jim not having an affair, and then you claimed you didn't know who you were pregnant by. And I can't believe you knew Jim had someone following us and you didn't bother telling me about it?"

"I know, Anise, and I'm so, so sorry. I swear I am."

"So who saw me at Frank's?"

"I don't know. I swear to you Jim didn't tell me. I swear on my daughter's life."

"You are such a liar. And you had the nerve to be angry because I didn't confide in you about my relationship with Frank?"

"I was wrong, and I know it. And I'm so sorry, Anise. I'm so sorry, I don't know what to do."

"Well, I don't want to hear it. All I want is for you to stay the hell away from me and to never dial this phone number again."

"But, Anise, I—" she said, but I slammed the phone down.

I was so enraged. This betrayal was like a bad habit, and I'd had enough. I needed my mother so badly, but I hated calling to disturb her so late. She worried about me all the time, and I didn't want to upset her when she had to be at work in the morning. I needed someone to talk to, but at the same time I wanted to be alone.

I wished I could pack my bags and leave this horrid life of mine forever.

CHAPTER 24

AYLIGHT APPEARED much too soon, and I felt as if I hadn't slept more than twenty minutes. It was 2:00 A.M. the last time I'd glanced at the clock on the nightstand, but I dragged myself out of bed when the alarm clock sounded at a quarter to seven. I felt drained, and if it hadn't been for the memo I was working on now, I wouldn't have thought twice about calling in sick.

At work I'd seen Frank already, but we purposely didn't speak because we both knew it was better to keep our contact low-key from here on out. We hadn't even discussed it before I left his house, but somehow we were on the same wavelength.

My office door was closed for the second day in a row, and I could tell my staff members wanted to know why I was so preoccupied. They must have known this wasn't my normal managerial style, but unfortunately I couldn't tell them what was going on. I couldn't tell them that major fireworks would be skyrocketing in a day or so.

I was reading the outline when my phone rang. I debated

answering it because I didn't want to be bothered with anyone inside the company. But since the caller might be Mom, I succumbed and picked it up.

"Hey, sweetie, it's Mom."

It was so good to hear her voice.

"Hi, Mom."

"How come you didn't call me back last night?"

"I didn't know you called."

"I called twice. You didn't see my number?"

"No, I guess I didn't scroll through all the calls far enough," I said, realizing I'd stopped viewing the numbers when I discovered how many times Lorna had called.

"It's so unlike you to go two days without calling, and I was starting to get a little worried. I even called you on your cell phone."

"I know, Mom. Things have been so crazy for me the last couple of days."

"David isn't harassing you, is he?"

"No, not since he was at the house on Saturday."

"Then what's wrong?"

"There's so much going on here at the company, it's best that I tell you in person. But the one thing I don't want to put off any longer is telling you about Frank."

"Who's Frank?"

"He's a guy that works here. I've been seeing him since last Thursday."

"Really, now? And you didn't tell me?" she said in a teasing tone.

I was elated that she wasn't upset about it.

"I didn't feel comfortable."

"Why, because you know how I feel about adultery?"

"That's exactly why."

"I'm not happy that you've become involved with someone else before your divorce is final, but sometimes things just happen and we don't have any control over them."

"Is this the real Emma Hill I'm speaking to?" I said, laughing for the first time in what seemed like weeks.

She laughed with me. "Honey, I know you've been going through a lot lately, and I know it hasn't been easy living alone in the process. And even though, I raised you to be strong, I know that every woman has her breaking point and sometimes needs someone to be with."

"This is true. But Mom?"

"Yeah?"

"There's something else I need to tell you about him."

"What's that?"

"He's white."

"Yeah right," she said, laughing again.

"He is."

"You serious?"

"Yes. Very."

"Well, the world certainly must be coming to an end, because I've never known you to even consider dating a white man before."

"I know, but I was attracted to him. And, Mom, I think I'm in love with him, too."

"My goodness. Don't talk to you for two days and you have a whole life story to tell."

"I have even more than that to tell you, but like I said, I'll tell you about what's going on here later."

"Okay, well, my break is almost up, but I just wanted to make sure you were okay. I figured you were, but you know how I worry."

"I know you do, and I'm sorry I put you through that."

"Give me a call when you get off work."

"I'll pick up some ribs and stop by instead."

"I'll see you then."

"Bye, Mom."

"Bye, sweetie."

I felt better already. It was so amazing how my mother's voice brightened my spirits the way medicine fixed an illness. She was the light of my life, and I didn't know what I would do without her. I hadn't seen her as much lately. Sometimes we saw each other seven days straight, and I knew she missed that, because I did. But things would return to normal as soon as I remedied this Reed Meyers situation. Things were going to be better for me all around when this was over.

The morning passed by as quickly as the night before, so I picked up a sandwich from the cafeteria and came right back to my office to finish the memo. I'd gone over it more times than I was willing to count, and then faxed it over to Monica so she could review it. She found a couple of typos, but that was it. I read through it one final time and then printed out five copies.

DATE: August 1, 2001

TO: Tom Peterson, President and CEO of Reed Meyers
Lyle Mason, Vice President of Operations
Jim Kyle, Vice President of Human Resources

FROM: Anise L. Miller, Manufacturing HR Manager

I would like to take this opportunity to share with you some very serious issues pertaining to the ill treatment of "protected class" employees here at Reed Meyers. As you know, I am a black female who began employment with Reed Meyers on January 10, 1999, as a benefits specialist for human resources. During my first year of employment, I discussed my career goals with Jim Kyle in terms of management, and he stated that there was much room for advancement in the department.

So eight months ago, when the position of corporate HR recruiting manager became available, I interviewed for it. However, I learned a few days later that Jason Massey had been promoted into the position, even though he had an associate degree with no previous HR experience. I, on the other hand, had a master's degree and four years of solid HR experience. Then, six months later, on May 29, 2001, Jason decided to leave the company, and the position was reposted. On May 31, 2001, I reapplied for it, and on June 11, 2001, I interviewed with Jim again.

On June 22, 2001, Jim told me that the position was being placed on hold because he needed to restructure the entire department. On June 27, 2001, the position of manufacturing HR manager was posted, and since the corporate position was still on hold, I applied for it. Then, on July 24, 2001, the first day in my new position, Kelli Jacobson, who was not as qualified as me, was promoted to corporate HR recruiting manager. The job was suddenly released from hold, although Jim never restructured human resources.

This is only a general summary of what has happened, but a more detailed outline is enclosed for your convenience. Also, I think you should know that I also have documented information that will prove continual racial and gender discrimination with other employees here at the company as well. Therefore, based on the humiliation, frustration, mental and emotional distress, and many sleepless nights, I feel it is not unreasonable to expect Reed Meyers to produce a separation agreement that shall include financial remedies equal to the damages mentioned above.

It goes without saying that the laws Reed Meyers have ignored, and the, not glass, but concrete "ceiling" it has created for women and minorities, would not be tolerated in a federal court or by the Equal Employment Opportunity Commission (EEOC). I think you will agree that it is in all of our best interests to bring this tense situation to an amicable conclusion in an expeditious manner.

Thank you in advance for your attention to this matter.

cc: Ray Stevens, Attorney

Enclosure

When the last page of the last copy printed, I stapled each set, slipped them into interoffice envelopes and distributed them to the secretaries of each addressee. I'd lost hours of sleep because of the way they'd treated me, and I wondered how much sleep the three of them would miss after reading my memo. I doubted they'd ever rest comfortably again, and something deep inside me was happy about it. They wouldn't believe for a minute that I had any real evidence, and I couldn't wait to produce everything if they asked me to back up my claim.

I walked back into my office and called Monica to let her know the countdown had begun. I wanted to call Frank as well, but decided I would wait until I was home. For all I knew, our phones were under surveillance.

Although after today, I wouldn't care about which of my conversations they heard.

CHAPTER 25

ANISE, Tom would like to know if you're available to meet with Jim, Lyle and him in the executive conference room this afternoon at four," the CEO's executive assistant said.

"Four o'clock is fine."

"I'll let them know, and thanks."

It hadn't taken them a full twenty-four hours to summon me to a meeting. I was glad they knew I meant business. I wasn't sure if they were going to try and weasel out of what I'd asked for, or if they were going to ask me what type of separation package was acceptable. The latter seemed too easy, and I knew it was time for me to prepare responses to possible questions. I hoped they wanted to keep our meeting as cordial as possible, and that they weren't planning to badger me. I wouldn't tolerate cocky attitudes from any one of them, and I would walk straight out of the conference room if I detected any rudeness. I wasn't going to tolerate it, because I no longer had to, and it was a great feeling. I still had some distance to travel, but I was finally starting to see the end of this tiresome journey.

I spent the rest of the morning and the first part of the after-noon catching up on work I'd ignored all week. Today was already Thursday, but I hadn't worked on any projects that weren't con-sidered crucial by my definition. I'd allowed most of my responsi-bilities to fall by the wayside, and now I felt guilty because of the three women who reported to me. It wasn't fair that they'd had to improvise without my guidance, but I hoped they would forgive me in the future.

It was now ten minutes to four, so I picked up the manila folder from my desk and walked out of my office and down to the conference room near Tom's office. I saw Lorna in passing, but I averted my eyes. I still wasn't speaking to her, and it was safe to say that I probably never would again. When I walked by Frank's office, he pointed his right thumb toward the ceiling and winked at me for good luck. I'd spoken to him on the phone last night for two hours after arriving home from Mom's, and couldn't wait to spend some quality time with him again. I missed him so much, but I knew the day would come when we could be together more frequently. I still wasn't so sure that getting mar-ried was the right thing to do, but I no longer had any doubts about his feelings toward me. I believed his love for me was gen-uine, and once my divorce was final, we'd be able to discuss our future in much more detail.

When I entered the room, the Big Three were already seated next to each other on one side of the table. I closed the door and took a seat across from them. They were seated in ranking order, from left to right starting with Tom, then Lyle, then Jim.

"Thank you for coming," Tom said.

I nodded but didn't speak.

"I have to say, Anise, I'm a little disappointed that you thought it necessary to put all of this in writing when we all work right here in the same building," Tom said.

Jim and Lyle kept their tails tucked.

"And I'm extremely disturbed by the accusations you've made against this company," Tom continued. "So much so, that we are prepared to deny any allegations you have made in any court of law. You may not like the way we run things here at Reed Meyers, but we all have choices. And if you're not happy with the decisions being made by the three of us, you're free to leave at any time."

I knew he'd eventually say something I couldn't resist responding to.

"First of all, Tom, going to work somewhere else simply because you've discriminated against me is not an option. I have the right to work anywhere I choose and be treated fairly. And the fact that you're prepared to deny all allegations means nothing to me because I have all the evidence I need in black and white. I have salary comparisons of other employees and proof that I was the most qualified candidate both times you passed me over for that promotion to corporate manager. And there's not a court in this country that will tolerate your blatant discriminatory practices. I know what my rights are, and I also know what the consequences are for people like you who break the law."

"You're playing way out of your league, girl, and if I were you, I'd be very careful," Tom threatened.

He was trying to intimidate me, but it wasn't working. I knew there was a time when black people had to cower to men like Tom, but this wasn't the 1800s or the 1960s. So it wasn't as if I had this great fear of being hanged or hosed down in the street.

Which is why I didn't even bother responding.

"And even if you did have any so-called evidence, which we know you don't, we still have legitimate reasons why we hired or promoted certain employees or why we gave certain raises to certain people," Tom continued.

"What do you mean I don't have any evidence?"

This was the highlight of the show. It was what I'd been waiting for.

"We know that you're just bluffing, Anise," Tom said. "I mean, did you actually think we would fall for something like that when we know for a fact that you only have access to the manufacturing side of the system?"

"So in other words, I don't have anything? Is that what you're saying?" I asked.

"That's what we know," Tom said in a louder tone than what he'd used before. I'd pressed the wrong buttons, and he was becoming belligerent.

But I didn't bother responding. Instead I opened the folder I'd brought with me and passed them each their *own* individual salary histories that dated back to the day they started with the company.

"Where did you get these?" Tom raised his voice even higher.

"That's the least of your worries," I answered.

"This is confidential information," Tom declared.

"And it will stay confidential if you provide me with a separation package that makes me happy."

"This is bullshit," Jim yelled.

I leaned back in my chair and stared at him. "You know, Jim, I wonder if Tom and Lyle would be interested in knowing about that little soiree you had going on in the training room on Tuesday. What do you think?"

He turned candy apple red, and I knew from that moment he wouldn't be voicing any other opinions so readily.

"If you've used an unauthorized ID or password to get this information, you'll be fired on the spot," Tom announced.

"Fire me if you want, but that won't stop me from going public with the information I have. So don't be surprised if you open the *Mitchell Post* in a few days and see your names plastered all over it."

"What is it that you want from us?" Lyle asked, speaking for the first time since the meeting began. But I wasn't surprised. He didn't like black people, but it was obvious that he never wanted to be an obvious villain.

"I want damages equal to the pain and suffering I've experienced the entire time I've worked here."

"Which is?"

"Three hundred and fifty thousand dollars tax free."

"That's absolutely insane," Tom insisted. "Even if we had a reason to pay you a settlement of some sort, which we don't, how would we go about paying you money that would leave you with no tax obligation?"

"The same way you break the law with everything else around here but end up making it look legitimate."

"We might be willing to offer you something so we can end this problem you've created, but it won't be six figures," Tom added.

"No, I don't think you understand. My request isn't negotiable. After printing out everyone's salary history, I've already found fifteen cases of racial discrimination in terms of pay and ten that are related to gender. You have consistently paid minorities less than white employees who are less qualified but doing the same job. You've done the same thing with women by consistently paying men much higher salaries when the women are just as qualified and in some cases, have more credentials. So you can either pay me the money I'm asking for now or the seven figures a judge will force you to pay me when we get to court."

"I don't think we have anything further to discuss," Tom said.

"No, I don't think we do either," I said, standing up. "But when the trial begins, don't say you weren't warned."

I left the room without a care in the world, because I knew I had them. Jim had told me so with that petrified look on his face. There was no doubt he would convince them to do the right thing, because he couldn't take the chance that I might expose his perverted ways or the sexual favors he was securing from Lorna, not to mention what he was probably doing with other women in the company.

I smiled openly as I strolled back to my office.

My coworkers stared at me like I was crazy.

What they didn't know was that I was only smiling to keep from crying.

What they didn't know was how degraded I felt as an African-American woman having to go head-to-head with three white men who cared nothing about me as a person.

CHAPTER 26

"EXACTLY WHAT LITTLE SOIREE was she talking about Jim?" Tom asked when Anise left the room.

"It's nothing. I was in the training room with Lorna the other night having a conversation, and Anise assumed something else was going on," Jim tried to convince him, but he knew Tom thought it might be true, or he wouldn't be asking for more details.

"So all you did was talk? And nothing happened that we're going to have to hear about somewhere down the road?" Tom wanted confirmation.

"Anise is just exaggerating the same way she did in this letter she wrote, but I will say she's crazy enough to make people believe it," Jim said. *We've got to get that black bitch out of here no matter what it costs.*

"Well, as much as I hate saying this, her letter does make me a little nervous, and it troubles me even more to know that she has access to the entire HR system," Lyle continued.

"But what right does she have telling us how to run this company?" Tom asked.

"I don't think it's about that," Lyle explained. "This is about how her accusations will look in a court of law. Right or wrong, no judge is going to simply overlook the fact that she has superior performance reviews, has two degrees and more than enough HR experience. Yet we gave the position to someone who is white and much less qualified, and then we paid them more. And what I'm concerned about the most is that she's found information regarding other employees that could lead to a class action lawsuit."

"I still don't think she has anything," Tom said. "Some disgruntled asshole inside this company may have given her pay information for the three of us, but I really don't think she has anyone else's. If she did, she would have brought them with her. No, what I think she's trying to do is bully us, and if we let her get away with it, we'll have every Joe Schmo in the company waltzing in here demanding thousands whenever they feel like it."

"You know, Frank could be our culprit," Jim suggested. "Because you know they've been seeing each other."

"That's another son of a bitch we've got to get rid of," Tom said.

"This is a tough one, but I think we have to offer her something, because right now the important thing is to get her out of here before she stirs up trouble with other employees," Lyle said, getting back to the matter at hand.

I agree, and I've got to make them realize how important it is for us to pay her that money, because the last thing I need is to have some sex-related rumor floating around about Lorna and me. Next thing you know, that black bitch will try convincing Lorna to have that damn baby. And then she'll be placing all the blame on me for not getting that fuckin' promotion.

"Look," Jim said to Lyle, "I cringe just from looking at Anise, but at this point I agree with you, because it's probably in our best interest if we give her a little hush money, along with her walking papers all at the same time."

"I just don't see it," Tom said. "And, Jim, I'm surprised that you're throwing in the towel so easily, because you've never liked this woman from day one."

"That's true, but I do think it would be better for everyone involved if we get rid of her. She's a troublemaker just like every other black person I know, and we need to get this taken care of. The sooner the better," Jim said. *I hope they're not going to try and give her less than what she's asking, because that uppity black bitch will never go for it. Lyle and Tom have no idea that I really don't want to give her one red cent, but I know if she doesn't get exactly what she wants, she'll try to crucify me.*

"Well, I think we need to think this through, because three hundred and fifty thousand dollars is a shitload of money. And we can't even be sure she has everything she says she does," Tom said.

"What we can do is ask her to bring us the originals of anything she's printed as well as any copies she's made," Jim proposed.

"Maybe. But still we're talking about making a large transaction that'll have to be executed under the table. Which means we'll have to handle every aspect of this with extreme care," Lyle said.

"I still don't agree, but if that's what both of you think we should do, then so be it," Tom said. "But we will *not* under any circumstances pay her what she's demanding. Maybe a hundred thousand, but I'm thinking it should even be less than that."

"Look, Tom," Jim said carefully, "I think she's full of shit the same as you do, but we have to consider the amount of bad publicity we'll get if she goes to the newspaper. She's already threatened to, and I believe she'd actually do it. It angers me that these affirmative action laws have made it possible for somebody like her to make such a threat, but this is the reality."

Tom didn't say anything else.

I can see he doesn't get what I'm trying to say, but I've got to keep encouraging him to do the right thing before next week. I've got to make Tom see that we can't afford not to pay her, and that if she goes public, he'll take the biggest fall as CEO of this company.

"What I think we need to do is take all of tomorrow and the weekend to think about our options and then try to arrive at some decision by Monday morning," Lyle said.

"Fine," Tom said. "But I still say we shouldn't give her a thing until we see what proof she has. No one is more worried about the laws than I am, but I just don't believe she has anything that could hurt us."

If only she hadn't seen Lorna and me in that conference room, I could force Lorna to talk some sense into that bitch. But now Lorna claims Anise won't speak to her. Which means I've got to figure out a way to make Tom give her what she's asking for, and then I've got to make sure Lorna has that abortion I gave her the money for. Because I'm not about to let two stupid women ruin everything I've worked so hard for, unless it's over my dead body.

"Mom, you would have been so proud of me for standing up to them the way I did," I said.

Mom and I were sitting on her screened porch on the west side of town eating sub sandwiches and chips that I'd picked up after work. They weren't as good as the ribs we had yesterday, but they were filling.

"I'm proud just because you decided it was time to call them on what they were doing."

"That Tom was so cocky, though, and if anyone tries to play hardball, it will be him."

"The way you've spoken about Jim, I would have expected him to be the problem."

"He would have been if I hadn't caught him and Lorna in that training room."

Mom laughed. "I've been thinking about that ever since you told me. It would be wrong for any man to sexually harass a woman, but somehow you just wouldn't expect that a vice president at a company would stoop so low."

"I know. But if you want to know the truth, I think something's wrong with him. He hates blacks in the worst way, but I've come to realize that he hates women just as much. And that means he hates me for two reasons."

"Well, I hope you get your money soon so you can get out of there and move on with your life."

"I do too, Mom, because even though I enjoyed seeing them squirm in that conference room today, I still feel so humiliated. I feel like I'm always going to have to deal with the same thing, no matter what company I work for. I'm always going to have to prove that I'm not just some whiny black woman who doesn't know her place or another black person screaming discrimination for no legitimate reason. And I'm so tired of that."

"I know you are, sweetheart, but hopefully this will all be over soon."

"I don't know, maybe it would be better if I commuted to Chicago to work. I've never wanted to do that before now, because it would take so many extra hours from my day, but maybe it's something to think about."

"Do you think you'd be treated more fairly than you have been around here?"

"I don't know. It's just so hard to say one way or the other. But there are more companies there."

"Maybe what you need to do is think about starting your own business."

"Actually, I've never really given that much thought, but maybe you're right. Maybe that's what I should do with the settlement package if they give it to me."

"I think you would do real well, and that way, you'd have money to pay your bills and funding to get your business up and running."

"You know, Mom, that's really something to consider. Because whether I want to admit it or not, I don't think I will ever find any real success if I don't go out on my own. Starting a business will take a lot of research and marketing, but I think it's worth trying."

"I *know* it is. We didn't have a whole lot of options when I graduated from high school back in the sixties, so the only logical choice was to go work in a factory. But at least you had the opportunity to get a good education, and now you have the option of doing something on your own. You'll still have to prove yourself twice over, but at least you'd be doing it for yourself."

"That's true. And I think what I'll do is take some time to clear my mind. Then I want to start thinking about the type of business I should start."

"A break will be good for you, because it won't be easy dealing with a divorce, being in a new relationship and then having to find a new place to live."

"Especially since David isn't being fair about anything. I haven't heard from him since we had that big blowup when he came to the house, but I can tell that things are going to get worse before it's all over. He is so angry with me, and I don't understand how he could be, because he's the one who decided he wanted someone else."

"But you know that's how it always is," she said. "It was one thing when David left you to be with another woman, but it's another now that he knows you don't care."

"The reason I don't care is because there was nothing I could do to make him love me. He found another woman, and I learned to accept it."

"I know, but what he wanted was for you to shed a bunch of tears over him. And when you acted like you didn't care one way or the other, he couldn't take it."

"Yeah, that's exactly why he's so upset. I've thought that all along, and he would die if he knew about Frank."

"Yeah, I'm sure he would."

"He'd never guess in a million years that I would end up dating someone white. Actually, I didn't ever think I would myself. But it just goes to show how funny life can be. I practically despised white men when I realized how racist Jim and Lyle were, and now I'm seeing one."

"Love is love, no matter what color a person is. You can't fight the way you feel about someone when it's meant to be. And with the way you always said you'd never date a white man, I know for sure that you must be head over heels about Frank."

I laughed. "I am. I don't know how it happened, but I really am. He's so considerate of my feelings and my needs, and he goes out of his way to make sure I'm happy. I never experienced that with David. So I finally had to ask myself, is it better to be with a black man just because he's black, even though he treats you like crap, or would it be better to live the rest of your life in peace with a man of any color who loves and respects you?"

"Love is much more important than someone's racial background."

"I realize that now, but you know Monica isn't happy about my relationship with Frank at all."

"She'll get over it. And if she doesn't, then she's not really your friend, and she doesn't care one thing about your happiness. I love Monica like a daughter, and I know you've been best friends with her forever, but it's during times like these that you discover who your real friends truly are. Because it's not Monica's job to decide what's right for you. Her job is to support you no matter what."

"I just hope she sees it that way pretty soon, because our conversations have been a little on the tense side ever since I told her about Frank. I called her a few times when I wanted her to read that memo I put together, but I could tell things weren't the same between us."

"You'll have to see how things go, but I wouldn't feel bad about being with the person I love regardless of who has a problem with it."

"I know, but I just don't want to lose Monica's friendship. She's always been like a sister to me, and the thought of us not having anything to do with each other really hurts."

"I understand how you feel, but it's like I said, she's not really the friend we thought she was if she doesn't support your decision. Especially when it's pretty obvious that Frank makes you happy."

"He does, Mom."

"Then I wouldn't worry about what anyone else has to say."

"I wish it were that easy for me."

"As time goes on, it will be. Don't get me wrong, you will always come across people who don't approve of your relationship, but in the end you still have to do what's best for you."

"Mom, thanks so much for always understanding me and for loving me the way only a mother could," I said, reaching for her hand and holding it against my cheek. My eyes misted.

Darkness spread across the sky, but we didn't go in the house until after ten o'clock. After another half hour or so, I drove home to get my clothes ready for work the next day. Then I called Frank. I'd given him a few details about the meeting before we left work, but I wanted to thank him again for everything he'd done.

"Hi, beautiful," he answered.

"How are you?" I asked, and smiled when I heard his voice.

"So how does it feel to be queen of the mountain?"

We laughed.

"Yeah right," I said.

"Well, you are. It took a lot of courage to stand up to the three of them in that meeting."

"Yeah, it did, but I have to say I'm glad it's over with, and I hope the rest of it is over very soon."

"I'm sure it will be. What they're doing now is trying to figure out how they can get away with paying you a smaller amount than what you're demanding."

"Well, I'm not taking less than three-fifty, so they can just forget about it. Actually, they should just be happy I'm not asking for more, because in reality, there's no specific dollar amount that could possibly equal the way they've treated me. And the only reason I'm asking for money at all is because that's the only remedy available to the victim when it comes to racial discrimination."

"Good for you, and if they don't do what you expect, then you have to go straight to the newspaper like we discussed. Then we'll go over to EEOC to get the ball rolling with them."

"I'm hoping it doesn't have to come to that, because, like you said, the publicity would totally destroy my chances of working anywhere else in the city. But if I don't have a choice, I agree with you that I have to move on to Plan B."

"So how was your mom?" he asked.

"She was fine. I hadn't spent that much time with her in a while, and it felt good."

"I'm glad to hear that."

"I do think she's lonely, though, and I wish she could find someone to share her life with."

"It's never too late."

"No. It's not, but she's almost sixty."

"Some people meet and get married in their eighties."

"Yeah, I've read about a few in the past, but I hope my mom doesn't have to wait that long."

"So what are you doing for lunch tomorrow?"

"Nothing, why?"

"I thought we could grab something quick and drive out to the forest preserve."

"I don't know if we should take the chance of being seen together now that Jim knows about us."

"I don't care who sees us, because I decided tonight that I'm turning in my letter of resignation as soon as you leave the company."

"I hate to see you doing that because of me."

"Don't worry about it for one minute, because Reed Meyers is no longer the type of place I want to work for. And you can bet that I'm never going to be promoted now that they know I'm dating you. They hate that sort of thing, so I'm out anyway, even if I continue working there."

"That's really too bad, and it makes me so angry to know that they have that much control."

"Well, they do."

"Frank, I'm so sorry that you had to get involved with all of this."

"Don't be. I would do it all over again if I had the chance."

"I love you so much," I confessed.

"I love you more," he said.

An hour passed before we ended our conversation, but as soon as I hung up, my phone rang again. My blood flowed rapidly when I saw that it was Lorna, and I couldn't help wondering how she could possibly have the audacity to be calling.

My first notion was to answer and see what she wanted. However, I soon decided against it, and waited to see if she was bold enough to leave a message.

She did, and I dialed the access number to retrieve it.

"Anise?" she began in a distraught voice. "I was really hoping you would be home so that I could speak to you directly. But I guess leaving this message will have to do. I'm so, so sorry for everything. I'm sorry for everything I've done to you. I'm sorry for lying to you and for betraying you the way I have. I know you probably hate me right now, but I'm still hoping that you will find it in your heart to speak to me again. Please let me make all of this up to you, Anise. I'm not just asking, but I'm begging you. I can't explain why I did what I did, except that Jim promised me a promotion and more money, and I really, really needed it. I needed it more than you could possibly ever know. And I guess I was just hoping that Jim would make good on his promise if I slept with him and didn't tell you that he had someone following you. I know it probably sounds sick, but there's no other way I can explain it. I don't know how long I have left on your voice mail, so I'll just say again that I'm sorry, and whether you believe me or not, I'll regret all of this for the rest of my life. I really do care about you, Anise, and I realize now that I've never had a more genuine friend than I had in you. I can't believe I was so stupid," she said between sniffles. "And if it's the last thing I do, I promise I will make things right with you. I don't know quite how, but I promise you I will. My life is so screwed up, and while I know that doesn't justify my actions, I hope you can try to forgive me one day. Bye, Anise."

I saved the message and found my emotions caught between blinding anger and inexplicable sadness. I was angry because I had wholeheartedly believed that Lorna was my true friend, but I was saddened because our friendship had been shattered through our association with Reed Meyers. I knew Lorna was responsible for her own disloyalty, but I couldn't help but wonder if she would have undergone such an eerie change in personality if Jim hadn't been sexually involved with her.

Lorna sounded so depressed, and I wondered if maybe she had aborted the baby she was carrying. She sounded as if she really needed someone to talk to and that she really was sorry for everything. But I couldn't find enough sympathy to call her. I didn't know if I would feel any differently in the future, but right now I just couldn't do it.

I stretched across the bed and rested my eyes, replaying my meeting with Jim, Lyle and Tom. I thought about every moment of it and tried to prepare myself mentally.

There was no telling what they were planning to do next.

I tried to prepare myself for the worst-case scenario.

CHAPTER 27

ANISE, THIS IS Tom," he said when I answered my phone. I couldn't believe the CEO himself was calling me directly.

"Yes," I said.

"Do you have those other salary histories you spoke about in our meeting last Thursday?"

"Yes."

"Then what I'd like for you to do is bring them to my office. There's no need to stop at my assistant's desk, and I'll let her know that I've given you permission to walk right in when you get here."

"I'll bring them to you in about ten minutes."

"I'll be here," he said, and hung up. He sounded more aggravated than when I'd met with them a few days ago, but something told me that he still didn't believe I had anything that could hurt them.

I pulled a stack of copies from my briefcase, secured them with a thick rubber band and headed down to Tom's office. Once again, when I arrived, I saw Lorna staring from a distance, but I pretended I didn't see her. Tom's assistant looked up at me and smiled, but continued working at her computer. At first I wondered if she knew what was going on, but I was sure Tom wanted to keep this little problem of ours completely confidential.

When I opened the door and walked in, I saw Tom positioned behind his desk with Jim and Lyle sitting in front of him. The atmosphere was tense. I knew immediately that there was no reason to speak to them, and that it was best to simply pass the infamous documents to Tom and leave. Which I did.

"Thank you, and we'll get back to you this afternoon or tomorrow morning," he said.

I turned and walked out of the office without making any eye contact with Jim or Lyle, but I couldn't help wondering what they thought of me now. I wondered what they thought now that they knew for sure that I hadn't been bluffing.

"Where in the hell did she get these goddamn printouts?" Tom yelled shortly after thumbing through the first two pages of information.

"Unbelievable," Lyle said. "I had a feeling all along that she was telling the truth."

"I knew it, too, because Anise is not someone to underestimate," Jim said. "And you'd better believe, just like she produced these printouts, she *will* go to the newspaper if she doesn't get what she wants."

Maybe now Tom understands that we have to pay her and get her out of here.

"Whoever helped her with this is going to suffer unmercifully," Tom said. "Just look at all of this," he said, passing the stack to Lyle. "Just look!"

Jim shook his head in disgust.

"She has information on every office employee we have, and if this gets out, we are going to be destroyed," Lyle said.

"Who in the world do you think would betray the company like this?" Tom asked both of his subordinates.

"I don't know," Jim answered, "but I'd be willing to bet that

Frank Colletti had something to do with it. I have no idea how, since he doesn't have access to the payroll system, but you can believe he helped her."

"He's lost his natural mind," Tom said. "Anise let him stick his dick in her a few times, and now he's gone insane."

"That's exactly what it sounds like to me," Jim added.

Lyle sighed in distress and passed the evidence back to Tom.

"We're fucked!" Tom said, slamming it down on his desk. "And I can't believe we've sat back like children and allowed this shit to happen."

"Now you understand why I don't like hiring them in the first place," Jim said.

"It's not like we have a choice," Lyle insisted.

"Yeah, but if we hadn't hired a black in human resources, we wouldn't be sitting here in turmoil like this," Jim said. "I knew Anise was trouble as soon as I heard she had an M.B.A., because when they go that far in college, they quickly forget who they are. Not to mention, we probably paid for that M.B.A. with our own tax dollars."

"Three hundred and fifty thousand dollars down the drain," Lyle said.

"I just don't see how we can give her what she's asking," Tom said. "Do you realize how much money we're talking about?"

"Yeah. But I don't see how we can avoid it, given the situation," Lyle said. "Especially since she's made it very clear that her terms aren't negotiable."

"Never in the history of my career have I had to deal with something so outrageous," Tom said. "And it pains me to think that we're going to sit back and let this woman rape us financially because she didn't get the job she wanted."

I thought Tom was beginning to realize the seriousness of this, but now I see I'm going to have to spell it out for him.

"I understand how you feel, Tom," Jim said, "but there's something else I think you need to consider: She mentioned in that memo that she had information on past employees, too. And if we end up in court, you can bet EEOC or some attorney will sue us on their behalf as well."

"That's a good point," Lyle agreed. "And what about the applications we were coding up until three years ago when that one secretary we hired refused to do it, because she said it was illegal. Don't forget we fired her a couple months later, so you can guess she'd be more than happy to testify against us."

Tom leaned back in his chair and breathed deeply. "We really don't have a choice, do we?"

"No, I don't see that we do," Lyle said.

"I know we don't," Jim commented.

"Then I guess all we can do is bite the bullet and call Jack," Tom said, referring to their lead counsel. "I've already informed him about what's going on, but I was really hoping we could see our way out of this for less than a hundred thousand. I've suggested that he draw up a contract which will obligate her to release all originals and copies in her possession, and I want a specific paragraph incorporated which will prevent her from discussing any information she has pertaining to any aspect of the company or the details of her settlement agreement."

It's about time he finally realized what we have to do.

"It's unfortunate, but the quicker we move this along, the better off we'll be," Lyle said.

"I agree, and I say we have her out of here by tomorrow afternoon," Jim said.

"We'll try, but that's only if accounting can do what they need to before then. We do have money available for severance packages and small settlements, but Larry is saying that he'll have to move a few things around to make this work," Tom said, speaking of the company comptroller. "And I suspect he'll have even more maneuvering to figure out now that we're talking the entire three hundred and fifty thousand dollars tax free."

"Well, let's just hope by the time we go to bed tomorrow evening, Anise Miller will be out of our lives for good," Lyle added.

"And what a relief," Jim said, but paused when Lorna stormed into the room.

"You cruel, conniving son of a bitch," she screamed, staring at Jim.

"What the hell . . ." Tom shouted, standing up.

"Good Lord," Lyle added.

"You've bullied me since the very beginning, and I'm not taking it anymore," Lorna continued, all the while glaring at Jim.

"What is this all about, Lorna?" Tom asked angrily.

"This is about Jim sexually harassing me, and his baby—which I've been carrying for three months now. *That's* what this is all about.

"Jim, is this true?" Tom asked.

"No . . . no. She's lying. She's . . . she's a lying sack of shit. I don't know why, but she's lying about all of this."

"No, I'm not lying, and here's the hush money you gave me for the abortion," she announced, tossing a stack of loose bills against Jim's chest. "I'm keeping my baby whether you like it or not, and that means you can expect a petition for child support real soon," she declared, and walked out without shutting the door behind her.

Lyle hurried to close it.

"I tell you she's lying," Jim said, trying to sound convincing.

"Then we have nothing to worry about," Lyle assured him.

Tom didn't comment one way or the other.

CHAPTER 28

I T WAS SO HARD to believe that a little black girl who grew up on the west side of Mitchell had stood up for herself and was going to be paid $350,000. Tom had called me this morning with their decision and asked me if I could meet with them at three o'clock to sign a separation agreement. I told him I'd be there, but that I wanted a copy of it two hours before so I could fax it over to my attorney. Tom had hesitated at first, but then told me he'd notify me when the document was ready.

Ray Stevens had reviewed it and told me that everything looked to be in order, and now I was entering the same conference room I'd dropped the bomb in last Thursday. When I closed the door and sat down in front of the Big Three, I wondered why Jim was still working for the company even though everyone had heard about Lorna's accusations. But for some odd reason I wasn't completely surprised. I wasn't surprised because I knew they were going to stand behind Jim until the end if they had to.

I waited for one of them to speak, but since their attorney was present, I knew right away that he'd be speaking for everyone except me.

"We've thought about this long and hard, and we've decided that it is in your best interest, as well as ours, for you to leave the company with a mutual agreement," Jack began. "It basically states that you will return all confidential originals and copies in your possession that pertain to this matter, and that you will not discuss the nature of this separation agreement, nor will you discuss any of your claims against the company, with another soul."

He slid four documents over to me. I'd already read my copy a number of times, and so had Ray, but I scanned it again just to be safe.

Then I signed all four copies and passed them back across the table.

Tom and Lyle signed above their names, and Jack gave me one copy of the agreement to keep.

"And here are the originals and copies you wanted," I said, although I still had one complete copy at home. But I wasn't planning to use it unless I had to.

"Here's the bank draft," the attorney said, passing me an envelope.

Tom, Lyle and Jim hadn't said one word, but I could tell they wanted to reach across the table and rip me out of my chair. I ignored them, though, because they owed me every dime of what they were paying me.

"So is there anything else?" I asked.

"As a matter of fact, there is," Tom said. "We'd like you to end your employment effective today. We're going to pay you through the end of the week, but we don't see a reason for you to stay. So if you need boxes, we will have one of our secretaries find you some, and maybe you can get someone to help you pack and carry them out to your car."

"No, actually, all I need is to grab my purse and briefcase," I said, because I'd never decorated my new office anyway. Not to mention the fact that I'd taken a few personal items home each day over the last week, anticipating that they would escort me out when the time came.

But I was still shocked. I knew I shouldn't have been, but I felt like a criminal. I felt like this was their last chance to try and humiliate me in front of my coworkers, because they knew I wouldn't be able to openly defend myself. My colleagues would think I was being fired because of some terrible thing I'd done, and I wouldn't be able to tell them any different. I'd been sworn to lifetime secrecy, and now I wondered if $350,000 was enough. I wondered if I'd done the right thing by negotiating my settlement, even though I hadn't looked out for all the other innocent employees Reed Meyers was still abusing. I wondered how I could sell out so quickly, even though deep down I knew this was the best option for me personally.

I stood and walked back to my office, Jim and Lyle followed me, and one of the security guards waited patiently outside my doorway. My coworkers stared as expected, but I couldn't look at any of them directly.

This was what I'd asked for, but right now it didn't feel so good. I thought I'd won the battle, but I was starting to see that no dollar amount could take away my pain and humiliation. It certainly would never stop discrimination in the workplace. All I wanted was for them to do what Martin Luther King had asked. I wanted them to judge me by the content of my character and not the color of my skin.

But now I knew that this was impossible. I knew Jim, Lyle and Tom would never rid themselves of that racist mentality they'd been taught by their parents and grandparents. I learned the hard way that I could never change that.

This was my taste of reality.

EPILOGUE

I T WAS HARD to believe that three months had already passed since I'd left Reed Meyers. I didn't miss the way they'd treated me, but I did miss having a career, the one I had worked so hard to build. Although, thanks to Mom's advice, I'd moved on to greater things. I'd decided to start a medical recruiting firm for in-home patients who were seeking private-duty nurses and certified nursing assistants. I was extremely excited about my vision, and now that I'd finalized both my business and marketing plans, I was ready to search for proper office space. Mom had told me she'd help out anytime I needed her, and had decided to go back to school to obtain her nursing assistant certification. That way, she could fill in whenever I couldn't find someone for a particular assignment.

Lorna had phoned me a couple of times, but I still hadn't returned her calls. She'd left one message telling me that she was glad she'd blown the whistle on Jim to Tom and Lyle, and that she wasn't going to get rid of her baby. She'd mentioned that she truly wanted to keep it, but eventually decided that adoption would be best once the baby was born. She didn't feel she could support the baby financially and couldn't dismiss the fact that Jim was married. I told myself that I would call her back sometime, but I still couldn't say when that would happen.

My divorce was still in the works, but surprisingly, David had toned his hostility down a few notches and had agreed to split everything fifty-fifty. So I did the right thing and relinquished any claim I had on his 401(k) account. I hadn't wanted it to begin with, and I think he finally realized that in the end. I hadn't seen all that much of him, but there were still times when I thought about the day we met and how things had been between us during happier times. But whenever I had those thoughts, they were soon replaced by all the hurtful statements he had made to me. I didn't hate him, but I was glad that our divorce would be final before the year was over.

Monica still hadn't totally accepted my relationship with Frank, but our friendship had finally returned to normal. We were like sisters again, and she had spent a lot of time helping me with the research for my business venture.

Frank was every bit of what I thought he was, and I was thankful to have him in my life. He'd left Reed Meyers shortly after I did, and was now working as an independent contractor for another company. He'd even kept his word and mailed salary printouts to EEOC and every woman and minority at the company. I still couldn't believe it, but we'd already heard that claims had been filed one after another, and that EEOC was finally ready to do something about it. I knew Jim, Lyle and Tom had to believe that I was behind all of this, but with Frank printing the information after I was gone, there was nothing they could do. The date listed on each document conveniently fell *after* my last day of employment.

On a personal note, Frank had been spending most of his time trying to convince me to marry him, but I still wasn't sure. I loved him from the bottom of my heart, but I wanted to slow things down just enough to sign my divorce decree and move out of the house David and I finally had an offer on. Frank couldn't understand why I wouldn't just accept his proposal, so I spent many hours explaining to him that I didn't want to drop any unwanted baggage on our new life together.

But today was a special day. It was his thirty-ninth birthday, and we were going out to dinner to celebrate. He'd been looking forward to it all week long, and although he didn't know it, I was planning to surprise him with two tickets to Ocho Rios, Jamaica. He'd told me more than once that the Caribbean was his favorite place to vacation, so I'd scheduled a trip for us next month.

My other gift to him was a bundle of balloons, but since he still hadn't called to thank me, I was starting to wonder if they'd been delivered. So I decided to check. If he didn't thank me as soon as I heard his voice, then I would call the shop I ordered them from to see what the problem was.

I dialed Frank's number and waited for him to answer.

"Hello?"

"Hey, how's it going?" I asked.

"I'm fine. Oh, and thanks for the balloons. I was completely surprised when the doorbell rang," he said, but sounded as if he was a thousand miles away.

"Since I hadn't heard from you, I was starting to think you hadn't gotten them."

"I know. I kept meaning to call you, but I just hadn't gotten around to it."

"So have you decided what you're wearing to dinner?"

"Yeah, but it won't be anything too dressy," he said, and at that moment I knew something was wrong. It wasn't what he said as much as the way he said it.

"Okay, Frank. What's up? Why are you acting so withdrawn?"

"Anise, we need to talk," he said.

I swallowed a lump that came out of nowhere.

"About what?" I asked, and felt my hand shaking.

"Not in a million years did I expect something like this to happen. And of all days, on my birthday."

I didn't like the tone of his voice, and my intuition told me that he was going to devastate me in some unbearable way. I knew he was going to feed me something I wouldn't be able to digest, so I didn't comment.

"My ex-wife is back in town, and she came by to see me today."

My heart collapsed instantly.

"What did she want?" I finally asked.

"She wants us to get back together."

My body entered total paralysis. I prayed that I was only dreaming.

"Anise?"

I heard him but I couldn't respond. How was I going to compete with an ex-wife he'd still been in love with long after they were divorced?

"Anise, are you still there?" he practically pleaded.

"Yeah, I'm here."

"I'm sorry about all of this."

"That's fine, but what did you tell her, Frank?" I asked.

"I didn't tell her anything, because I was too shocked about seeing her."

"But how do you feel about what she's asking?"

"I honestly don't know."

"You don't know?" I repeated in sorrow.

"I know it sounds crazy, but I don't. I mean, I thought Tracy was completely out of my system, but after seeing her, I really don't know."

"Well, if that's true, Frank, then where does that leave you and me?"

He paused for a few seconds.

"Anise, as much as I hate saying it, I don't know that either."

"Frank, you know what . . . I'm hanging up now."

How could he *not* know? was all I could think. How could he pursue me, claim that he loved me and then have second thoughts about it? How could he go on and on about us being married one day and now feel uncertain? I asked myself question after question, trying to figure out why this was happening to me, but in the end there weren't any answers. I wondered what Frank was thinking at this very moment.

But the more I sat there wondering, the more I realized that I'd been through way too much over the last two years to let Frank or anyone else control my destiny. Not that I wasn't hurt by his words, because I was. But at the same time, I started to remember everything I'd accomplished over the last three months. I'd uncovered years of discrimination at Reed Meyers, which would hopefully help current employees as well as those hired in the future, and against all odds I got a big settlement. I'd opened my eyes and accepted the fact that my husband didn't want me, and was almost happily divorced. Best of all, I'd taken the initiative to start my own business and couldn't be more satisfied with it.

I'd done all these things by drawing on my mother's love and the inner strength that God had given me. This new situation would be handled no differently. I wasn't sure what would happen between Frank and me, but what I did know was that every obstacle I'd ever encountered was only temporary.

Which meant I would be fine.

My history guaranteed it.

And just knowing that gave me a wonderful sense of peace.

ACKNOWLEDGMENTS

I am sincerely thankful to God for always guiding me in the right direction. You continue to bless my career year after year and my life as a whole. Truly, nothing would be possible without Your love and grace.

Much love to my husband, Will, for still being the love of my life as well as my greatest support system. You are the best, and I love you from the bottom of my soul.

Much love to my brothers, Willie Jr. and Michael Stapleton, for being so caring. Mom is no longer with us, but know that she is very much alive in our hearts.

Much love to my nephews and niece, Michael Jamaal Young, Malik James Stapleton and Alanna Denise Lawson; my stepson, Trenod Vines-Roby, and my step-grandson, Lamont Woods.

Much love and gratitude to Peggy Hicks, for being more like a blood sister than you are a best friend. You are always there for me, and I am extremely grateful for all the hard work you do as my publicist. Much love to the rest of your family (my family), Steve and Lauren.

Much love to Lori Whitaker Thurman for being so willing and dependable. We became friends just over sixteen years ago, but we are now sisters in every sense of the word. Much love to your mom, Mary Whitaker, who has made sure I still have a mom to turn to.

Much love to Kelli Tunson Bullard, my friend and sister for thirty-one years and still counting. Much love to Brian, Kiara, Kaprisha and KaSondra.

Much love to my aunts and uncles for being such loving and caring people. I'm so grateful to have all of you to depend on for anything at anytime. Fannie Haley, Ben Tennin, Mary Lou and Charlie Beasley, Clifton Jr. and Vernell Tennin, Ada Tennin and Luther Tennin. Much love to my uncle Robert Tennin, who has been ill for a long while.

Much love and thanks to Susan Saylor and Evelyn Barmore for always working around my sometimes hectic schedule and for being great friends and confidants.

Much love to E. Lynn Harris for always standing in my corner. Your loyalty and friendship have been unwavering, and I sincerely appreciate you from the bottom of my heart. Much love to you, Rodrick, as well.

Much love to Victoria Christopher Murray, who has always been my sister in publishing, but who now has become one of my closest friends. Your visits have been a blessing.

Much love to my friend and fellow author, Shandra Hill, for the many phone calls we share.

Much love to some of my author friends: Eric Jerome Dickey, Patricia Haley, Travis Hunter, Lolita Files, Tracy Price-Thompson, Jacquelin Thomas, Colin Chaner, Yolanda Joe and Franklin White.

Much love and special thanks to the following bookstore owners and staff members: Emma at Black Images Book Bazaar in Dallas; Frances at the Cultural Connection in Milwaukee; Jim at Zahra's in Los Angeles; Brother Simba at Karibu in Hyattsville, M.D.; Scott at Reprint in D.C.; Robin at Sibanye, Inc; Anika Sala at Shrine of the Black Madonna in Houston; Nkenge Abi at Shrine of the Black Madonna in Detroit; Sherry at Apple Book Center in Detroit; Sonya at Black Bookworm in Fort Worth; Joyce of Mitchie's Fine Black Art & Gallery in Austin; Andre at Our Story in Plainfield, NJ; Larry at Cultural Plus in New York; Jerry at Alexander Book Company in San Francisco; Desiree at Afrocentric in Chicago; Nia at Medu Bookstore in Atlanta; Marcus at Nubian Bookstore in Atlanta; Joi and the other two owners of Hue-Man Experience in Denver; Blanche at Marcus Books in Oakland; Rick at Barnes & Noble in Rockford; Jeremiah at Waldenbooks at Cherryvale Mall; and Reenie at Borders on 95th in Chicago.

Much love to all of the other African-American bookstore owners throughout this country who go out of their way to sell my books. Without you, I would not exist as a writer.

Much love and special thanks to the following for promoting my work year after year: Julie Snively (Congrats on your much deserved retirement!) and the entire staff at the *Rockford Register Star,* Steve Shannon and Stefani Troye at WZOK in Rockford; Andy Gannon at WIFR-TV in Rockford; Tommy Meeks at Rockford Cablevision; Dede McGuire of *The Doug Banks Show;* Cliff and Janine at KJLH in Los Angeles; Tom and Gwen Pope of *The Tom Pope Show;* Jay Butler at WQBH in Detroit; Huey Moore at WDTR in Detroit; Patrik Bass at *Essence* magazine; Shawn Evans Mitchell for *Atlanta Good Life* magazine; Glenn R. Townes for *Upscale* magazine; and Tamlin Henry and Nicole Bailey-Williams at WDAS in Philadelphia.

Much, much love and admiration to my agent, Elaine Koster, who represents me in the most dedicated and honorable fashion, but who also cares about me personally. For that, I am forever grateful.

Much love and a huge amount of thanks to my editor, Carolyn Marino, at HarperCollins/William Morrow for being so knowledgeable in terms of editing. It is every author's dream to find an editor who will work extra hard at making their work the best that it can be, but also one who will allow him or her the opportunity to write straight from the heart. Now I know why you have been in the business for as long as you have and why you hold the position you do. Thank you, Carolyn, for everything.

Much love and thanks to Jennifer Civiletto and the rest of the HarperCollins/William Morrow family. I am completely indebted to all of you.

Much love to Black Expressions Book Club for promoting and selling thousands of African-American titles.

Much love to the OT Book Club in Rockford of which I am a member (Tammy Roby—founder, Lori Thurman, Regina Taylor, Virginia Givens, Valerie Hanserd, Cathy Watkins, Lesia Smith, Mattie Tate and Sandra Wright). I truly enjoy the time we spend each month discussing books and everything else we can think of! Also, much love to Nicole Redmond, who now lives in Texas, but who we all miss a great deal.

Much love and thanks to ALL of the wonderful book clubs throughout this country. There are hundreds of you who I have met personally, and I can only imagine how many I haven't. You continue to make an amazing difference in terms of getting the word out about my books, and I am totally grateful.

Much love to Pastor John F. Senter, Minister Deniece Senter and every member of the Providence Missionary Baptist Church—a place I've called home since the day I was born.

And finally, to you, my readers. You make this thing we call writing so worth the while, and I appreciate the support you always give each time my books are released. You make all the difference in the world and no matter how many books I write, I will always remember that.

DISCARD